He Don't Play Fair

He Don't Play Fair

CLIFFORD SPUD JOHNSON

www.urbanbooks.net

Urban Books, LLC
78 East Industry Court
Deer Park, NY 11729

He Don't Play Fair Copyright © 2013 Clifford Spud Johnson

ISBN 13: 978-1-60162-543-4
ISBN 10: 1-60162-543-X

First Trade Printing February 2013
Printed in the United States of America

10 9 8 7 6 5 4 3 2 1

This is a work of fiction. Any references or similarities to actual events, real people, living or dead, or to real locales are intended to give the novel a sense of reality. Any similarity in other names, characters, places, and incidents is entirely coincidental.

Distributed by Kensington Publishing Corp.
Submit Wholesale Orders to:
Kensington Publishing Corp.
C/O Penguin Group (USA) Inc.
Attention: Order Processing
405 Murray Hill Parkway
East Rutherford, NJ 07073-2316
Phone: 1-800-526-0275
Fax: 1-800-227-9604

CHAPTER ONE

Papio had a frown on his face as he listened to his girlfriend continue to talk to him in a disrespectful manner. *This bitch has got to be out her ever-loving mind if she thinks I'm going to let her get away with this shit,* he said to himself as he continued to listen to her rant and rave. He chose to remain quiet and let her continue to dig herself a deeper hole. *Keep on, you silly bitch; you think I'm washed up but your ass will have a rude awakening real soon,* he thought as his frowned turned into a smile.

It had been years since he had been convicted for conspiracy to distribute forty-five kilos of cocaine. The Feds threw the book at him for going to trial. He actually thought he would win his case, especially after his $100,000 attorney caught several of the government's confidential informants in different lies. But it just wasn't meant to be. The Feds don't be playing: when they come scoop you, believe it, they got your ass.

After receiving a thirty-year sentence from the judge, Papio smiled. He was smiling on the outside but he really wanted to scream. He refused to give the US attorney the privilege to see him fall weak like that. Instead, his mind was busy turning, trying to come up with a way to get himself out of this gigantic mess he'd gotten himself into. He turned his head and gave a slight nod to the fat Cuban who was sitting and watching the proceedings inside of the courtroom. I didn't snitch, you fat bitch; go tell your boss that, you fucking flunky. You think I'm done, but best believe Papio will be back stronger than ever. *He turned and faced the judge when he asked him if he had anything to say for himself. Papio stared at the judge with so much contempt in eyes that the judge actually felt intimidated by his hateful glare. Papio smiled as two US marshals came and led him out of the courtroom and downstairs to the holding tank.* A fucking million-plus-dollar nigga and I got washed up because a bunch of soft-ass Oklahoma City niggas fell weak on those punk-ass Cubans. Damn, I know I should have never fucked with that bitch-ass nigga Charlie. I knew his ass was weak any-fucking-way. Fuck it, that's a wrap, time to execute your exit plan, Papio, *he said to himself as he stepped inside of the holding tank and sat down in the freezing cell.*

The telephone beeped, snapping Papio back to reality. He cleared his throat and stopped his girlfriend's tirade and said, "Check it, we only got one minute left, Mani. Calm down and don't panic. I'll have some more ends brought to you, so stop fucking tripping."

"Stop tripping? Nigga, if you would have left me with the ends like you said you was I wouldn't be having none of these issues! You got that fat joke-ass nigga Hugh telling me he's going to bring me some ends but every time I call that bitch he comes up with one lie after another. I'm telling you, Papio, I can't keep going through this shit."

"I told you Hugh's been busy taking care of shit for me. My appeal is coming up and he's got to make sure that everything is good with that."

"For real, Papio, do you know what the chances are that you're going to get a time reduction? Be realistic, nigga; you done for a minute."

The telephone hung up before he could respond to her. He started laughing as he hung up the phone and went to his cell. His celly, a Jamaican man who had been down since the late nineties, was sitting on his bunk reading the latest *King* magazine. He looked up and smiled at Papio as he entered their cell. "Wah you do, mon?"

"Just chilling, Kingo. What up with you?"

"Me good, mon. Just checking out these American women; you know me love them big battys they have." They started laughing as Papio took a seat at the small desk inside of the cell.

Kingo noticed that Papio's mood seemed sour. "Something on your mind, mon? Wah is it? Talk to Kingo."

They had been living in the same cell for the two and a half years Papio had been at the Federal Correction Institution of El Reno, and over the years Kingo gave Papio some very solid advice. It was rare to trust fellow inmates but Papio had grown to trust Kingo. Kingo looked at Papio as a young man with plenty of potential to make something of his life after he was released, so he chose to school him as much as he could. Their bond was solid so Papio knew that he could talk to him about anything.

Papio sighed and said, "Man, that dumb bitch Mani tripping about money again. I make sure she continues to live in my pad, pushes a fly whip, and keeps her stank-ass in the top-of-the-line clothes as if I was still out there doing me. Now she thinks she can talk to a nigga like I'm some type of chump or some shit. She's going to get it as soon as I touch; my word that bitch will never get away with talking to me like she just did."

Kingo shook his long gray dreadlocks from his face and said, "American women got that bad, mon, but it's no one's fault but you 'Shotta,' 'Top Rankin,' 'Rude Boys.' You spoil them without keeping them in their proper place. If you would have made sure she knew her place she would never disrespect you now. But you was so busy being top rankin' that you let her have her way." He shook his head slowly and continued, "Right now, mon, you have to stay focused on your appeal and hope for da best. Don't let her interfere with your mind, mon. It will do nothing but drive you crazy with madness."

"What about you? You been down, what, twenty years now? How the hell do you and your wife remain on good terms?"

Kingo smiled and stared at the picture of his very beautiful, very white wife and said, "Me girl know her place; she know that if she ever disrespects Kingo she will not live long enough to see her next earth day."

"Fear? That's how you keep her in check then?"

Kingo shook his head and said, "No fear, mon, respect. She respects me for being a mon, a real mon. She has watched me do wicked things to people who have tried to disrespect Kingo and she knows that I will kill or die before I am ever disrespected by anyone."

"I know you were out there having some serious paper and your finances are still good even after all of this time you've done, but do you really think she's not out there fucking?"

Kingo started laughing and his Jamaican accent was even more pronounced when he said, "So wah! She need to go to the rompin' shop just like everyone else, mon. Me no mad at her for dat. Shit, me wish I could get me hood sucked and make love long time in the rompin' shop. I cannot ask her not to take care of her needs, mon. Respect Kingo and make sure that me needs are taken care of and me good. I have four more years to go and I'm back; then she will be treated as royalty because she has done everything Kingo has asked her to do. She takes good care of me sons and she loves me in a way that you American men can only dream about." He started laughing again as he stared at his celly.

"I know one thing: I'm about to be out this bitch any fucking day and that dumb bitch Mani don't even realize she's out of there. I can't wait to hurt that slick-mouthed broad."

"Wah you know? Wah make you t'ink you gon' be out of here any day?" Kingo answered with a smile. Kingo frowned and said, "The twenty years I've been in federal prison, the only way I've seen anyone get out of a thirty-year bid, mon, is snitching. Don't tell me I've made a friend who's weak like that, Papio?"

"Come on with that shit, Kingo. If I was going to snitch we would have never met. I would have done that shit from the be-gin. That ain't in me. Let's just say that I got some moves being made in my favor that's going to have them gates opened for me real soon like. So don't worry, old man, by the time these next four years float by I'm going to be out there, back on millionaire status, and you will be looked out for as soon as you get at me."

Kingo touched his heart with a closed fist and said, "'Nuff love, Papio. Me hope all of your dreams come true, me really do. But I don't want you around here looking all sad because of your blood-clot American woman done talked down to you, mon. We have to keep our heads held high through all this time."

"I got you, old dread. Don't worry about ya boy, I'm good," Papio said as he climbed onto the top bunk and closed his eyes. *Handle your business, Hugh; handle your fucking business,* he said to himself and smiled as he opened his *DuPont Registry* car magazine. He turned to a page with a brand new black Aston Martin coupe on it and his smiled brightened. "You're going to be mines, baby," he whispered.

The next morning Papio and Kingo were on the rec yard, working out. It was amazing for Kingo to be in his mid-fifties and have the wind and stamina of a twenty-year-old. His long dreads were tied in a long ponytail as he stepped up to the pull-up bar and began to do his set of twenty-five pull-ups. He finished his set easily and dropped off of the bar and watched as Papio stepped up to do his set. Papio, at twenty-seven, wasn't a slouch himself. Since coming to prison he made sure that he kept his body in tiptop shape. Thanks to Kingo's intense workout plan, his six-foot frame was slim, yet muscular. Abs were right, chest was tight, arms and legs were big and firm; his smooth features made him one handsome young man. His intense light brown eyes with his bronzed skin complexion showed his Puerto Rican side; what stood out most was his long hair. He loved his hair. He kept it pulled in a tight ponytail tapered on the sides. Some consider Papio the pretty boy type, but in Papio's case looks were truly deceiving. He could be as deadly as any cold-blooded killer. Just as he was finishing his set he heard his name being called over the prison's PA system. "Preston Ortiz! Preston Ortiz, report R&D now!"

Papio smiled at Kingo and said, "Well, looks like I get out of this one, old dread."

Kingo shook his head and said, "No, you haven't, mon. When you get back we will finish, you lazy blood clot."

Papio slapped him on his sweaty back and laughed as he grabbed his workout bag and headed toward the receiving and discharge room. He had a smile on his face because he knew that he was about to receive the news he had been anxiously waiting for. *You did that shit, Hugh. I knew you would hold me down, you soft-ass nigga,* he said to himself as he picked up his pace.

When he made it to R&D, a white correctional officer frowned and told him to have a seat in the holding cell while they finished getting things ready for him. *Ready for me? What the fuck is this?* he thought as he sat down on a hard bench and tried his best to remain calm. *Don't panic. You know the business. You can't miss on this. As long as Hugh handled up you good, no way can this shit backfire on me, no fucking way,* he said to himself.

Twenty minutes later the same white CO came to the holding cell and said, "Come with me, Ortiz." The CO led him into a case manager's office and left him alone with a pretty sister who Papio had seen only in passing around the prison. He knew that Ms. Wickerson wasn't no joke; he heard how she would curse a nigga out for trying to pop too slick with her. He was going to make sure he kept everything real smooth with her.

Ms. Wickerson looked up from her PC and said, "Have a seat, Mr. Ortiz." After Papio was seated she smiled at him and said, "Today is truly your lucky day, young man."

"Lucky day? How can any day be lucky for me and I got all of this time, Ms. Wickerson?" he asked, playing the part as his heart was beating out of control. *It worked! Hugh did that shit!* he thought as he waited for her to continue.

She passed him some papers to read and said, "I think you'll change your mind after you've read that," as she sat back and smiled.

Her smile was so damn beautiful that he was momentarily mesmerized. He shook his head, stopped staring at this beautiful case manager, and started reading the papers she passed him. A huge smile slowly spread across his face as he read that he had been exonerated of all the crimes he had been convicted for. The felony scar would be removed from his name and he was to be released immediately. He took a deep breath and made the sign of the cross across his heart and smiled. He looked up at Ms. Wickerson and calmly asked, "Is this real, ma'am?"

She nodded and said, "Yes, yes, it is, Mr. Ortiz. You're about to become a free man. The staff secretary is in the process of taking care of the necessary paperwork as we speak. You will be released in the morning at nine A.M."

"No probation or anything?"

"That's right, nothing. You will be a free man in every sense of the word. I hope you take this blessing for what it's worth, Mr. Ortiz, and take advantage of this in a positive way. It's not every day that a convicted felon gets an opportunity like this. You've been given a second chance; don't become another statistic and come back to prison. Do the right thing and enjoy your freedom."

Papio smiled at her and said, "Believe me, ma'am, I will."

She smiled at the handsome man in front of her and wondered what his sex game was like. *Mmmm, he's been down for three years so I know he has a lot of pent-up frustrations he's ready to release. Stop it, Brandy, you know better,* she scolded herself. "So, what are you going to do when you go home? Are you going back to Oklahoma City? Or are you going to California? That's where you're from originally right?"

"Yeah, that's where I'm from but I have to go back to Oklahoma City to take care of some business; then I'll be off to the West. I got to sell my home and get some other finances in order first. Tell me, since I paid my fine when I was sentenced, will I be reimbursed since my conviction has been overturned?"

"That was exactly what I was about to explain. All you have to do is give me an address and you will receive a check within ninety days."

"Ninety days? Damn, that's a long time. I mean I need those crumbs for real."

Crumbs? She stared at the financial report she had in front of her and thought, *Did this man just call $150,000 crumbs?* "Well, I'm sorry but that's the normal procedure when something like this takes place. And since this is a very rare circumstance the proper procedure has to be taken. You will receive a check from the Treasury Department on or before ninety days. Sorry."

He shrugged and said, "No biggie; that was going to be my shopping money anyway."

Shopping money? This young man can't be serious, she thought as she stared at him. When she saw the look on his face she knew that he was, in fact, dead serious. *Wow. Impressive.* "Well, since you have the luxury to spend that kind of money shopping you shouldn't have a problem maintaining your freedom then. You're obviously financially secure. So, again, I ask, what are your plans?"

He gave the sexy case manager a very flirtatious grin and said, "Whatever I want, Ms. Wickerson, whatever I want. If you want specifics why don't you give me a way to get in contact with you so you can see for yourself," he stated boldly.

"Be careful, young man, you're not free yet," she said sternly.

"True. But I will be in the morning," he countered with a smile.

I am dead wrong, but technically he is a free man and he is no longer a felon. I wouldn't be breaking any rules if I had contact with him. With that thought she said, "While we're waiting for your paperwork, humor me and tell me exactly how you'd show me."

What the fuck? This bad-ass bitch is straight choosing? Well I'll be damned! You got action at Ms. Wickerson! Wait until I tell Kingo this shit! he thought. He kept his poker face on as he said, "First, I would fly you out West and take you on a shopping spree to show you that as far as the material things go there's nothing you couldn't have be being with me. After that we'd eat at the finest restaurants and drink the best wines. Whatever you would want to do would be done."

"Is that right?" she asked, amused.

"You think I'm playing?"

"Yes, I do."

"Give me a number and watch my get down then."

"I'm thirty-eight years old, young man, and I don't have time for games."

Before he could respond the staff secretary came inside of the office and gave Ms. Wickerson Papio's release papers. Ms. Wickerson in turn gave them to Papio and told him where to sign. After he finished signing for his freedom he stood and smiled. "Can I go now?"

"Yes, you can. You'll be called to R&D in the morning around seven A.M."

"Seven A.M.? I thought you said I was getting out at nine."

"You are, but there is some more paperwork that has to be done and a warrants check has to be made. By the time all of that has been taken care of it should be close to nine o'clock."

"That's what's up. Well, I guess this is good-bye then, Ms. Wickerson."

"I guess it is. Good luck, Mr. Ortiz," she said as she stuck her hand out.

He shook her hand gently and said, "Don't cheat yourself, treat yourself, *mami*." He turned and walked out of her office with his swagger in full swing. Papio was about to be back in the game and the world was in a whole bunch of trouble.

CHAPTER TWO

Kingo was sitting on his bunk when Papio came into the cell with a smile on his face. "Wah you got that big goofy smile on your face for, mon?" Papio gave him his release papers as well as the papers that showed that he had been exonerated of all his crimes. He continued to smile as he watched Kingo read. When Kingo finished he sighed and said, "Damn, mon, I never seen no shit like this before. Wah you do, Papio? Wah you do, mon?"

Papio sat down next to his celly and said, "Check it, this clown-ass nigga I got out in OKC is like super loyal to me; I mean there's nothing he wouldn't do for me. I had him make some moves for me when I first got knocked because I had a feeling that I was about to get fucked. No way in hell was I going to let them punk Cubans get away with crossing me out."

"Wah you do, Papio?" Kingo asked again with a frown on his face.

"I gave Hugh all of the information needed to get me out if it came to it. He gave the investigator for the US assistant attorney information on about twenty-five hundred kilos of cocaine and about five thousand pounds of weed. Purple, that good shit."

"Ahh, mon, not the ganja!" Kingo said with a smile on his face.

"Calm down and listen, you damn bud head. Anyway, I told him to make sure that he made a deal that would get me back on the streets with no felony scar or anything. It took way longer than I expected but everything came through like I knew it would. They went for that shit."

"Did they knock the Cubans?" Kingo stared real hard at Papio as he waited for him to answer.

"Nope. Hugh didn't know anything about anybody to tell shit. All he knew was the location of the drugs. Oh, and there was like $4.5 million in cash there, too."

Kingo slapped his forehead and said, "You do know they are going to kill you, right, mon? Those Cubans will know that it was you who gave up that information as soon as they hear that you're back on the streets."

"Pretty much. But fuck them. I got plans and as long as I make the moves necessary I'll give them all of their money back, with interest. Shit, they left me for dead, they should let me make it. But since I know that ain't going to happen I have to get out and make moves and make them like fast."

"Wah you gon' do, mon? That's serious money you speaking on."

"I know. That dope boy shit is over, so I got some more shit on my mind to score those kind of ends. Whatever it takes, Kingo I got to do. I got a little under a million out there, so I'm going to go back West and make some moves and play it by ear from there."

"Dope game can get you bread like that quick but there's plenty of others ways, mon."

Just like he figured, Kingo was going to lace him and help him get the kind of money he needed to keep those Cubans at bay. Even though he had the money already his mind was on bigger shit; no way was he going to pay them all of that fucking money back. *Fuck that shit.* As far as he was concerned that shit was nothing compared to the thirty fucking years he would have had to do. He knew once he explained everything to Kingo the old dread would help him.

"Explain your get down to me, mon. What are you willing to do to get money? I mean serious money, mon."

Papio stared at his celly directly in his eyes and said, "I'm a dope boy by right, but I'm also a magician because I got more tricks of the trade than any other nigga in the game. I trust no nigga and damn sure don't trust no bitch. I'm an assassin for this money because I damn sure will kill for it quick about my business. Whatever needs to be done I will do to get money. I'll rob, steal, and kill, Kingo, true story."

"I can put you in a position of power but you have to be able to handle this power, Papio. You have to be able to hold on to it by the most heinous means necessary."

"I don't want power, Kingo. I want money. Period."

Kingo shook his head and said, "Power is money, mon."

"Fuck the power; all that shit will do is get a nigga caught back up. I roll solo and that's that."

Kingo nodded. "Understood. You will still need assistance from time to time."

"True."

"I will give you three numbers: one in the 876 area code, one in San Diego, and one in New York. Call these numbers when you're ready to make your move. You will have the assistance you need to get money. Can you do a takeover?"

"A what?"

"Takeover, mon: full and total control. Banks."

"Robbing banks? I never got down like that but I don't think I'd have a problem getting down like that."

"When you're ready call the 212 area code first. You will have to go to New York and visit me family. My brother will train you. He will show you that way to do takeover properly."

"Banks, that's what's up. But I got more on my plate than just hitting banks. I know a lot of niggas who got that fucking money and they're about to come up off that shit for Papio."

"You going back to Oklahoma City?"

"Just long enough to get some shit square with my pad and tie up some loose ends."

"Mani?"

Papio smiled and said, "Exactly."

"Wah you gon' do to her, mon?"

Papio frowned for a second and then said, "Make her regret ever disrespecting me."

Kingo saw the look on his face and knew that Mani was going to be visiting the hospital real soon. He hoped it was in fact the hospital instead of the morgue. "So, you gon' rob old associates as well as what?"

"I'll put some work on the streets somewhere in the South or Midwest, too. Ain't no money in the West unless I fuck with the pills. Ain't no telling; whatever I go to do I'm doing it."

"I thought you said that dope boy shit was over with."

"I did. That shit is over for me but I know how to find niggas who are hungry enough to get a nice run out of they ass. See I got caught up in that shit deep because I was slanging them bricks and shit. The richest rewards in that game go to those lowest on the chain. You know trapping and shit. They take the most risks but they eat real good if they handle that shit right. I'm going to touch money from every fucking level on them streets. I got too comfortable in OKC; that's why I got knocked. None of that shit now. It's all about hit and move. I'm going to have spots every-fucking-where! I'll never get stagnant with my moves."

"Good. But you must never underestimate those Cubans, mon. A classic mistake is to underestimate; when you underestimate anyone the percentage of you losing becomes ninety percent. I don't want to lose, Papio, so listen to my words, mon. You won't understand the words now but eventually you will. Find true love; real love balances you. It gives you the necessary that's needed to make things go smooth in your life. If it's not with Mani then so be it. Find that love of your life and cherish her. Demand our respect but respect her as well. Life has taught us that love does not consist of gazing at each other but looking outward in the same direction. Find that true love, Papio, and you will find true happiness. As long as you're happy out there your moves will become easier and easier, mon."

"I feel you and that's some real talk right there, but right now love gots to get put on fucking standby, my dreaded friend. All I'm thinking about is the fucking money!"

Kingo shook his head and smiled at his friend. "You are too silly, mon."

"Check it, if I need some muscle can you help me out?"

"These last few years I have looked at you as a son. I care for you, mon, and I will do whatever you need of Kingo. No worry about muscle. You will have the numbers to get any help you may need in that wicked world."

They talked late into the night, planning and making sure that they touched every base. Before they fell asleep Papio made Kingo a promise: "I promise you this, Kingo. By the time you come home I will have the table set for you in a way that would make a king envious. My word."

"I know you will, Papio, and I give you my word that I will help you as much as you need, mon. Remember this: do not be careless, impatient, nor reckless. Take your time and you will get everything you want."

"I'm going to get this money, Kingo, any and every way I know how to. Those nigggas played the game the way they chose to and now it's my turn to play the game the coldest way ever. My way. And believe me, my dreaded confidant, I don't play fair."

CHAPTER THREE

"Preston Ortiz! Preston Ortiz, report to R&D now!" the R&D officer yelled over the PA system. Papio and Kingo were standing outside of their cell, waiting for that announcement. Papio smiled at his friend and said, "Come on, old dread. Let's roll."

With teary eyes Kingo shook his head no and said, "Me nah go wid you, Papio. Good-bye is too much for me, mon. Send me a letter when you have a number and me will call." He gave Papio a manly hug and said, "Remember: do what has to be done and be careful as well as patient, mon. When you ready call the numbers and you will get the assistance you will need." He then turned and went back into his cell and let his tears flow freely, making sure none of the other prisoners saw him crying. He would miss Papio greatly.

Papio picked up his small box with his possessions inside and stepped quickly toward R&D. A few of the homeboys from California came and escorted him down to the R&D building. They wanted to make sure that no jealous nigga would try to ruin Papio's release by sticking a shiv in his back. After making it safely to R&D and saying his good-byes he knocked on the door.

The same CO from the day before opened the door and scowled at Papio. "What, you don't want to go home, Ortiz?"

Papio ignored him and stepped inside of the room and went straight to the holding cell. The CO had a smile on his face as he came and slammed the door to the holding cell. Papio sat back and relaxed because he knew that he was trying to play head games with him. He didn't give a damn; in a few hours he would be out of this bitch and as far as he was concerned there was no looking back.

One hour later Ms. Wickerson came to the holding cell and told him to follow her to her office. Papio smiled as he grabbed his box and did as he was told. Once they were inside of her office she sat down and smiled. "You should be very excited, Mr. Ortiz. Today is your day."

He shrugged and said, "Yeah? I'll believe it when I'm on the other side of that razor wire fence. Ain't no telling what can pop off between now and nine o'clock."

"I highly doubt it. Your warrant check has come back clean. All we're waiting on now is for your ride to arrive, so you most likely won't have to wait until nine."

"My ride?"

"That's right, didn't you arrange for a man named Hugh Garrison to come and pick you up? He called about thirty minutes ago and said he would be here within the hour take you home."

"I didn't arrange for anything but that's my peoples though," Papio answered with a smile on his face.

"Good. Now, I brought you in here because I wanted a few minutes with you alone before you went home. This is highly irregular for me, Mr. Ortiz."

"Call me Papio."

She gave him a nod, smiled, and continued, "Like I was saying, Papio, this is highly irregular for me but there is something about you that has piqued my interest. I hope you won't disappoint me." She reached inside of her purse, pulled out a card, and gave it to him. "Call me when you're ready to show me that you aren't all talk."

He accepted her card and smiled. "Give me thirty days and be ready to take a week off. Can you do that?"

"I'll put in for it later on today." She stared at him for a moment and started laughing. "My God, what am I getting myself into here?"

"You don't strike me as a fool, Ms. Wickerson—"

"Call me Brandy."

He smiled and said, "You don't strike me as a foolish woman, Brandy. You recognize a boss when you see one. This job is comfortable with good benefits and all but you want to experience the finer things in life. By associating yourself with me you will experience all of that and more. But let me tell you now if you're looking for love you're looking at the wrong man. I don't need love at this point in my life. Now, if it's fun, relaxation, and some damn good sex you're after then Papio is your dude. I don't play games and I will remain straight up with you all the time."

"I respect that, and, believe me, Papio, love is over-rated as far as I'm concerned. Been there done that. I just hope that you're not all mouth. That would be very disappointing." Before he could respond the telephone rang. "Excuse me. Hello? He'll be right out, Carol." She hung up the phone and told Papio, "Your clothes are here. Go get dressed and come back so you can sign the release for your money on your account."

He stood and left the office without saying a word. Fifteen minutes later he returned to her office, looking official as ever in a pair of Armani slacks with a crisp white cotton Armani dress shirt, open at the collar, with a pair of expensive Italian shoes on his feet. He sat down and crossed his legs so she could see his shoes. The shoes spoke volumes as far as he was concerned; if she knew anything about clothing she would know that he was the real deal. The confident smirk on his face told her that, yes, Papio was authentic.

"Impressive. I see that my first assumption of you was correct."

"In thirty days you'll see that everything I've spoken on was real. Check it, Brandy, let's sign these papers 'cause for real, I got business to take care of. You get ready for the time of your life in a month."

She passed him his account papers and said, "You can cash this treasury check today if you like; everything has been taken care of."

He signed the paperwork and stood. "So, I guess this is it then."

She stepped from behind her desk and stood in front of him and gave him a soft kiss on his lips and said, "I'll be waiting to hear from you, Papio." With that said she turned and led the way out of her office and back into R&D.

Ten minutes later Papio was walking out of FCI El Reno's doors. He started laughing when he saw his man Hugh standing outside of his blue Ford F-150. Papio gave him some dap and said, "Good looking, my nigga. You did that shit, dog; you did that shit for real, G! Come on, let's get the fuck out of here," and climbed inside of the truck.

Hugh was smiling as he pulled out of the parking lot. "For a minute there I didn't think they were going to go for that shit, Papio. I think it was all that money that finally got them to deal. When they called me last week and told me to come downtown to their office I knew it was on."

"Yeah, I was in that bitch sweating because it seemed like they was going to fake on a nigga."

"Why didn't you get at me? You could have called me and I would have put you up on everything."

Papio shrugged and said, "Didn't want to stress you. I dealt with it just like I've always done; you know how I get down."

Hugh stared at Papio with admiration and said, "Yeah, you one cool mothafucka, Papio. So, what's the plan now? How we gon' get money? Work?"

"Work? I know you don't think a nigga like me gon' get a j-o-b! That ain't my get down, fool."

"You know what I meant: *work* work. We are going to pay the Cubans back right?" Hugh asked nervously.

"Calm down, my nigga; we gon' take care of everything. Right now the first thing I got to do is get to the West so I can get with Mama Mia and Q so I can get my ends together. I got some moves to make out there and then everything will fall in place. Those Cubans don't know what's what for now so I have to take advantage of that and get enough ends to calm their nerves. When they find out I'm out they'll put everything together and it might get crazy."

"You ain't gon' call them now? Man, that might be a mistake, Papio. They gon' kill our asses."

Papio stared at Hugh for a minute and thought, *Damn, Hugh, I was going to let you make it. Can't do it now, dog. Your scary ass gots to go.* But to Hugh he said, "Check it, baby boy, if I get at them now they will really be salty because I ain't got shit for they ass. By the time I get at them I plan on handing them their $4.5 million back. At least then they will give me a pass. I know how they get down; shit, they most likely will give a nigga some work to help me take care of that tab. If I come at them with nothing they will take that as blatant disrespect. Don't panic on me now, my nigga. You held your boy down so now it's time for me to get us rich."

"But what about the money that your man Q has for you? You could give them a little something. I mean you still got all that loot in the West."

Papio stared at Hugh and shook his head and asked, "You rolling with me right?"

Hugh smiled and said, "You know I am, Papio. I got your back all the way."

"Good. Now pull over at that gas station so I can get me some shit out of there real quick."

Hugh pulled into the gas station. As they were walking into the store Papio noticed that there was a bank across the street. He smiled and thought, *It's time to get money*. He entered the store and grabbed a cheap-looking OU Sooner hat and put it onto his head. He then went to the counter and grabbed a pair of cheap shades from a rack and told Hugh, "Pay for this shit, dog. I'm about to run across the street and cash my UNICOR check."

"Gotcha, Papio," Hugh said as he grabbed a six pack of beer.

Papio went back to the truck and opened the glove box and grabbed Hugh's Glock. He knew that Hugh kept a gun and it was right where he figured it would be. He slid the gun into the small of his back and quickly stepped across the street toward the Mid-First Bank of El Reno, Oklahoma. He entered the bank and smiled when he saw that there weren't many people inside of the bank. Three of the four counters were open and there was only one person at each of them.

He stepped up to the third counter just as a small, old lady stepped away from it. He quickly pulled out Hugh's Glock and said, "Do not scream nor try to push the alarm and you will live another day. Please give me all of the hundreds and fifties out of your drawer, ma'am, and everything will be okay. I know you have been trained not to disobey when something like this goes down, so follow your training and everything will be good."

The bank teller did as she was told and slowly stacked all of the money onto the counter. Papio watched her with a trained eye. When he figured there was close to $30,000 on top of the counter he told the teller, "Listen carefully. My friend to your left is going to watch you until I am outside. If you move to tell anyone what went down he will start shooting and you will be the first person shot," he warned.

The bank teller looked to her left and saw a black man waiting for one of the other tellers to become available so he could handle his business. When she saw that the man was wearing a similar-looking OU hat as Papio she figured that, yes, they were in fact together. There was no way she was going to disobey him.

Papio followed her eyes and knew that she was going for everything he told her. *Good.* He then scooped the money off of the counter and said, "Have a nice day."

When he was outside he jogged across the street and jumped inside of Hugh's truck and said, "All right, dog, let's roll. I really need to see my bitch."

Hugh started laughing and said, "Yeah, after three years I bet you do!"

Papio smiled at Hugh, not because of what he said but because there was no commotion whatsoever at the bank as they drove by. *Ain't been out the Feds fifteen minutes and already hit a bank. Damn I'm good,* he said to himself with a smile on his face.

Forty-five minutes later Hugh pulled into the driveway of Papio's home. There were over 3,800 immaculate square feet of quality features throughout. Papio's home in Oklahoma City was one of his most prized possessions. There was an elevator inside of the four-car garage as well as a fireplace inside of the master suite, and a media room with the top-of-the-line LCD televisions with some very expensive furniture imported from overseas. All of this plus a state-of-the-art indoor gymnasium.

Papio's smile brightened when Hugh stopped his truck and he saw Mani as she came outside, looking absolutely gorgeous dressed down in a pair of shorts and a wife-beater. Even with rollers in her hair she looked fucking beautiful to Papio. He turned toward Hugh and told him, "Give me a couple of hours and meet me at the Tree Lounge. I got some moves we need to make."

"All right. You need some ends? I know that small-ass UNICOR check ain't gon' hold you off."

Papio smiled and said, "Nah, I'm good. I'm going to hit the mall and do some shopping, then make some calls because we got to get shit right out here before I bounce."

"When are you leaving?"

"In a day or so, depends on what goes down tonight. I'll put you up on everything when we hook up later. Let me go as you can see I got some pussy to go tear up." Papio gave Hugh a pound and then jumped out of the truck.

Mani couldn't believe her eyes when she saw her man jump out of Hugh's truck. Her heart was beating so fast she felt as if she was about to have a heart attack. *Oh, my God, oh my God, please, God, don't let this nigga fuck me up,* she thought as she held her small hands over her mouth and watched Papio stroll confidently toward her. When he was standing in front of her she stared into his light brown eyes, trying to gauge his mood. When he smiled at her she gave a sigh of relief and said, "Hi, babe." She then got onto her tiptoes and gave him a soft kiss on his lips. She then wrapped her arms around him and gave him a tight hug. "Boy, how in the hell did you get out of the Feds?"

He pulled from her embrace and stared at her for a moment and said, "I told you Hugh was making moves for me. My man handled that shit and I got my immediate release papers yesterday. While you were so busy talking shit on the phone my release was being handled."

"Come on, Papio, don't even go there," she said and dreaded that conversation as she led him inside of the house. *No way am I going to let this nigga get to tripping the fuck out on me. I'm about to fuck his brains out and everything will be good,* she thought as she led him upstairs to the bedroom.

Papio was grinning mischievously as he followed her upstairs. He knew what she was thinking and he was all the way with it. After three years he needed to get his nuts out of the sand. He'd been deprived for too damn long. After he fucked the shit out of her she was going to be in for one hell of surprise. He thought as he stared at her firm ass, *Yeah, this is going to be a nice welcome home shot of pussy.*

As soon as they were inside of the bedroom Mani let go of his hand and pulled off her wife-beater and let Papio get a good look at her firm D cups. She knew how much he loved her big titties. She then got extra with it as she slowly pulled her shorts off. She put her hands on her hips when they were off and said, "You miss this, babe? 'Cause I sure as hell been missing that," she said as she pointed toward the bulge that was inside of his Armani slacks.

"Take those rollers out of your hair," he said and began to undress. He smiled as he stared at her long, silky jet-black hair with blond streaks running through it. *It's a damn shame this bitch ain't shit. I would love to keep her around but she gots to go,* he thought as he stepped to her and gave her a kiss with so much passion she felt as if everything was going to be A-Okay with them for a very long time. Little did she realize the reason that kiss was so passionate was because it was his way of releasing her from his system.

He pulled back and told her, "Lie down." She took a few steps backward and lay on top of the huge bed and smiled seductively at him. He climbed on top of her and began to kiss her slowly. He started from her lips and worked his way toward her toes, making a short stop at her pussy and began to devour it. He bit, nibbled, and sucked her clit until she was in a frenzy. She came several times before he stopped and put his very well-endowed dick deep inside of her. He thought he would come quick especially after not having sex for such a long time. He was mildly surprised as it took him over twenty minutes to release his first nut. Mani was loving every minute of their sexing because she knew that she kept her pussy nice and tight. She was really glad that she hadn't wasted her time by fucking with any of those scrub-ass niggas in the city. That was the best decision she had ever made. It had been three whole years she went without having sex; just her and her sex toys got her through the hard, lonely nights. Now that she was getting the real thing she went ballistic. After Papio finally came she turned him over onto his back and began to suck his dick as if her life depended on it. Papio was in heaven as he watched her suck the hell out of his dick. When he came again it felt even more powerful than the first nut he busted. Mani's head game was still vicious and she still loved to swallow. He smiled and watched her swallow every drop of his semen. When she was finished she wiped her mouth and climbed on top of him and inserted his dick back inside of her soaking wet pussy.

"Yeahhhhhhh, ooohhhhh, babe, you don't know how bad I've missed this dick," she said as she gyrated her hips and worked her pussy slowly on top of his manhood. She came quickly and her orgasm triggered another one from Papio. They came together this time and fell asleep in each other's arms totally spent.

A couple of hours later Papio woke up and went and took a long, hot shower. After he was finished he came back into the bedroom to see Mani was still sleeping soundly. He stepped to the bed and slapped her on her ass hard and said, "Wake the fuck up, Maroni."

"Ouch! Babe, that hurt; what you hit me so hard for?" she asked as she sat up in the bed.

"To get your ass up that's why. You gots to start packing your shit."

"Packing? Where are we going?"

He smiled at her and said, "We ain't going nowhere. Your ass is getting the fuck out of my house."

"What? What are you talking about, babe? You know I don't have nowhere else to go. You're all I got, Papio," she said and started to cry.

"Is that right? You should have thought about that shit when you was busy bumping all that fly shit to me on the phone." He shook his head in disgust and said, "I gave you everything I had, bitch. I made sure that you were taken care of in every possible way while I was done. And what do I get for that shit? Disrespect like I'm some chump-type nigga or some shit. You blew it, champ. Now get your ass up and take every last thing that I've ever bought you. The only reason why I'm giving that shit to you is because you did respect me enough not to fuck any of these clown-ass niggas. If Hugh would have told me any different you'd be getting kicked the fuck out without a damn thang."

"But, babe, I—"

Papio put his index finger to his lips and said, "Shh-hhh. No talking, bitch, you got packing to do. You are out of here. If I come back up here and you aren't packed in the next thirty minutes I'm going to start beating the shit out of you until you get the fucking picture. Now handle your business, bitch."

He spoke with such calm contempt that she knew he was serious and she was not about to test his gangster. Once Papio was angered a bitch could get hurt for real. She jumped out of the bed and started to pack her things. *Damn, I fucked up,* she said to herself as she slipped back into her shorts. *Fuck!*

CHAPTER FOUR

After Mani finished packing she asked Papio, "Are you going to drop me off at a hotel, babe?"

Papio started laughing and said, "Fuck nah! You can have the Charger, bitch. Never liked that cheap-ass car any-fucking-way."

She sighed and said, "For what it's worth, Papio, know that I still love you."

"Save it, bitch, and get to stepping."

With tears sliding down her face she grabbed her purse and started taking her stuff out to the Dodge Charger in the garage.

Papio watched her with a satisfied smile on his face. He checked his watch and saw that it was one in the afternoon. He grabbed the phone and called Hugh. When Hugh answered the phone he told him, "I'm on my way to the Tree; meet me there in thirty minutes."

"I'm there, dog," Hugh said and hung up the phone.

When Papio heard the Charger start up he smiled and said, "Good riddance, bitch!"

Thirty minutes later Papio and Hugh were sitting inside of the Tree Lounge, sipping some Patrón. Papio had his eyes on a cute light-skinned honey as she was walking around, asking everybody inside of the lounge if they wanted to purchase a book that her baby daddy wrote while in prison. Papio shook his head and told

Hugh, "Check it, we got to hit up the mall for a minute so I can snatch up stuff and get my gear back up to par. After that we got a lick to hit."

"A lick?"

"That's right. We gon' hit that punk-ass nigga Lee up. He gots to run that dough he owe, with interest. I want you to call his punk ass and tell him that you got some serious shit you need to holla at him about. If he gets funky with it let him know you got a hundred Gs to spend. That greedy mothafucka will tell you to come straight to his pad."

"Damn, Papio, you ain't wasting no fucking time huh?"

Papio heard Hugh but ignored his question, as he was watching the television mounted over the bar, as the news was reporting about a bank robbery that had taken place earlier that day out in the city of El Reno. He smiled when he saw the video footage of the robbery. There was no way he could be recognized with those cheap shades and hat he had on when he robbed the bank. He had a grin on his face when he told Hugh, "Time is money, my nigga. I've wasted the last three years; I don't have no more time to waste. Come on, let's bounce."

$36,000 wasn't shit to Papio but it was enough to get his gear right. It was a must that he looked good. As soon as they hit the Quail Springs Mall Papio got busy spending. Everything from expensive jeans, shirts, and tailor-made suits by the very best designers in the fashion industry. His everyday gear would consist of Ed Hardy apparel and a different fresh pair of Nike Air Forces or Jordans. But when it was time to get real fly with it, it was suits by ThomBrowne, Ralph Lauren, Ravazzolo, Calvin Klein and of course his favorite, Armani. Brooks Brothers, Italian loafers, and any type of Mauri alligator were his choices of dress shoe.

After spending three hours inside of the mall Papio bought so much stuff that he only had $3,000 left from his bank heist.

Hugh couldn't help but envy Papio; the man had some serious style. He hoped that just by being in his presence he would learn how to be as debonair as Papio. Not only was Papio a fly dude he was a straight gangster. At five foot nine and chubby the chances of Hugh ever becoming anything remotely close to being like Papio were slim and none. Some was blessed to have it and some wasn't. Hugh definitely fell under the category of not being blessed at all. Still, he had high hopes of changing that when they became filthy rich. And there wasn't a doubt in his mind that as long as he stayed down with Papio that would become a reality real soon.

Papio decided to stop at the food court to get a quick bite to eat. Hugh could then make the call to Lee to set up his next move for the day. They were sitting down, eating some BBQ wings from KFC, when Papio smiled suddenly and said, "Well, I'll be damned."

"What's up?" asked Hugh

"Nothing. Make the call. I'll be right back," Papio said as he stood and started walking toward Ms. Wickerson. She was standing in line, waiting to order something to eat from Chick-fil-A. When she saw him approaching her eyes lit up and she gave him a mega-watt smile. Papio stared at her looking all good in a pair of tight-fitting low-slung jeans, which showed the top edges of her black thong. The short baby tee she was wearing made her look as if she were in her twenties in-stead of her late thirties. Light brown skin, sexy brown eyes, and an ass that made him become semi erect just by looking at it.

"Look at you looking all jazzy this afternoon," he said.

"Hello, Papio. How does it feel to be a free man?"

He pointed toward all of the bags, where Hugh was sitting, talking on his cell phone, and said, "It feels real good to come home and blow thirty-plus grand on some new gear. So, what are you doing besides looking extremely fine in this mall?"

"Since today is Friday I decided to come to the city and hang out a little."

"Yeah? Where do you stay?"

"In Yukon. I'm renting a nice house not too far from the FCI so everything could be convenient. I like coming to the city because there's so much to do down here compared to Yukon."

"A lot to do? Is that right? Wow, that's a new one to me. If you think there's a lot to do down here wait until you get to Cali; you'll probably pass out."

"I can't wait. So tell me, have you had a chance to take care of yourself yet?"

He grinned and asked, "Do you mean have I got me some pussy yet? Yeah, I got my nuts out of the sand a little bit, why?"

She shrugged and said, "Just wondering."

"Wished you could have been my first huh?"

She shook her head from side to side and said, "You are a mess, Papio."

"That I am, Ms. Wickerson."

"Brandy."

"Brandy it is."

He checked his watch and said, "Check it, I have to take care of some business and after that I'm free. Why don't I call you say around nine o'clock so we can kick it for the rest of the evening?"

"The evening? Why not for the rest of the night?" she asked boldly.

He laughed and said, "Whatever you like, *mami*. So
stay around the town and don't go back your way and
I'll hit you up so we can hang out."

"You want me to hang around the city until you call
me? What am I going to do while I'm waiting for your
call, Papio?"

He reached inside of his pocket and pulled out the
$3,000 he had left and gave it to her. "Take this and
do some shopping and get something nice to wear.
We'll do dinner and hit the club or something later on.
I'll call you in a few hours after my business has been
handled."

She stared at the handful of one hundred dollar and
fifty dollar bills and smiled. *This young man don't be
playing,* she thought. She gave him a kiss on his lips
and said, "Okay, daddy, I'll be waiting for your call."

"Daddy huh?" He shook his head, smiled, and said,
"I like that. Talk to you in a little bit, *mami*."

He left her and rejoined Hugh. "You get that nigga
on the line?"

"Yeah. He want me to meet him at his house in a
hour."

"I knew that greedy nigga would play it like that.
Come on, I need you to get me a celly. After that I'm
going to my pad and get my strap. When you get to his
house let him know that you're waiting for your man
to call you with the ends. I'll hit you on your cell when
I'm down the street from his spot. If he's alone like I
expect him to be let me know that everything is good. If
someone else is there ask me do I have all of the ends.
Then I'll give you the adjustments to the play. Got me?"

Hugh smiled at his main man and said, "Yep."

"Good. Come on, let's get up out of here." Papio noticed Brandy as she got her food and stood there, staring at them, as they grabbed all of his bags and walked

out of the food court. He smiled and blew her a kiss. *If the boys in the Feds could see old Papio now . . .* he thought with a smile on his face.

Papio pulled his Range Rover into the garage and began to gather up his purchases from the mall. He went into his home and set his stuff down in the living room and ran upstairs to his bedroom. He opened his closet, moved some of his shoeboxes out of his way, knelt down to his floor safe and began punching in the combination to open it. When the safe was open he pulled out two 9 mm pistols and then grabbed two silencers, one for each weapon. He loved using silencers when he handled his business, kept everything real nice and quiet like. He closed the safe and stepped to the bed. He sat down and began twisting the silencers onto each weapon. He popped out each clip and made sure that each gun was fully loaded. He then jacked a live round into each chamber and smiled. He tossed the guns onto the bed and checked his watch as he went back to the closet. He grabbed a pair of black Red Monkey jeans and a black sweatshirt. He changed clothes quickly and grabbed his weapons, then went downstairs. The telephone rang just as he was grabbing his keys. He stopped in the kitchen and answered it. "Hello?"

"Hey, babe, I know you're really mad at me but can't we get together and talk about this some more?" asked Mani.

"Check it, ain't shit to talk about, Mani. You did what you did and you should know me good enough that once you cross that line, it's a wrap. So find you another nigga to take care of your ass."

"Babe, if there was someone else worthy of this pussy I would have moved on a long time ago. You my heart babe; where else will I ever find a man as good as you?"

"You should have thought about how good I was to your ass when you was being slick at the mouth. The only advice I can give your ass is to move on because we're through." Before she got all emotional on him he said, "I gots to go. I'll see you in traffic." He hung up the phone, wondering if he should give her another chance. By the time he was back inside of the Range he thought about how good Brandy was looking in them jeans she had on and started laughing. "Hell nah! That bitch can't get another chance. I got a older and way classier broad on my line. Fuck Mani!"

Papio pulled out his new cell phone and called Hugh just as he got to the corner of Lee's neighborhood. He let his eyes roam up and down the street to see if everything was cool. Satisfied, he smiled and waited for Hugh to answer. "What's good, my nigga?" he asked when Hugh answered the phone.

"Everything is good, dog."

"Get ready then 'cause here I come," Papio said as he hung up the phone. He tossed his cell phone onto the passenger's seat and once again did a quick survey of the neighborhood. He eased into Lee's driveway and parked the Range behind Hugh's F-150. When he jumped out of his truck he smiled when he saw Lee standing in the doorway of his home with a chrome 9 mm in his hand. "Damn, Lee, like that? What the fuck is the gun for, nigga?"

Lee had a shocked expression on his face when he saw who had pulled into his driveway. "What the fuck? How the hell did you get out of the Feds, nigga?"

Papio shrugged as he stepped toward him and said, "You should've known that they weren't going to be able to keep a real one like myself in a cage, fool. Now put that fucking pistol down and show a nigga some love."

Lee put his gun in the small of his back, opened the screen door, gave Papio a manly hug, and said, "I'm glad you're out of that bitch, Papio. These streets done got real fucked up since you've been gone. Some real niggas are needed out in this bitch for real."

"Yeah, I've heard. Hugh told me all about how wild these youngsters have been acting. Don't panic, nigga. You know it's time to get that fucking paper right?"

"You know it. So, what's this shit Hugh talking about? You know damn well your money ain't no good with me. I got you with whatever you need. I got them chips I owe plus I got a nice blessing for your ass too."

Papio touched his heart with a closed fist and said, "That's love right there, my nigga." He took a seat next to Hugh on Lee's couch.

"This is how we gon' do this: I'll hit you off with two bricks plus a hundred of that three I owe you. Then we'll go get our party on. They got some fly-ass clubs down in Bricktown so we should all go out and give you a proper welcome home party."

"Two bricks? A hundred Gs? Come on, Lee, you've had three years to flip those ends." He paused and took a look around Lee's home and added, "And from the looks of how you've redone you tilt you've flipped that shit several times. Don't insult me, baby boy. Give me mine and let me spend this hundred I got with you. You know I got to make my moves ASAP, dog. I ain't got time for any playing or partying. I got three years to make up for and I'm hungry."

"I feel that. But I don't have that other change right now. I got some shit in the streets I got to scoop and then I'll tighten you up. You know I ain't gon' try to play you, Papio."

Papio gave him a nod and said, "Hope not. All right, dog. That's cool. Tell me, who you getting your work from now?"

Papio noticed how Lee flinched when he asked that question. "Just like I thought; this bitch-ass nigga is fucking with those punk-ass Cubans."

Lee smiled and said, "Your Cuban connect came through and blessed me when you got knocked. The offer they put on the table was so sweet I had to jump on it, Papio. I know, now that you're back in the game they'll put you right back on, so it looks like I'm going to have to step up my hustle game."

At least this bitch-ass nigga didn't try to insult me and try to lie about shit, he thought as he said, "Don't panic, dog. There's enough money out here for all of us. It's time to eat good again, baby, believe that." Papio turned toward Hugh and said, "Ain't that right, my nigga?"

"Oh, for sure," replied Hugh.

"All right, Lee, let's handle this business so we can bounce. We got shit to do and money to make."

"That's right. I'll be right back."

Papio knew that Lee was waiting for this opportunity; he knew that Lee was about to go into the other room and call the Cubans to let them know that he was out. What Lee didn't know was Papio had no intentions at all of letting him make that phone call. As soon as Lee turned to go into the next room Papio sprang to his feet with the agility of a leopard, with both of his silenced pistols firing away. He hit Lee three times in the back and twice in the back of his head. Lee was dead before his body hit the carpet.

"What the fuck? Damn, Papio, what you do? Why you blast that nigga like that?" Hugh asked, scared out of his mind.

Papio turned toward Hugh and pointed one of his guns at him and said, "Shut the fuck up, nigga, and come help me find this bitch-ass nigga's money and work. Did you think I was going to let this nigga live so he could get at the Cubans and let them know I was back?" Before Hugh could answer his question Papio said, "Don't answer that, fool, just come help me get this shit so we can get the fuck."

Hugh stood nervously and followed Papio into Lee's bedroom and began to help him search for the drugs as well as Lee's money. Hugh felt as if he was going to be sick as he stepped over Lee's lifeless body and entered the bedroom. It took twenty minutes but Papio and Hugh found everything that they were looking for: ten kilos of cocaine and a little over $500,000. Papio smiled as he held up a large stack of one hundred dollar bills and waved them in the air. "See, that nigga did have the chips to pay me what he owed me. Just like I thought, that bitch was trying to stall so he could get at those Cuban mothafuckas. That's why he's a dead man now."

"Like always, you're right, dog. Fuck that nigga," Hugh said, trying to sound tougher than he really was.

Papio shook his head and thought, *Bitch. Fuck it, might as well hit two birds with one stone.* He got to his feet and put the money and drugs onto Lee's king-sized bed and pulled the comforter over all of it. He then told Hugh to take it outside to the Range. Hugh came and grabbed the money and drugs off of the bed.

As he turned to walk out of the bedroom Papio sighed, made the sign of the cross across his chest, and said, "Sorry, dog." Hugh stopped and turned around just as Papio pulled the trigger of his weapon. He shot Hugh two times in the throat. Hugh's eyes bulged and looked as if they were going to pop out of their sockets as he dropped the comforter and grabbed his throat. He fell to his knees and Papio watched as his life slowly ended.

After grabbing the money and taking it out to the Range, Papio came back inside of the house and began to clean up. He grabbed a towel from the bathroom and began to wipe down everything he touched. After that was finished he stepped over to where Lee's body was lying and put the silenced gun that he used to kill Hugh in Lee's right hand. He placed his finger on the trigger and laid it at an angle so it would look as if he shot Hugh. He then went to where Hugh was lying flat on his face and adjusted him so everything could look like there was more than one robber in this home invasion. Papio had it all thought out; he knew how the police would figure it so he made sure everything was just right. They would think that Lee had shot Hugh in the throat and then was shot by the second home invader. At least that's what he wanted them to think. *It doesn't really matter though, because there is no way they will be able to tie me to this shit anyway,* he thought as he stood and smiled. *Time to go see Brandy.*

CHAPTER FIVE

Papio was in a jovial mood as he drove toward his home. Everything was going just as he hoped it would and as far as he was concerned he had just gotten started. He grabbed his cell phone off of the passenger's seat and dialed the number off of the card Brandy gave him when he was in her office.

She answered the phone on the first ring. "Are you ready for me yet, daddy?" she asked sweetly when she answered the phone.

"Yeah, I'm ready. Where are you?"

"At this beauty shop on the east side."

"What's the name of it?"

"We Do Good Hair."

He smiled. "Okay, that's Kammy's shop. I know where you're at. I'll be there in ten minutes."

"What are we going to get into tonight, daddy?"

That daddy shit is getting me horny than a mothafucka, he thought. "We're going to go out to eat and then I thought we'd hit up this club called Broadway for a little bit. I need to see if I can bump into a few old associates and the chances are high that they will be there. After that it's back to my place so we can make it do what it do, *mami.*"

"All night long, daddy?"

He smiled and said, "Yeah, all night long. I'll see you in a few minutes."

Ten minutes later Papio pulled into the parking lot of We Do Good Hair and jumped out of the Range with his swagger in full swing. As soon as he entered the beauty shop he saw Brandy sitting in a chair getting a manicure. Kammy, the owner of the beauty shop, saw him and screamed, "Papio! When did you get out, boy?"

Kammy was a bad older broad. For her age she had a lot of the young niggas around Oklahoma City gone off of her thickness and those firm-ass fake titties she had done a few years ago. She and Papio had always been cool. She was a tad too much for his taste so he kept everything between them on the friendship level, even though he knew he could have hit that years ago if he wanted to.

"I got out earlier today," he said as he gave her a hug. "Damn, Kammy, your ass is still looking good I see."

She smiled and said, "You know I got to stay in the gym and keep it right with all of these big-booty girls out here sucking up all the good niggas."

"I know that's right." He turned toward Brandy and asked, "How much longer are you going to be, *mami?*"

"She's almost finished, daddy."

"All right, I'll be outside chopping it up with Kammy." He turned back to Kammy, who had a frown on her face as she stared at Brandy and then back at him. He grinned and said, "Come holla at me real quick, Kam."

Once they were outside of the shop Kammy said, "So, you're into older women now I see. What, the Feds changed your taste or something?" she asked with much attitude.

He laughed and said, "Something like that. But for real, look at her. She don't look like she's an old broad. She got a tight, banging-ass body just like you, baby."

Kammy smiled at his compliment and said, "You're so full of shit, Papio."

"Check it, give me the scoop on these streets real quick. Who's doing what, and who's making the best moves? I need a feel for shit before I get back cracking."

"For real, those Cubans got shit locked down as far as the yayo goes. They got your boy Lee working hard for they ass. That money is still good, bricks are going for eighteen or 18.5. But the real money out here now is those fucking X pills and the Purple weed. There's some young niggas out here from Dallas who are making a killing with the Purp and the pills."

"Yeah? They ain't tried to holla at your fine ass yet?"

"Kinda, but you know me, I ain't jumping at no niggas first move; they got to earn this kitty."

He laughed and said, "I know that's right. All right, do me this: find out as much as you can about those fools for the next couple of months so when I come back we can send those niggas back to Dallas. No need for no new niggas getting all this city money."

"I know that's right, Papio. But how we gon' send them back to Dallas, dead or alive?"

He stared at her hard for a moment and answered, "That will be their choice. Don't much matter to me how they make that ride back down I-35."

She shrugged her shoulders and said, "Me neither."

"That's my girl."

"Hmph. If I'm your girl why I can't get me none of that dick, you fine-ass mothafucka?"

"It ain't over until it's over, baby. Let's get this money right first. Feel me?"

"Yeah, I feel your ass. Tell me, where Mani ass at?"

"Dismissed. She got a little too big for her panties."

"What? Oh, that bitch is gon' get straight clowned as soon as I see her extra out ass. She was walking around this mothafucka like she was the shit for real. I can't wait to see her."

"Don't sweat that punk shit, just get on those Dallas fools for me. We got bigger shit to worry about than Mani's wack ass."

"Gotcha. Here comes your broad. You got a number yet?"

"Yeah." Brandy came out of the shop while Papio gave Kammy his cell number. After he finished he said, "All right, girl, hit me when you got something for me."

"I will. Be careful out here, Papio, these young, stupid niggas have been acting up since you've been gone."

"Do you really think they can keep up with a nigga like me?"

She smiled. "Hell nah!" She turned and went back inside of her packed beauty shop.

Papio turned toward Brandy and asked, "You good, *mami?*"

"Mm-hm. Good and ready for you, daddy."

He checked the time and saw that it was twenty minutes after nine. "All right, come on, follow me to my pad so we can change and go enjoy the rest of the evening."

"I'm with you, daddy."

Papio heard Brandy gasp as they entered his home. She couldn't believe her eyes as she walked around his living room looking at all of the expensive furniture. *I knew Papio was for real but daaaaaammmmmmnnnn,* she said to herself. She stepped into the media room and put her hands over her mouth when she saw the expensive LCD television and sound system.

Papio smiled as he watched her walk around his home. "Come on, *mami,* you'll have time later for a full tour of the spot. Let's go get dressed so we can get something to eat. I'm hungry as a mothafucka." He then led the way upstairs to the bedroom and pointed toward the bathroom. "You'll find some towels and everything you'll need in there. Go on and take a shower and get ready. I have a few calls to make real quick."

"Okay," she said as she grabbed the clothes that she bought earlier with the money he gave her. She smiled because she knew when he saw what she was going to put on he was going to be pleased, very pleased indeed.

Papio went back downstairs to the media room and turned on the television to SportsCenter and watched as Stu Scott got his sports reporting on. He grabbed the phone and made a call he had been waiting to make all day long. When his mother answered the phone he smiled and said, "Mama Mia, *que pasa madre mia?*"

There was a brief pause and then his mother asked, "*Eres tu mijo?*"

"Sí, it's me, *Madre.*"

"Where are you?"

He started laughing and said, "I got out this morning, *Madre.* I don't have time to explain everything to you right now so you're going to have to be patient. I'll be home in a day or so. Most likely Monday evening. I'll give you a call to let you know exactly when okay?"

"Sí. Do you need for me to do anything, *mijo?*"

"Is that money you have secure, *Madre?*"

"Sí. Every last peso. I haven't touched it at all. Your friend Quentin takes cares of everything just fine."

"Good. Okay, I'll give you a call after I've made my reservation. I have to go get my identification renewed and then I'll be on my way. Talk to you soon, Mama Mia."

"God bless you, *mijo.* Please be careful."

"Always, *Madre,* always," he said as he hung up the phone. Hearing his mother's voice always made him sentimental. He sat back on his comfortable Italian leather sofa and thought about his mother. No matter what he got himself into she was the one constant in his life; she never turned her back on him and always had his back. When he went to jail he told her he would never let those people take him away from her for too long. She begged to come see him but that was something he knew that he wouldn't have been able to handle. Now that he was out he couldn't wait to see that beautiful woman. He became emotional as he thought about all of the pain she endured by the hand of his no-good-ass father. An evil smile spread across his face as he thought back to the day that he took his black-ass father's life. Papio had witnessed his father put his hands on his lovely mother one too many times and for that his father paid with his life. That was a long time ago and he didn't regret it for one second.

Papio was done reminiscing about his past. He only wanted to focus on the future. He hopped off the sofa and went to the downstairs bathroom to take a shower.

By the time he finished showering Brandy was dressed and was sitting in the media room, watching television. She was watching ESPN highlights showing Kobe Bryant doing a spectacular slam dunk over some unlucky NBA player. Papio heard the television playing and stepped inside the media room with only a towel wrapped around his waist. When he saw Brandy sitting on the sofa looking like a super-fine model chick, video girl, and classy woman all rolled in one he smiled. *One of God's perfect creations,* he thought as he stood there, staring at her. She felt his presence, turned, and smiled. "I see you took a shower without me, daddy. Why?" she asked with a pout on her full lips.

"Because we wouldn't be able to go out and enjoy the night if I would have. Like I told you, I'm hungry. Give me a minute and I'll be ready so we can get up out of here."

"Okay. I'll come up and lotion that gorgeous phy-sique of yours."

He shook his head and said, "Only if you be good, *mami.*"

She glanced at his body with lust in her eyes and said, "I'll try."

Papio couldn't help himself once they were inside of the bedroom. He turned around and grabbed her around her waist and gave her some serious tongue action. After a full minute she pulled from his embrace and asked, "I thought you wanted me to be good. How can I be good when you're getting me so hot; daddy?"

He started laughing, took a step back from her, and said, "Turn around and let me look at how damn good you're looking."

She did as she was told and did a circle so he could take in the full effect of her outfit. She was wearing the hell out of an Inga dress by Herve Leger, which hugged her curvaceous body as if the material from the dress was a second skin. The split that ran up the right side of that dress showed off her well-toned legs. The Given-chy stilettos she had on her pretty little feet completed the outfit to perfection. *My God, I'm going to have a ball with this bad-ass female tonight,* he thought as he stared at her. Her shoulder-length hair looked so silky and smooth he thought she had to have gotten a perm it was so straight. He shook his head and said, "Damn, *mami,* you look hotter than Saturn. Let me get dressed so we can get the fuck out of here before I tear your ass up."

She started laughing as she said, "Go get the lotion so I can have a reason to put my hands all over that body, daddy."

He smiled as he went into the bathroom and came back with a bottle of his favorite scented lotion by Sean John. While she rubbed her hands all over his body he felt his dick become hard as a rock. "Uh-huh!" He jumped up and said, "Nah, *mami,* let me do that shit." He wanted to savor the build-up until they fucked later that night.

He laughed as he went back into the bathroom and finished taking care of his business. He came out and went into the closet and grabbed one of the suits he bought earlier. He chose the black pinstriped two-button wool suit by Ralph Lauren. He then went to his tie rack and chose a silk tie by Prada. Black Mauri alligator shoes completed his outfit.

"Mmmm. I'm going to do some damage to you, daddy. You look too damn good."

After adding a pair of gold cuff links to his sleeves he smiled at her and said, "We will see, *mami,* we will see." He stepped back into the bathroom and hit himself with some smell good. After a couple of squirts of his Dolce & Gabbana cologne he was ready to do the damn thing. He came out of the bathroom and led the way downstairs to the garage.

"You wanna choose our ride for the night, *mami?*" He smiled as he presented his collection of cars to Brandy.

Her heart felt as if it were going to stop when she stared at the cream-colored 8600 Mercedes-Benz sitting on twenty-four-inch chrome rims. She looked to the left of the Benz and had to catch her breath at the bright red convertible 750-series BMW, Range Rover 600, and a Beamer. *My God,* she said to herself. She turned toward him and said, "The six, daddy; we have to roll that."

"The six it is then. Come on, let's hit it."

They ate a good Cajun meal at Pearls on the Lake; then Papio took Brandy to Club Broadway, one of the

He Don't Play Fair 49

hottest clubs in Oklahoma City. As soon as they entered the club all eyes were on them. Papio loved the attention and he made sure that his swagger was on full blast. A few old acquaintances came up to welcome him back home. Though he was originally from California, Oklahoma was just like his home since he had been hustling out there since the late nineties. He took Brandy to the VIP section and ordered a bottle of Patrón as well as a bottle of rosé. They sipped champagne and took shots of Patrón. The tequila had Papio feeling the urge to get his groove on. He wanted to show Brandy off to the haters he saw watching him. He took her out onto the dance floor and they proceeded to get their groove on. They were both vibing each other. It was everything Papio could do to not tear Brandy's dress off right there on the dance floor. After four songs Papio was winded, thirsty, and horny as a motherfucker. He started to lead Brandy back to their table but she needed to go to the bathroom.

While she was gone Papio was sipping some water when Mani came up and got in his face. "You ain't shit, Papio. You shook me for that old-ass bitch you got up in here? That's real fucked up."

Papio smiled. "Please, you can't be serious. Have you really taken a good look at her? She's a dime times fifty, bitch. Get the fuck before I get to acting in this place."

Seeing that this approach wasn't going to work Mani changed her tone. "Please, babe, can we at least talk civilly?" She put her hand on his knee.

"Nope. Now get the fuck on. I'm not going to tell your ass again, Mani."

Mani was turning to leave just as Brandy came back to the table. They made eye contact and Brandy could tell that there was some history between the two. So in order to claim her piece she sat on Papio's lap. "Whew,

I'm tired, daddy; can we go back to your place now? I'm ready to make you feel real good."

Papio smiled at Mani as she stared at him because he knew what Brandy was up to. He finger waved good-bye to her and said, "Bye, Mani. Good luck with your wasted life, bitch." He took Brandy from his lap, pulled out five one hundred dollar bills from his pocket and set them onto the table. He grabbed Brandy's hand and said, "Yeah, let's go make some magic, *mami.*" He made sure to brush past Mani as they left the club.

An hour and a half of straight sexing had Papio feeling real good as they were lying down on the couch inside of the media room. Their sexing started on the staircase and somehow ended in the media room.

He didn't have a clue as to how this happened; all he did know was that Brandy was a fucking tiger! The pussy was the bomb with a capital B. *She is definitely going to be around for a little while,* he thought as he grabbed the remote and turned the television on to the news. They were wrapped in each other's arms, watching the news as a reporter was reporting on the bank robbery that had taken place earlier that day in the city of El Reno. After a commercial another news reporter was reporting a double homicide in the Wildewood neighborhood. The police suspected it was a botched drug deal/robbery. Papio smiled.

Brandy shook her head and said, "Dear God, this world is slowly going crazy."

A bank lick for thirty-plus Gs, a $500,000 lick plus ten bricks and, to top it all off, I've just finished fucking one of the baddest bitches in the city. Not bad, Papio, not bad at all. What a motherfucking day! What a motherfucking day! he thought as he started to play with Brandy's titties.

CHAPTER SIX

Papio opened his eyes with a shocked smile on his face. Brandy looked up from his crotch area with his dick inside of her mouth and smiled. She continued to give him one of the best blow jobs he'd ever had in his life. When he came he came hard and she swallowed every drop of his sperm. She smacked her lips and produced a condom out of nowhere as if she was a magician or some shit. She tore the wrapper open and gently placed it onto his semi-erect penis. She put him back inside of her mouth for a few deep strokes to get him fully erect and then climbed on top of him and rode Papio for close to twenty minutes, bringing herself to three very satisfying orgasms and one monster orgasm for Papio that put him back to sleep.

When Papio opened his eyes again it was close to noon. He got out of bed and went to the bathroom to get himself together. He smelled food being cooked downstairs and thought, *She cooks too? Definitely a keeper.*

Brandy had on a pair of Papio's boxer shorts and his wifebeater, looking like she was twenty-five years old instead of in her late thirties. When she saw him enter the kitchen she smiled and pointed toward the dining room table and told him, "Have a seat. I'll bring your food to you in two minutes, daddy."

He smiled and did as she told him. While seated at the dining room table he began to think about the moves he had to make for the day. He wasn't worried about the Cubans yet because it would take them a minute before they realized he was back on the streets. Those bitch niggas he saw at the club wasn't knowing the business with him and the Cubans so that was cool. *I gots to check a few traps and set shit up for when I come back to get at those Dallas fools.*

Brandy came into the dining room, carrying a plate of food smelling so good it made his stomach growl. She set a plate with a juicy steak, scrambled eggs, and some home-fried potatoes in front of him. She sat down across from him and watched him dig into his food vigorously. *I know this man is a bad boy but I can see myself loving him with all that I have, but I need to slow down. Papio isn't that type of man. Enjoy this and take it for what it's worth,* she reminded herself.

Papio noticed her staring at him, paused from eating his food, and asked, "What you thinking about, *mami?* You look like you got something heavy on your mind."

She shrugged her shoulders and said, "I'm good. I keep replaying yesterday and last night in my mind. It's so wild because I have been acting so out of character with you, daddy. You got me going way too fast for my tastes. This is kind of scary," she replied honestly.

"Baby, it is what it is. I'm feeling you, you're feeling me, so let's enjoy the moment and try not to get too caught up. I got plenty of moves to make for the next few months so shit is going to be hectic until I can get back acclimated with the world. My money has to get back right before I can even think about anything else seriously."

"So, money is what motivated you, daddy?"

Staring directly into her eyes he said, "Hell yeah, money! Can't you tell? I have to have the finer things in life and no one is going to give me shit, so I gots to do me."

"Aren't you worried about going back to prison? Is money really worth the risk of getting all of that time? You already know that the federal government won't have a problem taking you off of the streets for a very long time. You already miraculously beat a thirty-year sentence. I would hate to see that happen to you again, especially after I've just entered your life. I'm not trying to sound preachy or too clingy; I'm keeping it all the way real with you, daddy. I'm feeling you like crazy. It's something about you that has pulled me to you in ways that I cannot put into words. It feels . . . it feels scary good."

"Scary good huh? That's what's up. Check it, it's like this, my world consists of a lot of maneuvers. I'm not some penny-ante nigga hustling out on these streets. A miscalculation got me caught up, or should I say a poor decision on my part made me run into that wreck. That won't happen again. If you want to remain in my world the two things I demand of you are respect and trust. You can't respect my get down then we had fun, go on and bounce now. You can't trust me, then definitely leave as soon as you can go back up them stairs and get your clothes on. Now, if you can respect and trust me and the moves I have to make we can enjoy the very best the world has to offer. Now that you've seen a little bit of my get down you see that I'm not all mouth." He smiled and continued, "I won't sell you a dream, Brandy. I will respect you at all times and I will keep it real. I know no other way. Play your part and let's enjoy every day we're together."

"Play my part? What part do I have to play, daddy?"

Gotcha, he said to himself. To Brandy he said, "Right now, baby, all you have to do is continue to look cute and keep making me happy. You never know what might pop off down the line; just always be there for me if I call upon you. Be my ride or die, *mami*. And make damn sure you keep making me scrumptious meals like this!" They started laughing. "Seriously though, I may need you to do some things for me from time to time. My man Kingo is still in that hellhole job of yours and I want him looked out for at all times; that's a must."

With raised eyebrows she asked, "Looked out for how?"

"Like taking him some trees for me. That nigga loves the bud and I want to do that for him. He's a model inmate so the people up there won't be on him at all. Most important he's solid and if he did get knocked he'd never rat."

"Hmph. You'd be surprised what a man would do when he gets caught up. So, you want me to put my career in jeopardy by taking your friend some weed? You're sitting here actually asking me to put all that I've worked so hard for on the line just to look out for your friend?"

He chewed and swallowed the last of his steak, stared at her for a moment, and cockily answered, "Yep. I expect you to do as I tell you to because you respect me as well as trust me.

You know that those crumbs and security you have is nothing compared to what I'll bring to your life. I'm not a temporary nigga, *mami*. I don't live for the moment, I live for the long haul. You feel me?"

"How often would you want me to do this, Papio?"

"Not often. I want you to hit him off on some surprise shit and keep it moving. I may need you to relay a message here and there but other than that that's it. That is small and there is no way you can get caught up as long as you listen to me. Trust me, Brandy."

She was quiet for a few minutes as she thought about what he just told her. She smiled and said, "Okay, daddy. I guess I have to earn my spot in your heart, so I'm willing to move how you want me to. God, this is so out of character of me! It's exciting yet it scares the hell out of me."

He started laughing and said, "Don't trip, *mami*. It's time for your sexy goody-goody ass to live on the edge a little. We'll be all right, my word. Check it, go in the living room and grab that comforter that's on the sofa and bring it into the media room," he said as he stood up from the table. *It's time to lock this broad in; she's going to be a very nice asset,* he said to himself as he left the dining room and went into the media room.

Brandy retrieved the comforter and brought it into the media room. She set the comforter next to Papio on the sofa and asked, "What's in that, daddy?"

After she was seated on the opposite side of Papio he said, "This is just a part of what I'm about. I trust you and I feel you won't ever cross me. So I'm about to let you into my world, Brandy. Now is the time for you to step off or jump on board for the ride." He unwrapped the comforter and let Brandy have a look at the money and the drugs that he took from Lee.

She put her hand over her mouth and said, "Oh, my God! Look at all of that money! How much is that?" She grabbed a stack of hundred dollar bills and fingered them lightly.

He shrugged and said, "About five hundred Gs or so. Hamburger money for real."

"Hamburger money? Are you kidding me? Wow, you don't be playing do you?"

"Don't got time to play; there's too much money to get to be playing."

As if she had just realized the drugs were next to the money she asked, "So you're a major drug dealer, daddy?"

He shook his head no and said, "Nah, I ain't no dope boy. I'm a modern-day pirate, *mami*. I do whatever it takes to get the money. If I come across some dope along the way it is what it is. I'll put it out there and let it work for me. I'm not turning down no money. But that's not my get down. I do it all, Brandy. Whatever it takes to get the amount I want."

"How much money do you want, daddy?"

With a dead serious look on his face he told her, "$100 million. A million dollars ain't shit to me; I can fuck that off in my sleep for real. When I get a hundred million I'll leave everything alone and be on my merry fucking way. Now listen, this is what I want you to do: I'm about to go make a few runs and then I'll be back so we can chill for the rest of the weekend. I want you to count out $400,000 and take it to your house. Get a change of clothes and then come back here so we can kick back and relax. I'm leaving for L.A. Monday morning and I'll be gone for a couple of months. When I get things situated I'll send for you so we can have that week I promised you. You'll have the numbers you will need to get in contact with me so we'll stay in constant contact."

She smiled and said, "You really do trust me huh, daddy?"

"Yeah, my gut tells me you will be my ride or die. But please, baby, don't ever get it twisted. I'll take your life if you ever put mines in jeopardy. Don't make me show you a side of me that's nothing nice."

Any normal woman would have been terrified to hear words like this, but for some reason his words did exactly the opposite. She was extremely excited. She gave him a tender kiss and said, "I'll never give you a reason to hurt me."

He smiled at her and said, "I know you won't." He stood and gave her another kiss. "I'll be back after five. Cook us some dinner and get ready for the later rounds in our sex bout because we're going to go at it again for a real long time."

She smiled seductively at him. "I can't wait for that fight right here." She noticed the pistol he had in the small of his back as he left the room, and smiled. *I done went and fell for a straight gangster. Wow,* she thought with a grin on her face.

CHAPTER SEVEN

After two more days of sexing Brandy, Papio was ready for his trip back to his hometown. He slept the entire flight to Los Angeles and was truly excited to be going home. As soon as the flight landed in LAX he sighed. *Home. I'm back on my stomping ground,* he thought as he stared out of the window.

He had a suite reserved on the tenth floor of the Westin for a week. After he got his key card to his suite he stepped to the elevator bank, thinking about his mother. He couldn't wait to see her beautiful face.

He tossed his bag onto the bed, grabbed the phone, sat down, and made a call. When his man Twirl answered Papio told him, "You ready to get some fucking money, nigga?"

There was a brief silence on the other line before Twirl finally said, "I know those fucking dumb-ass Feds ain't let your ass out of the clink, nigga. Did they do that stupid shit for real? Papio? Tell me your ass ain't out, fool?"

Papio smiled. "Like I said, you ready to get some fucking money, fool?"

Twirl started laughing. "You fucking right! Man, you don't know how bad a nigga is doing out here in this wack-ass world. This recession shit is kicking everybody's ass."

"Recession? Nigga, fuck a recession. It's time to get that fucking money. Check it, I'm at the Westin, room 10047. Get here, we got business to discuss."

"Damn, fool, how long your ass been out?"

"I got out Friday and I've already got my Jesse James on, plus jacked a nigga for a nice chunk of change. I'm home now and it's time for moves to be made. So like I said, get here, nigga."

With a smile on his face Twirl told him, "I'll be there in thirty." He hung up the phone and quickly began to get dressed because he knew one thing for certain: Papio's scandalous ass was about to put some serious paper in his pockets.

Papio made another call. "May I speak with Quentin please?"

"May I tell him who's speaking?" asked the receptionist.

"Yes, my name is Preston, Preston Ortiz."

"One moment please."

Quentin came on to the phone and said, "Preston? As in Papio Preston?"

"Yep, that's the Preston you know and love, old boy. Whatup?"

"Whatup? How the hell did you get out, dude?"

"I got my David Copperfield on, fool. What does it matter? I'm home and I'm ready to get money. You got me or what?"

Quentin sighed and said, "You know I got you, Papio, but things aren't the same as it was when you left."

"Nothing stays the same, my favorite white boy. Don't worry, I ain't trying to hurt your pockets. You know how I do it. What you got for me?"

"That depends on what you want. The pills are the new thing out this way now. That yayo is slowly becoming a thing of the past out here."

"Yeah, that's what I've been hearing. Check it, I got some peeps who want a few bundles, so let me get with them and see what they trying to do and I'll get back to you in a day or so."

"That's the business. I'll let them go to you for five dollars a pill as long as you cop ten bundles or more."

"My man! Anything else you got for me? You know what I mean too, fool?"

Quentin shook his head from side to side and said, "Still the same huh? I see you're still the fucking same dude."

"You know how I get when I'm hungry. I gots to have the entire entree plus a hefty dessert. What you got? Because I can hear it in your voice you got something for me, white boy."

"You have a nice vault. Why don't you relax for a bit, Papio? I mean, dude, what's the rush?"

"You've been my man for way too long to even think like that. You know what my goal is and I'm nowhere near where I need to be. You've handled my business for me and for real, Q. I really appreciate how you have taken care of my business concerning Mama Mia. But it's time to get back on the grind and I'm not stopping until—"

"I know, I know, until you get a hundred mil. Give me a few and get back," he said and hung up the phone.

Papio hung up the phone, laughing. He knew that Quentin would turn him on to some serious licks and he loved it. Ever since he started fucking with the crooked accountant his money multiplied. Quentin was his money man as well as his link into the world of the easiest robberies. He had eyes and ears everywhere. Not only was he an accountant but he sold everything from cocaine, X pills, guns, and anything else his greedy ass could sell for a profit. The white man was about his money; that's why they got along so well.

Papio called Brandy back in Oklahoma and told her that he made it in safely and that everything was moving along as he planned.

"That's good, daddy. I can't wait to come out there and be with you. I'm missing you like crazy already."

"It's all good; you'll be here before you know it. Check it, make sure you hit me when you bring Kingo into your office to break him off that thing. I want to talk to him before you give it to him so he won't be super spooked."

"Okay, I will. I'm going to give it to him tomorrow, so I'll call you around lunchtime. That way there won't be too many people floating around R&D."

"Good thinking, *mami*. I'll be expecting your call between nine and ten my time."

"Okay."

"I'll hit you back this evening. Be easy, *mami*."

"I will. Bye, daddy."

Just as Papio hung up the phone there was a knock at the door. He jumped and went to open the door for Twirl. Twirl had a smile on his face as he shook hands with Papio and gave him a manly hug. "You're one hard nigga to keep down, dog."

"Can't stop, won't stop, my nigga. Come on in so we can put this thing together." Twirl followed him into the living room of the suite.

After they were seated Papio wasted no time. "I got my man about to set something real sweet up for us. He told me something with seven figures so it's going to be real right. I don't have the particulars yet but I will in a minute. In the meantime I got this chump nigga who wants to spend a cool piece of change for some X."

"What's a nice piece of change?"

"A couple hundred Gs. I got at him over the weekend and it's solid."

Twirl smiled knowingly and said, "We're going to give him the one-two?"

"You know it. When he hits me I'm going to tell him I can get him the love for five dollars a pill. He'll get excited and then we'll set up the meet. You know the business somewhere in the open so he can feel comfortable."

"Yeah, stupid mothafuckas think 'cause we out in the open they safe. Damn shame."

"Their stupidity is our advantage, my nigga. Once we meet up you come and do what you do. We meet back here and split the proceeds. After that I want you to become the X man for a minute. If you start dropping that shit with the love you will be able to keep your ears to the street for future moves."

Twirl shook his head and said, "You still the same huh, nigga? Always playing the game three moves ahead of yourself?"

"Gots to play it that way, baby; never know when shit may go left, so I have to stay ahead of the game."

"That's right. Since I'm going to be the X man, who am I going to cop from?"

"My man Quentin is going to hook you up. After we snatch these chips from these suckas I'm going to introduce you to him. We'll get a few bundles for five a pop and let you drop them for ten a pop and make some loose money as we wait patiently for the next available sucka."

"And what do you get out of this for showing me so much love?"

"Every five hundred Gs you get you put two hundred Gs aside for me. Cool?"

"Definitely!"

"After we get at my man Quentin we'll find out what he has for me on that seven-figure lick I told you about. We'll split that fifty-fifty; that is, after we break Q off."

"That's the business, but, tell me, when are you going to get your man Quentin for his life savings?"

Papio shook his head and said, "Nah, that's my man. He's held me down with my finances and a bunch of other shit way too long for me to do him dirty like that." Papio shrugged and smiled. "Then again you never know what may pop off later in the game," he said with a shrewd smile on his face.

"You one cold-hearted nigga, Papio."

"Compliment accepted with a smile, my nigga. I will not lose, dog, you know that. That's why you love fucking with me."

"I fuck with you because you are the one nigga I know who will always help a nigga keep ends in his pocket. I also know that your ass ain't loyal to nothing but that fucking money. I can respect that because I'm the same mothafucking way. Let's make it happen, dog."

Everything went exactly as Papio expected it to. He went to go meet the men who wanted the X pills for five dollars a pill at a shopping center located in Inglewood on the corner of Crenshaw Boulevard and Imperial. As soon as Papio got inside of their SUV with a duffel bag that was supposed to have the X pills inside of it, Twirl came out of nowhere and snatched open the door and aimed his gun at everyone inside of the SUV.

He grabbed the duffel bag Papio was holding first, then turned his aim toward the two men sitting in the front seat of the SUV and said, "Now, where's the fucking money? Not asking again." One of the men slowly raised another duffel bag and passed it to Twirl. "Good. Now, lie the fuck down in the seat or y'all are all dead." Papio did as he was told and so did the men in the front seat. Twirl slammed the door to the SUV and vanished just as quickly as he appeared.

Papio waited three minutes and then raised his head from the seat and said, "All hell the fuck nah! What the fuck was this shit, Grass Hopper? You niggas got me fucked up! I can't go back to my niggas without they fucking money! You niggas trying to get me killed or some shit?"

"Come on, Papio, you know I don't play no games like that shit."

"You picked this fucking spot, nigga! Who else the fuck you tell?"

Grass Hopper was about to say "no one" until he remembered that he did tell his girl before he left that he was about to go take care of some serious business at the Crenshaw Shopping Center. "Damn, that punk-ass bitch set me up. I'm going to kill that bitch!"

To Papio he said, "Look, Papio, man, I would never put you in a bind like this; we've always done good business. Give me a week or so and I'll get back with you so you can toss your peoples something for this loss. I just need a minute to go back to my out-of-town spot to get some more ends. I'll spend the same as I was going to today and toss you a cool chunk. Just don't get all crazy with it, cool?"

Papio paused for theatrical purposes and said, "I can cover this shit, but on the real, it's going to be tight for me, Grass Hopper. Don't be on no bullshit and try to shake me."

Grass Hopper gave a sigh of relief and said, "I got you, Papio, I got you."

"All right. You find out who put this shit down. You make sure you let me know because a mothafucka gots to die behind this shit."

"No fucking question," Grass Hopper said as he thought about what he was about to go do to his trick-ass girlfriend.

***

Papio and Twirl finished splitting the $200,000 from their successful robbery and started laughing. "Damn, nigga, you make this shit be so fucking easy it makes me wonder how the fuck I've been out here barely making it since you been gone," Twirl said seriously as he stuck his money in a small paper bag.

"Let me roll, my nigga. I'll get with you in a couple of days."

"What you about to get into?"

"Going out the way to spend some time with Moms until Q gets at me. Stay ready, dog."

Twirl smiled and said, "You better fucking believe it. You keep a nigga eating too damn good for me not to stay ready, dog!"

CHAPTER EIGHT

Thanks to light traffic on the freeway Papio was able to make the drive from Los Angeles to the city of Riverside in little over an hour. He had a smile on his face when he pulled his rental car into the driveway of his 7,200-square-foot home. Surrounded by enchanted-looking gardens, and impressive outdoor dining and living areas made to enjoy fun in the sun, his home was his safe haven. A place for him and his mother to live in peace. After all they'd endured he felt she deserved this home more than he did. When he stepped inside he smelled something delicious being cooked in the kitchen and he knew that Mama Mia was preparing his favorite meal: her homemade enchiladas. He went into the dining room and smiled as he stared out the glass window at his Olympic-sized swimming pool. *Home. . . home is where I belong,* he thought as he turned and went into the kitchen to give his mother something he had been wanting to give her for the last three years: a kiss.

Mama Mia, a small, light brown–skinned woman of Puerto Rican descent, possessed the same light brown eyes as her son. She wore her hair pulled tightly in a long ponytail just as Papio wore his. There was no mistaking that he was her child. She was pulling a pan out of the oven when she heard him enter the kitchen. When she turned and saw her only child, a smile slowly spread across her lovely features. She calmly set the pan on top of the stove, made the sign of the cross across her chest, raised her eyes toward the ceiling, and said, "*Gracias,* you, Virgin Mother, for bringing my *mijo* back home to me safely." She then ran to her son's waiting arms and gave him a tight hug accompanied with a big fat kiss on his lips. "Welcome back, Papio. Please, *mijo,* don't ever let them take you away from me again. I couldn't take it without you with me anymore."

Papio smiled lovingly at his mother. "Don't worry, *Madre.* I'll never let anyone ever take me away from you again. I'm home for good."

With tears sliding down her face she asked him, "*Te hudo?*"

He wiped her tears from her face and said, "*Yo te hudo, Madre.*" *I promise, Mother.*

"Good. Now, come and sit so we can eat together." She led him back into the dining room and sat him down at the dinner table and ran back into the kitchen. She came back a few minutes later, carrying the food she prepared, and Papio smiled and thought, *Home. Definitely where I need to be.*

After polishing off several enchiladas along with rice, refried beans, and a super hot homemade salsa his mother specialized in, Papio felt as if he had died and gone to heaven. In between bites of his food he told his mother all about his immediate release and how he was no longer a felon. He also told her about Mani and how he put her out of his home in Oklahoma City. "I'm through with her, *Madre;* she's around me no more."

Mama Mia nodded her head and said, "Good. She was no good for you, *mijo.* All she wanted was what you could do for her. She would constantly call here and ask me for money because she needed this and that. She would tell me that you wanted her to have the very best. I knew you cared for her but I remember what you tell me and I give no one nothing. Even when your friend come out here to see me, I do as you say do and told him I didn't have any money. I could tell that he didn't believe me but I never give in. I do the right thing, sí, *mijo?*"

"Sí, *Madre.* You did good. Don't worry about any of that now. I'm home and I'm going to make sure everything is good all of the time. Come, let's go into the living room and sit for a bit." He led his mother into the living room and they sat down on one of the expensive sofas.

"I'm going to be busy taking care of my business, *Madre.*" He saw the concerned expression on her face and knew he had to put her mind at ease quickly. "Don't worry; everything is good. I have to get everything better than good, *Madre.*" He spread his arms wide and continued, "This, all of this, is nothing compared to how we're going to be living. I'm going to give you the world, *Madre,* because you deserve it all."

She shook her head slowly and told him in a stern voice, "Don't you realize that I already have the world? As long as I have you I am just fine. This house is nice, very nice, but it means nothing to me without you here with me, *mijo.* I know I can't stop you; you are stubborn just like your father was, God rest the dead."

Papio frowned at the mention of his father; he hated being compared to the man.

"You will do what you feel you must. Just make sure that you keep your promise to me, *mijo.* You've never broken a promise to me yet and I don't expect you to start now. Relax now and let me go clean up the kitchen and then we can sit and watch television, sí?"

"Sí, *Madre*. But can I ask you why didn't you hire a maid like I told you to a long time ago?"

She grabbed him by his cheeks and said, "Bah, you know me better than that, *mijo*. I can keep my own home clean, even a gigantic house like this one. It keeps me busy. Go, I'll be finished in a little bit."

Papio did as she told him and went upstairs to his bedroom. After taking a shower and going through his clothes he realized that he was definitely going to have to do some more shopping. None of his shirts fit properly and he didn't feel like getting them refitted. *Fuck it, got to get some new shit. It ain't like my paper ain't right,* he said to himself. He sat down on the bed and thought about the game plan he came up with during the drive from L.A. to Riverside. *After I get that Aston Martin no more big spending. Well, after I get a few more threads then it'll be all about the stack. I got to get a nice chunk to throw those greedy fucking Cubans; they should know I'm out in a few weeks or so. No way in the fuck I'm touching my vault for them hoes, fuck that shit. They won't be able to put that shit with Lee on me, even though they'll damn sure think it was me when they find out I'm home,* he said to himself and smiled. *Fuck them bitches. Left me for dead. I shouldn't give them hoes shit. Nah, can't go out like that. The first thing they'll do is come back out here looking, and if they even think about getting at Mama Mia it's on. Can't go that route; got to give them dogs a bone. And fast.* He pulled out his wallet and stared at the three numbers that Kingo gave him. New York was calling him. He would get in contact with his man Harlem Nick and see if he had anything for him. If he did he would hop a flight east and check out that business.

CHAPTER NINE

The week went by rather quickly. Papio and Mama Mia spent most of it shopping and enjoying one another's company. They went and saw a different movie every single night. He received the message from Q that he'd been waiting for. He had a smile on his face as he pulled his brand new 2009 Aston Martin DBS coupe off of the car lot. Stratus white metallic over obsidian black leather with silver stitching. He had the dealer put some twenty-inch ten-spoke chrome-alloyed rims on the sleek car. Every feature he could think of was added to the $318,000 vehicle. Sapphire ECU push button starter system, alarm system and a full engine immobilizer. Satellite navigation, Bluetooth, HID headlights, parking sensors, 700-watt Aston Martin audio, USB, and iPod. "The works" would have really been an understatement. Papio went all out to get his dream car and now that he had it, it was time to get back to work.

He stopped back home to get his clothes and told his mother that he would be back Sunday at the latest. After giving her a kiss good-bye and grabbing a bag with a few different outfits inside he was off. Mama Mia watched as her son jumped into his car and made the sign of the cross across her chest. *Keep your hand on my* mijo, *Virgin Mother,* she prayed silently as she turned and went back into the kitchen.

Papio was speeding on the freeway as he headed down to L.A. He called Q and wasted no time. "What you got for me, Q?"

"Do you feel like partying tonight?"

Papio checked the time on his $19,000 IWC Aquatimer watch and said, "I don't have time for fucking partying, Q. I gots to get my money right. So, like I said, what you got for me?"

"First off, let me thank you for that move you made with your man; we will definitely do some good business. I like Twirl. I think he will get that paper, dude."

"If he wasn't about his business I would never have introduced you."

"Cool. Okay, here it is. This Italian cat—and I mean for real straight out of Rome and shit, accent and all—is out here really getting money. He's a big dog for real. But trip this, he is strictly solo, no serious crew or anything like that. He has a flunky here or there for delivery purposes and all but that's it. He's caked up and just waiting to get got."

"What it look like?"

"My first estimation was way off, at least three mil or more. His money is longer than the 405 freeway and he has the X by the ton."

"Your take?"

"The X. You keep the money; all I want is the X."

"What if I can't get the X?"

"We split what you do get straight down the middle. I know your ass don't want to do that so get me that X."

"What did you mean about that partying shit?"

"You know how the Italians love the women right, well, this guy fucking loves to party. He's having a big wingding at this old mansion out in Hollywood, you know, one of those old movie star's shit. Your invitation has already been delivered to your hotel. I sent two because I figured you might need an extra one."

"Good. Weaknesses?"

"I already told you, women. He loves a gorgeous woman. So if you got any on your team they might be very useful with this one."

"Does the party boy get down?"

"Yep. He does the X, snorts, and smokes the bud. Drinks champagne only."

"What time does the party start?"

"Ten, ten-thirty would be a nice time for you to arrive. He most likely won't be there until well after midnight. The address is on the invite and you're going to like this one; you must be dressed to impressed. That's another thing about this guy: he hates for anyone around him to be looking shabby. He takes that shit as an insult. I guess that's some more of his Italian customs and shit. So, I guess you can use this time to wear some of those expensive threads you're known for wearing."

Papio smiled. His mind was on a possible $3 million move. "When we speak again it will be at my suite at the Westin. Either we'll be splitting that three million or I'll be giving you your X."

"I'll be waiting for your call," Quentin said as he hung up the phone.

Papio called Twirl and told him, "Got some more money for you to get, dog. Do you have a suit?"

"Nope, that's your style, not mines, my nigga. But I damn sure can buy one. What's the business?"

"We're going shopping. I got to get you looking nice; you're playing my bodyguard tonight while we go see how we're going to get this Italian sucker."

"I'm with it. Where are you now?"

"Just got on the 405. I'll be at the suite within the hour. Time to get a whole bunch of money, my nigga."

"Fucking right!"

Papio and Twirl arrived at the old mansion of some Hollywood starlet and realized that they were going to be rolling with the big dogs of Hollywood for real. Twirl noticed some heavyweights in both worlds: the entertainment industry as well as the criminal underworld. Major players like the Orumuttos, the Japanese lockdown boys. It was rumored that Danny Orumutto murdered his father as well as his two uncles to take over their very enterprising X pill drug ring. Twirl flinched when he saw Taz, an Oklahoma nigga who was also rumored to be the leader of the infamous and super low-key power group called the Network.

"Whoa, this is some big boy shit going down in this piece," Twirl said. He checked Papio and could see the dollar signs swirling around in his eyes. He shook his head and followed him at a discreet distance, playing the bodyguard role to a tee. Papio had Twirl dressed in an expensive tailor-made Versace suit with some extra-comfortable Italian loafers.

After Papio found himself a seat he gave Twirl a nod toward one of the many bars located around the first floor of the mansion. Twirl, playing his part, went and took a stool at one of the bars and kept his eyes on Papio at all times.

Papio was taking everything in as he sat down and let his eyes roam all over the party. Just like Twirl he noticed the bags that were at the party and wondered exactly how he was going to pull off this caper. He was clueless at the moment but one thing he was certain of. *The Italian, Nicoli, is getting got for his riches this night,* he thought with a smile on his face.

It was a tad bit after midnight when the host of the party made his entrance. Nicoli was wearing a perfectly tailored suit by Neil Barrett with a tie by Dolce & Gabbana and some shoes by Salvatore Ferragamo. He received a silent nod of approval from Papio because he was wearing that suit exactly like any well-dressed man should. Suit fit right, a quarter inch of cuff showing, just the slightest break in his trousers with a crisp white dress shirt. Papio appreciated his style. It made him check his appearance and smile. He knew he was looking good in his Armani suit and nothing or no one was going to outdo him in this place. *Not even the Nicoli,* he thought with a wry grin on his face. As he watched Nicoli stroll confidently around the mansion speaking to everyone, Papio's eyes fell on the most stunning woman he had ever seen in his life. She was standing by the bar, sipping a drink with alert eyes, following Nicoli everywhere he went. He grinned because that awesome specimen had her sights locked on the big prize for the night. *Sorry, honey, you're beautiful and all but this clown belongs to Papio tonight,* he said to himself. He eased toward the bar and spoke to the beauty dressed sexy but elegant in a Donna Karan dress and Jimmy Choo pumps. Her golden skin complexion turned him on like crazy. He set his drink onto the bar and asked her, "Please tell me you don't have your eyes set on the man of honor this evening?"

The fine woman turned toward him and took in his appearance before she spoke. After confirming by his dress that he was no scrub type she said, "Excuse me?"

"I've been watching you watch the host and I had my fingers crossed that you wasn't hoping to become one of his many conquests." She smiled and Papio felt as if his heart were going to melt. She was absolutely gorgeous. Her smile made his heart actually skip a beat. She had a slight gap between her front teeth and that imperfection perfected her smile instead of flawing it. *Wow,* Papio thought as he continued to smile at her.

"You do know that the statement you just made sounds like some serious hating."

Papio shrugged. "It is what it is." He reached out his hand and said, "My name is Papio, Papio Ortiz. And you are?"

She ignored his question as she continued to watch Nicoli.

After she saw that Nicoli had stopped and was speaking with the leader of the Network she turned back toward Papio and grinned. "My name is Special, Special Pearson."

"Special, well, you do have the perfect name, love."

"Thank you. Now, since you have learned my name and interrupted me and my business is there anything else that I can do for you, Mr. Papio?"

Papio was intrigued. "Your business? It's your business to lightweight stalk that Italian guy? You're too beautiful to be on that page, sweetheart."

This cocky nigga just won't leave me, ugh! But damn he is one fine fucker. Wrong time, baby, wrong time, she thought. "You have no idea what my business consists of, Mr. Papio."

"Well, please enlighten me."

She smiled at him and thought, *I should tell this pretty nigga the truth and watch him freak the fuck out. Nah, how my luck's been running lately this fool could be the fucking Feds.* She sighed and said, "Excuse me, Papio, but I have to go."

He grabbed her lightly by her elbow and he could have sworn there was some sort of electric shock when his fingers lightly touched her skin. "Wait, you didn't enlighten me on your business. Maybe I can be of some assistance."

She stared at his hand holding on to her elbow, and she wondered if she had some type of static cling, because when he touched her she felt as if there were something electric around her. She shook the thought off and thought, *fuck it*. She stared directly into his light brown eyes and said, "You in this bitch. One way or the other it's going down tonight."

CHAPTER TEN

"Well, I'll be a mothafucka," Papio said softly as he watched Special work the room. *She's checking that fool like a fucking vet. She's good, too,* he said to himself as he continued to watch Nicoli's movements around the party. *She's in the game? Wow, that's going to make this lick all the more fun,* he thought as he noticed Nicoli leave a few people he was conversing with and head toward the staircase. He remembered what Twirl told him: the party girls were downstairs doing their thing and some of the big boys were down there also. The third floor was where the orgy was cracking. *Mmmm, looks like the man is ready to get his freak on. And there goes Special making her move.* He stopped and watched as Special stepped to Nicoli and sparked conversation. They chatted briefly and then Nicoli whispered something in her ear and Papio could tell that is was an offer to go upstairs because Special hesitated for a moment and played the shy role to a tee. A moment later Nicoli grabbed her hand and lightly pulled her toward the staircase. When they started climbing the stairs Papio realized that this was his time to move. He turned and let his eyes roam over the entire room quickly until he spotted Twirl standing by the bar. As if feeling Papio's eyes on him Twirl looked his way and their eyes locked. Papio gave a nod toward the staircase and held up three fingers indicating the third floor. He then gave Twirl the thumbs-up

to let him know that it was about to go down. Before he
turned to go up the stairs he held his right palm in the
air, telling Twirl that he needed five minutes before he
was to come upstairs to the orgy. Twirl gave him a nod
in understanding, downed his drink, and set the empty
glass onto the bar.

Papio climbed the stairs quickly and hit the third
floor with his mind racing. He knew the next part of
this move was going to be crucial. He was confident
they would able to pull this off, simply because this
rich clown was stupid enough not to have any security.
A joke for real, he thought as he stepped toward a door
where he heard music and laughter on the other side.
*We're going to have to snatch this nigga as smoothly
as possible without alarming the party people,* Papio
said to himself. *Fuck it.* Now, there really wasn't too
much in this life that could shock Papio, but what he
was staring at when he opened the door to the room
shocked the shit out of him. There were about twenty
men and women inside of the huge room getting their
freak on something vicious. Women on women, two
women on one man, two men on one woman, even
fucking men on men! This shit was off the fucking
chart. No drugs were in view, just some good old serious fucking was going down up in there. There were
big throw pillows scattered all over the floor where the
freaky people were getting theirs on. Papio stepped
inside and as soon as he closed the door a short, blond
white woman who looked like she had to be over fifty
grabbed him by his hand and told him, "Ooohh, more
black cock. Come on handsome, come give me some of
that black cock."

He smiled sheepishly and said, "Sorry, baby, this
ain't my groove. I'm looking for someone." Before she
could say another word he moved on. His mind was on

one person, well, two actually. When he saw Special and Nicoli sitting on a throw pillow in the back of the room he smiled. *Gotcha.* He was about to approach but stopped in his tracks when he saw Special stand and begin to peel off her dress. *My God! Look at those firm-ass titties! D cups, too! Damn, look at that fucking body!* Papio said to himself, totally fascinated with what he was staring at. He felt some stirring in his groin and groaned as Special bent over and began to undress Nicoli. He was so mesmerized with what he was looking at that he almost forgot that he couldn't afford for her to get the Italian naked; that would fuck up shit and make him have to wait until they were finished. He had to stop that. Plus, on the real he didn't want to watch Special have sex with Nicoli. He reached into the small of his back and pulled out his pistol and held it down by his thigh as he stepped toward them. Special had just undone Nicoli's trousers when Papio said, "Excuse me, you two, I hate to disturb you but I have some very pressing business to discuss with you, Nicoli."

Nicoli looked up at him with an expression on his face like, "you got to be kidding." "Who are you? I don't know you. Wait, before you answer, can you give me twenty minutes here please? Then we can discuss whatever you like, yes?"

Papio shook his head no, raised his 9 mm and told the Italian, "Sorry, Nicoli, but we have to talk now, yes?"

With courage that Papio wasn't expecting Nicoli stood, fastened his expensive trousers, and said, "So, you will shoot me here in front of all of these people? Come now, man, you couldn't be that stupid."

"He couldn't but I could," Twirl said as he stepped in front of Papio with a big .45-caliber Glock in his hand. "Now, do we make this messy or do you come with us so we can have that discussion my man asked you about? Please don't try me because you will die if you do," Twirl said in a no-nonsense tone.

Realizing that Twirl was not to be tried Nicoli gave him a nod yes and let Twirl grab him loosely by his right arm and lead him out of the room. Papio took a quick peep at Special's gorgeous, perfect body and shook his head. "Sorry, Special, you missed this one."

Without any shame in her nakedness she stood and slipped her dress back on. "Whatever game you're playing, you really need to watch yourself because you're way out of your league, Papio. Fucking with my moves can get a nigga fucked off."

He let his eyes roam all over that luscious body one final time and said, "Baby, you can fuck me off anytime you want. But right now, I got money to get. See ya, sexy!" He turned and stepped quickly and caught up with Twirl and Nicoli just as they made it to the door of the freak room. What was so crazy was that not one person inside of that room other than Special realized what was going on right in front of them. They were so caught up fucking and sucking that they didn't see anything that had just transpired. *Good,* thought Papio as he looked over his shoulder and saw Special staring at him with a frustrated frown on her face. Before he turned to leave she gave him the finger. He laughed as he stepped out of the door.

Papio stepped in front of Twirl and said, "We're taking you out of this place now, Nicoli. If you resist in any way you are a dead man. If you do as you're told you'll live to see another sunrise." He didn't wait for a response; instead he stepped toward the staircase with them following him. They made it downstairs and through the crowd without incident. Once they were outside of the mansion Papio rushed and got the rented

XF Jaguar that Q supplied for the night. Twirl opened the door and let Nicoli sit in the passenger's side while Papio got into the driver's seat. When Twirl was inside of the car Papio slowly pulled out of the mansion's long, winding driveway. After they were safely moving in the Hollywood traffic Papio said, "Okay, now that wasn't so bad now was it?"

"Fuck you! What do you want, you peasant? Tell me and I will give you what you ask for. I just want to hurry and get this over with."

"Good. That's exactly what we wanted you to say. What I want is for you to take me to your main spot and give me everything. When I say everything, I mean everything, Nicoli. All of the X pills you have as well as all of your money. And please, before you insult us let me tell you that saying no isn't an option for you. You will die if we don't get everything we want."

Nicloi took a look over his shoulder and stared at Twirl for a second and realized that he was indeed fucked. He sighed and said, "My home in San Fernando valley, we go there and I give you what you ask for."

"Humor me and tell me exactly how much is there," Papio said with a smile on his face.

"A little over three million and eighty-five bundles of X pills," Nicoli answered in a defeated tone.

Twirl's eyes almost bugged out of their sockets and Papio laughed. "Good, Nicoli, very good."

"You won't let your man kill me, okay? You said I live another sunrise if I do as you tell me, yes?" he asked nervously.

"That's right, Nicoli. You give, you live."

Twirl reached up from the back seat of the Jag and slapped Nicoli hard on his shoulder and said, "You gon' live, my man! You gon' live!" Then he started laughing.

CHAPTER ELEVEN

Two weeks after the successful robbery of the Italian, Papio received the call he'd been waiting for from the East Coast. His man Harlem Nick finally returned his call and informed Papio that he needed to get to the NY ASAP. Papio packed his bags immediately and then called Brandy. When he had her on the line he told her that he would be in New York for two weeks and he wanted her to make some reservations so she could fly out there to be with him the following Friday. She screamed she was so happy for the upcoming trip east. The excitement in her voice put a smile on his face; just the thought of that body on top of him made him feel horny. It had been three weeks since he had some sex and it was past time for him to get some. After he hung up the phone with Brandy he called Kammy to see if she made any progress yet. When she came on to the line he wasted no time. "What's the business, *mami?*"

"Slow motion right now. I've seen those fools a few times and the head youngsta is definitely feeling a bitch, he just hasn't made a move yet. I heard they went back to Dallas so as soon as I hear that they're back in the city I'll turn this shit up. When are you coming back this way?"

"I should be there by the end of the month. Anything else cracking out there?"

"That nigga Lee was found dead in his house with that nigga Hugh you used to fuck with."

"Is that right? Who did that shit?"

"I don't know, I was wondering the same shit. Word on the streets is that some young niggas jacked they ass."

Good, thought Papio. "All right, let me roll. I got a flight to catch to the East Coast. Hit me if you have anything important to get at me about."

"Will do. Hey, Papio."

"Huh?"

"You do know that you're going to have to break a bitch off right?"

"Why mix the business with pleasure, Kammy? I mean you are definitely one bad-ass female, but business is business."

"Fuck that business bullshit, I'm trying to fuck the shit out of your fine ass. And that's that, Papio. I'm serious. You got me?"

He smiled into the receiver and said, "Yeah, I got you. Let me go." He hung up the phone and grabbed his bags. After loading everything into his car he went out back where Mama Mia was busy fussing at the gardener. He stepped to her and told her that he was leaving and that he would be gone for a few weeks.

"Be careful, *mijo.*"

"Always, *Madre.* If you need to get in contact with me make sure you don't hesitate to call okay?"

He gave her a kiss and let her get back to fussing.

During the drive down to Los Angeles Papio called Twirl to let him know that he would be MIA for a minute and that he would get back with him when he returned. He gave him his cell number and told him if he needed to holla at him he could call anytime.

"Nigga, I'm so fucking good right now. But by the time you get back I may have something for us."

"Yeah?" Papio asked, interested.

"Yeah, my nigga E.T. hit me the other day and told me that he was working on setting up something real nice for me. I thought about you and figured if it was cool enough we'd fuck with him and make it do what it do. I mean, man, you blessed a nigga something lovely off these last two licks. I got the X shit cracking already. My homie K-Mack is on his way from Vegas to holla at me; with him on my team I will keep this shit on just like you want me to."

"That's what's up. Handle that shit, my nigga, and we will continue to eat. Keep your ears open for any future moves; we gon' keep eating off of all the suckas. Feel me?"

"Do I? You better fucking believe it! The streets is watching and I'm that nigga who ain't missing a thang."

"Check it, I'm pulling into the airport now. I'll hit you in a week or so. Be safe, fool."

"Fa sho'. You be safe, my nigga."

"No doubt," Papio said as he hung up the phone. He got out of the car and grabbed his bags and gave the key to the valet and told him that he needed his car held for at least a month. He always paid for longer than he thought would be needed just in case. After he finished taking care of the finances for his car he turned and took a look at his pride and joy and smiled as he headed toward the entrance to LAX.

Papio checked his bags and went to the bar to get a drink. He was sipping a Crown and Coke when he thought he saw someone very familiar. He jumped out of his seat and stepped to the entrance of the bar and saw Special walking quickly toward one of the boarding gates. He stepped back inside of the bar, downed his drink, and grabbed his carry-on bag. By the time he came out of the bar and went in the direction where he last saw the gorgeous woman she was nowhere to be found. He checked the time on his diamond bezel Patravi T-Graph by Carl F. Bucherer and saw that he had less than twenty minutes to find the stunning beauty. He knew she was going to be super pissed to see him but he had to take that chance; he wanted to talk to her something terrible. After about ten more minutes of walking around the terminal he gave a frustrated sigh and headed toward the gate for his flight to New York.

Special was seated in the waiting area of the same boarding gate of the flight that Papio was now boarding. She frowned as she watched him quickly disappear onto the airplane. *Now, ain't this something; that pretty-ass nigga is headed east. I know one thing, his ass better not be anywhere near my next move, because God as my witness if I see him anywhere near this one I'm going to dead his ass,* she said to herself as she stood to board the same flight.

Due to some bad weather the flight from L.A. took a little over six hours to New York. By the time the plane landed Papio was more than ready to get the hell off of that plane. As he waited impatiently for the slow passengers in front of him to deplane he could have sworn he saw Special exiting the plane in front of him. This made him more impatient. He was dying to meet up with that fine piece.

By the time he made it off of the plane he still had hopes of seeing her at the baggage claim area. He wanted her bad and just the thought of speaking to her gave him an extra pep in his step as he maneuvered his way through the crowded airport. By the time he made it to the baggage claim area Special was nowhere to be seen. "Damn." He let his eyes roam all over the area but nope, it wasn't meant to be. He waited for his luggage to come sliding down the carousel as he thought about what could have been if he had known Special was on his flight.

Special could tell that he was looking for her, that's why she purposely kept herself shaded in the back of the baggage claim area. Just like she figured that pretty bastard was trying his best to get at her. *Should've let that nigga holla just to see what kind of weak shit he was going to pop to me,* she said to herself as she watched Papio grab his luggage and step out of the airport. *If I see you again, nigga, it won't be pretty,* she thought as she stepped to the carousel and retrieved her own luggage. *Time to get some of this East Coast money.*

After Papio checked into the Crowne Plaza hotel located in Times Square, Manhattan he called Brandy. "Hey, *mami,* you good?"

Brandy had a huge smile on her face as she said, "Mm-hm, missing you, daddy. How was your flight?"

"It was cool. Did you make those reservations?"

"Yes, I did. I'm so excited! I've never been to the East Coast. Will I be able to do some serious shopping?"

"I already told you, you will be able to do whatever you like. So make your list now because all of your wishes will come true as soon as you get here."

"Wow! I don't know what I've done to deserve you in my life, but I'm sure glad I did it."

He started laughing and said, "It wasn't you who done anything, *mami,* it was your mama."

"Huh?" she asked, confused.

"Your mama blessed you to have one hell of a face and body that turns me on in the worst way. So make sure you give her all the credit for these blessings because it's because of her genes she passed to you!"

It was Brandy's turn to laugh as she said, "So you saying I got it from my mama?"

"Exactly. Check it, I want you to go by my pad and make sure that everything is okay out that way. I don't want that crazy-ass broad Mani to come over there acting. Do that for me?"

"I got you, daddy. Anything else you need me to do for you?"

"Nah, that's it. Is my nigga good?"

"He's fine. I saw him earlier today coming out of the chow hall. He smiled and kept it moving, most likely in a rush to go back to his cell so he could get tight with that good."

"Get tight with that good? Look at you talking slang and stuff. Where that come from, college girl?" he teased.

"I may be a college girl, daddy, but I know what's up."

"That's right. All right, baby, it's late out here. I got to get some rest. I'll hit you tomorrow some time. If shit ain't right at the house make sure you get at me."

"I will, daddy. Sleep well. See you in a week."

"Believe it," he said and hung up the phone. Just as he made himself comfortable on the huge bed the telephone started ringing. He smiled because he knew it was Nick. "Whatup, Harlem Nick, you funny-talking-ass nigga?" Papio asked when he answered the telephone.

"Funny talkin'? Son, you the proper-talkin'-ass nigga, B. What's good? You ready to make a whole bunch of that loot, B?"

"That depends on how much loot you talking about."

"Seven figures, son, multiple seven figures."

"I like that type of loot. What's up?"

"Sleep for now, B. I'll hit you up in the A.M. and then we'll get everything out on the table. One question though."

"Whatup?"

"There may be some vicious shit with this one, B."

Papio started laughing and said, "So the fuck what! In the morning, son!"

Nick hung up the phone, smiling. He knew that he called the right man for this job. Papio's murder game was no joke, especially when it came to getting money.

CHAPTER TWELVE

The next morning while Papio was getting dressed, Kingo called him and was surprised yet happy to hear that his friend was in New York. "Make sure you give my brotha a call, mon. He may even have something for you to do while you're out there," said Kingo.

"Yeah, I was going to give him a call later after I finish taking care of some business with my man Nick."

"Nick? Isn't that the guy who you told me about who had you on some wild wild west shit, mon?"

Papio laughed. "Yeah, that's him. He's a good dude so I'm going to listen to what he's talking about and see if the rewards are worth the risk. After that I'll get at your brother and see what's up with him. So, what's up with you, you good?"

"Ahh, mon, everyt'ing bless, mon, you got me right in here, Papio. Tell me, mon, did you put your buddy in that bumpa yet?"

Papio laughed again and said, "You good, right?"

"Yah, mon, me good."

"Well, that answers your question then."

"She 'ave do glamity?"

"Some of the best nookie I've ever had."

"You sound as if you're in love, mon."

"You know better than that, old dread. I'm feeling her but that's about as far as it can go, at least for now. I kind of met someone though, and, man, let me tell you, she is so beautiful."

"You out there top rankin' and you tell me you kinda meet a woman? I don't understand that one, mon."

"It's a long story and I don't have the time to break it down right now. Just know this, when it pops off you will be in the know."

"Okay, mon, you be careful out there and do what needs to be done. Have you spoken to them blood clots yet?"

"Nope. But soon. Give your brother a call and let him know that I will get at him later on this evening if everything is good on my end."

"'Nuff respect, mon," said Kingo as he hung up the phone.

By the time Nick arrived Papio was starving. Nick smiled and told him that he was going to take him to one of the best soul food restaurants in New York. They took a cab to Harlem and even though this wasn't Papio's first time in New York he was still amazed at all of the people walking around. Yellow Cabs filled the streets and people of all shapes and sizes filled the sidewalks. By the time they made it to Sylvia's soul food restaurant in Harlem, Papio felt as if he'd seen over a million people walking around.

As they sat at their table waiting for their food Papio asked Nick, "So, what's the business?"

Nick sipped some water, smiled, and said, "Some fuckin' boy Indians up in Niagara are slipping big time and it's time they come up off that loot, son."

"Niagara? As in Niagara Falls?"

"Exactly."

"Isn't that like fucking six or seven hours from the city?"

"Seven hours and twenty minutes to be exact, B."

"So, you want me to go with you to put down some possible murder shit seven hours away. You need to break this one down to me real good, Harlem Nick. Because I can tell you I am not feeling anything I've heard so far."

"You will, son, you will." Before Nick could continue their food was brought to them.

As they ate Nick said, "All right, son, it's like this. These Indians are slipping out that way. They got work all over the fucking place but all of their moves come from Niagara. I got word from this cool bird I fuck with and she tells me that they are caked up nicely."

"Can this bird be trusted for good intel?"

"Definitely, B. Like I was saying, they got everything from pills, heroin, and that shit them fools from Texas be copping all the time."

"What, codeine?"

"Yeah, that syrup shit. She told me that the money as well as the work is at the same spot. Can you believe that shit, B? I mean those fools are so comfortable out that way that they have all of their cakes in the same oven, son."

"The take, as close to an approximate as you can give me, Nick, no bullshitting."

Nick smiled and said, "B, milly or better."

Papio gave him a nod of his head and asked, "How many is in this shit with us?"

"Me, you, and the bird. Fuck we need more than that for, B? I'm not trying to have to split this shit more than three ways."

It was Papio's turn to smile. "Come on with that shit, Nick. If you want me in on this shit you gots to keep it real with me, B," Papio said, mimicking his friend perfectly, New York accent and all.

"What are you talking about, son? I've given you the real."

Papio shook his head from side to side and said, "If you really think I'll even begin to think you would split this shit three ways and give that bird a even split then you gots to be getting soft on me. And I know damn well there ain't a soft bone in your body. With that said, it's either a even split between me and you or I'm not with it. Especially if we have to dead somebody."

Nick smiled and said, "Can't get nothing past you huh, Papio? Yeah, on the real, B. You already know I'm gon' body that bird; she wouldn't do nothing but run her fucking mouth anyway. So, fitty-fitty it is then. But you gots to murk the bird."

"Why, the pussy that good, nigga?"

"Something like that, B."

"Whatever. When do we make this happen?"

"Next Saturday morning. We'll drive out to Niagara and hook up with the bird at the Falls and get everything put in the proper perspective. From what she gave me those fools are slipping like a bitch. We hit 'em hard, get that shit, and get the fuck."

"That's a long ride back here to be that dirty, Nick. I know you got something better in that wild-ass head of yours."

"But of course, son. We ain't leaving at all. We're going to get some suites at the Seneca Niagara Casino. After we make the move we're going to go right back to the hotel and do some tourist shit for the rest of the weekend. Monday afternoon we'll hit the road and raise the fuck up outta that piece. No way would I even try to bounce like that; too much risk in that shit, son."

Papio sat back in his seat and ran the scenario through his head and said, "Okay, I got a broad flying out here next Friday from Oklahoma City and I think she'll fit right into this equation."

"Give it to me, B."

"After we hit the lick we come back to the room and get on some chill shit. Late that night though after everything is everything we put her onto the highway and let her make the move back down here. That way we can be extra safe with it, feel me? You give her the directions where you want her to go and she'll go sit with everything until we make it here the next day. Fuck that Monday shit; won't be no need for us to kick it out there that long."

"For real huh? I'm with that shit, son."

"And, Nick, you know there ain't no room for any faulty shit. This broad is a square bitch; she has absolutely no gangster in her whatsoever."

Nick touched his heart in mock pain. "I can't believe you would even think some shit like that, Papio. I am wicked when it comes to the cake but I would never cross you like that, son. Word to mother, B."

"Had to put it out there, Nick. I know ain't no punk in you and I respect that. Just like I hope you know there's no punk in me either. The respect must remain all the way across the board or one of us will die," Papio said seriously.

"Get the fuck outta here! Nigga, we about to be some rich-ass niggas in one quick and easy-ass lick. Ain't got time for that rah-rah bullshit, B."

"I'm already a millionaire, Nick, a million or two ain't shit to me no more. It's a hundred million or better for me, son," Papio said with a smile on his face.

"Damn, I guess I've set my standards a li'l too low then huh, son?"

"Not if that's all you want. Me, I got a much larger scheme. I can fuck off a million on clothes and travel, dog." They both started laughing.

CHAPTER THIRTEEN

Just as they were about to split up and take separate cabs Papio asked Nick, "What about weapons for this caper, we good?"

"You know I got everything we need, son, that and some. I'll give you a holla in a day or so. You good or do you want me to send a bird or two your way to keep you company?"

"I'm straight. I got some family I need to holla at later on. I'll hit you up in the morning."

"That's what's up, B, holla back," Nick said.

Papio jumped inside of the cab and told the driver to take him to his hotel. He sat back in his seat and began to replay everything Nick told him. Nick was a good dude but he was a greedy nigga, so Papio knew that he would have to make sure that he was on top of his game at all times. *The first sign of that nigga pulling any bullshit and he will be dead.* Papio watched the bustling city pass by as he headed back down Times Square.

Papio awoke from his three-hour nap feeling refreshed. He was still kind of full from the soul food he had earlier at Sylvia's. Before he went and got his chill on in the Big Apple he called Kingo's brother. Papio thought he had the wrong number because he was expecting to hear someone with a heavy Jamaican accent like Kingo, but instead a very American-sounding man answered the phone.

"Hello."

"Excuse me, but my name is Papio and I'm calling to speak to the brother of Kingo."

Kingo's brother smiled. "I've been waiting for your call."

"Yeah, well I've been kind of busy today. Hope I didn't catch you at a bad time."

"No time is a bad time when it comes to a friend of my big brother's. So, do you have any plans for the evening?"

"Actually, I don't. I was about to get dressed and go do a little sightseeing."

"We can't have any of that. There's a club between Forty-ninth and Fiftieth on Broadway called Caroline's on Broadway. Be prepared to have some fun; this is a comedy club of sorts and the comedians are well known for harassing the customers. We can eat, sip a little something, and talk about some things. Cool?"

"No doubt. I can be there within the hour."

"Fine, I'll see you then."

"How will I know who you are?"

"You'll know because I'm the younger version of my brother, long dreads and all."

"And your name is?"

Kingo's little brother laughed and said, "Kango. See you in a little bit, Papio."

Papio hung up the phone, took a shower, and put on an entire Ed Hardy outfit: T-shirt, jeans, and sneakers all Ed Hardy and all with loud, gaudy designs on them. No jewelry except for his watch and his two-karat earring in his left ear. He grabbed his wallet and put a couple of thousand dollars inside of it, then stuffed it in his back pocket. He checked himself out in the mirror one last time and smiled as he ran his fingers through his long hair, which was hanging loose tonight. "Damn, Papio, you are one handsome man!"

As soon as Papio entered Caroline's he saw four men with long dreads standing at the bar, laughing at the comedian, Jason Andors, who was on stage talking real greasy to a sister with an extremely long and ugly weave in her hair. The entire club was in tears as Jason continued to rip into the sister. *Damn, he's funny for a white boy. I wouldn't want him ripping into me,* Papio thought as he made his way to the bar.

He scanned the room before getting to the bar and couldn't believe his good fortune when he spied Special sitting at a table in the rear of the club. She was sitting with two men who looked like they were of Indian descent. They each had real long hair hanging loose, similar to how Papio had his hair. He stared at Special for a moment in hopes that she would look his way. She didn't. *She's not getting out of here tonight without me getting at her sexy, fine ass,* he said to himself. When he made it to the bar he said, "Excuse me, gentlemen, any chance either of you Kango?"

Kango extended his hand. "What's good, Papio? Glad you could join us this evening. Come in, I have a table reserved for us so we can have a touch of privacy." Kango led the small group toward the rear of the club.

When they were seated Papio smiled as he locked eyes with Special. They were seated about three tables from where she was sitting. *Gotcha,* he said to himself with a confident smile on his face. Special frowned in return. She continued to laugh and talk with the Indians like Papio didn't exist.

"My brother tells me that you are a very interesting individual, Papio. He speaks highly of you and that is something very rare for him."

"Kingo is my man. We held each other down in there and he knows my pedigree. He's one on a very short list of men who I can say I truly respect."

Kango nodded. He looked to his right and said, "This here is my first cousin, Steven." Steven gave Papio a nod of his head and in perfect English said, "Pleased to meet you, Papio."

Kango turned to his left and said, "This man right here is my dear friend Macho, and next to him is his brother, Brad." Both men gave Papio a nod in greeting but remained silent. "Please excuse those two; neither likes to do much talking. They're men of action. Tell me; are you a man of action, Papio?"

"Most definitely. Especially when it comes to getting money. I play no games and I do what I must in order to make that dollar."

"Good, very good. Have you ever participated in any bank jobs?"

Papio thought about the bank he robbed in Oklahoma. "As a matter of fact I have. One to be exact."

"How did it go?" After Papio gave him a detailed account of how he robbed the bank only minutes after being released from federal prison Kango burst into laughter. "Please tell me you are joking."

"Nope, I'm dead serious."

"I like that, balls of steel," said Steven. Macho and Brad both gave nods of approval.

Papio shrugged off the compliment. "Just wanted to see what it felt like. Kingo told me that there was no better feeling in the world than hitting a bank, and for real he was right. It was like taking candy from a baby."

"This is true, but $36,000 is nothing; chump change for real. No disrespect."

"None taken."

"How do you think you would feel if you did a take-over with us and came away with a few million?"

Papio became very serious as every pair of eyes sitting at the table was waiting for his response. "I would love it; that shit can get addicting for real. I would definitely want to keep putting those kind of moves down."

"Good. I won't waste words because time is money. We're doing a takeover the day after tomorrow and we need a fifth man. Your part of this will be to ensure that Macho, Steven, and myself are covered while we hit the safe and the tellers. Brad will be watching your back as well as holding everyone in place until we're finished. Any questions?"

"How long will we be inside of the bank?"

"Three to three and a half minutes tops."

"Means of escape?"

"When we exit the bank we will jump inside the car we arrive in. We will then proceed for two blocks where we will have another SUV waiting for us to switch to. After that we will drive to a final destination where we will once again switch vehicles and be on our merry way. Takeover complete."

"Cool. I'm with that. But I have one last question."

"Yes?"

"Why do you guys call the bank jobs takeovers?"

Kango gave a wicked smile. "Because that's exactly what robbing a bank is, Papio. When we go in we go in hard, any resistance is met with immediate pain. We don't shoot unless we absolutely have to. We have no problems slapping a few people around to make it clear to the people inside of the bank that for the next three to three and a half minutes that bank belongs to us and us only. In essence it's a—"

"Takeover," Papio said to complete Kango's sentence.

"Exactly."

Papio noticed that Special had gotten up from her seat and was heading toward the restrooms. He stood and said, "Could you excuse me for a minute, gentlemen? I see someone I have to meet."

Kango also noticed Special. "No problem." He watched as Papio quickly stepped toward the area where the restrooms were located. After Papio was out of his sight he asked the men at the table with him, "What do you think, should we give him a go?"

Steven grinned and said, "I like his nuts. If he has the heart to pull off the shit he said he did right after getting out of the Feds he has tremendous nuts. He gets my vote."

"Kingo's stamp of approval is good enough for me," said Macho.

"As long as he doesn't fuck anything up I don't care. If he does, he dies. Make sure that your brother understands that, Kango," Brad said seriously.

Kango smiled at his crew and said, "My brother would never approve of someone who wasn't loyal enough to deal with me. He also knows how we do, so there's no need to explain that. So, Papio is in?"

Each man gave Kango a nod.

"Good."

Papio was waiting patiently for Special to come out of the ladies' room. He wanted to talk to her so bad it hurt. He couldn't believe how nervous he was. *Calm down, nigga, you gots to be cooler than this,* he said to himself as he wiped his slightly sweaty palms on the side of his expensive jeans. When Special stepped out of the ladies' room she saw Papio standing there. Before she could speak he said, "I know you are like really salty at me right now, but can you give me three quick minutes to try to explain what went down out in Hollywood?"

She held up two perfectly manicured fingers and said, "You got two."

"Thanks. That move was designed for us to put down days before. If I would have thought you were serious I would have backed down and aborted so you could do you," he lied. "I thought you was on some joke shit. By the time I realized you were for real the wheels were already in motion and there was no turning back. I hope you can accept my apology."

"Whatever. Just don't let no shit like that ever happen again. You see me anywhere, odds are I'm working, so that means back the fuck off."

"You working now?"

"I'm always working. So back the fuck off."

"One more thing before you leave my life, Special."

She checked the time on her expensive diamond bezel Cartier. "You have twenty-two seconds, Papio."

She remembered my name; good sign, he thought. "Can you please give me a number so I can have the opportunity to stay in touch with you?"

"For what? You wanna go out on a square date or some shit? Come on with that shit, you know what the business is; if it ain't about money it ain't about shit else with me."

"Okay then, let me get at you on some business shit. I got several moves in the works as we speak."

"Time's up, Papio." She began to step away from him, then thought better of it. She turned to face him and said, "Give me your number and pray that I use it."

He smiled and pulled out a card from his wallet and passed it to her. "I'll be out here for another two or three weeks. After that I'll be in Oklahoma City; you can reach me wherever I am with that number. Use it, Special, it will be worth it."

She smiled at him and he swore that he fell in love right at that very moment. "Maybe I will, Papio; then again, maybe I won't." With that said she stepped back inside of the club area and left Papio to watch her firm ass sway from side to side in a motion that made him have an instant erection.

He regained his composure and rejoined Kango and his crew of bank robbers. It was time to finish listening to how he was about to participate in his first takeover.

CHAPTER FOURTEEN

Papio and Kango's crew pulled in front of Bank One in the Bronx at 11:45 A.M., dressed in all-black army fatigues. Each man was armed to the teeth, carrying a fully automatic AK-47 assault rifle along with two 9 mm pistols. Since every member of the crew had extremely long hair they had on black skull caps to cover their hair. They checked their weapons, cocked the hammers, and pulled the ski masks down over their faces. They took a moment to all get on the same page, then jumped out of the brown Chevy Tahoe and entered the bank at 11:47 A.M. Kango was the first man to burst through the doors and enter the semi-crowded bank.

"Everyone put your hands in the air now or die!"

Kango, Steven, and Macho wasted no time hopping over the counter. Steven and Macho went straight to the open vault while Kango proceeded to empty every drawer in front of each bank teller. Papio stepped to the middle of the bank and watched their backs as Brad stood by the door, keeping an eye on the streets. When Kango emptied every drawer he tossed his large duffel bag over the counter to Papio. Papio let the bag drop by his feet without taking his eyes off of anyone inside of the bank.

Brad was impressed that Papio remained focused and didn't take his eyes off of the people inside of the bank. He checked the time and saw that they had been inside of the bank for three minutes and fifteen seconds. "'Time!" he yelled.

Kango grabbed two more duffel bags, jumped over the counter, and headed straight toward the door. Macho and Steven were right behind him. Brad watched as Papio knelt and picked up the duffel bag that Kango tossed him without once taking his eyes off of the crowd inside of the bank. Once Steven and Macho were out of the bank he watched as Papio calmly stepped toward him. Brad and Papio exited the bank last and joined the others inside of the Tahoe. Kango eased into the light traffic and they were on their way at exactly 11:51 A.M. *In and out without any problems.* Papio slid his ski mask off and watched each man as they did the same. Two minutes later they switched SUVs and were now driving down the street in a black GMC Denali. Papio didn't relax until they entered Brooklyn and once again switched SUVs. This time they were inside a red Escalade. Thirty-five minutes later they pulled into the garage of a house in a suburban area of New York. Once they were inside of the house Kango went into the bedroom and Papio heard him speaking to someone on the telephone.

"How did it go? Good. I'll get with you later, baby," Kango said as he hung up the phone and came back inside of the living room with the others. He had a smile on his face when he told them, "Everything went cool. No one came out and tried to get the tags or anything. Well done, gentlemen."

Brad, known for not saying much, stepped over to where Papio was sitting and gave him some dap. "You do have nerves of steel, my man. I loved how you were so cool under the gun."

Papio smiled and said, "Man, I may have been calm on the outside but if anyone would have moved they would have gotten shot the fuck up! I was scared out of my fucking mind!" All of the men started laughing.

"That's the adrenaline rush of a takeover, Papio. There's nothing else like it in the world, my man."

"I hear you, Brad, that shit was wild! How many of them do you guys pull a year?"

Steven shrugged and said, "Two, maybe three. Don't worry, you will be notified when we get down again."

"That's what's up. Now, can we split all this fucking money!" Everyone inside of the room started laughing again as they began to empty the duffel bags of hard green currency. The takeover was complete.

Four hours later Papio was sitting down in the living room area of his suite, watching the news on the television. The news reporter was reporting how five masked gunmen robbed the Bank One of the Bronx and got away without a trace. He smiled as he grabbed his cell phone and called Brandy. After speaking with her for a few minutes he called Nick to see what he was up to. Nick told him that he was planning on going to the club since it was Friday.

"I'm telling you, son, you haven't experienced shit until you go clubbing in the Apple. You Cali niggas don't know how to party like we do out East."

"Is that right? Well, come and show me how it's done, B." Papio started laughing as he looked down at his duffel bag that contained his cut from the takeover. *$1.5 million for three and a half minutes. Shit, I can get used to this type of change,* he said to himself.

"The limo will be there to pick your ass up at midnight, so be ready to kick it real live, son, because you won't be coming back to your hotel until the sun comes up."

"Midnight? Damn, that's what time we're going to the fucking club?"

"That's right, B, shit don't even start jumping off for reals until around one A.M. anyways. Told you, ain't nowhere in the world like the Apple when it comes to getting your club on, B. Get some rest, you're going to need it. Oh and, Papio, dress fly. I mean really fly, son."

"Pssst." Papio knew that wasn't going to be a problem. After he hung up the phone with Nick, Papio started doing some quick calculating. *Okay, with 1.5 from this lick added to the 1.5 I got from that Italian move, I'm three tickets strong. That other shit with Twirl will pay dividends on the back end so I won't even count that. The chips I got from the work from Lee will hold me down for a good minute. Now all I need is for this shit to pop off with Nick and I can get at those fucking Cubans.*

Papio figured he better get some rest if he was going to be kicking it all night at the club so he headed to the bedroom. When he heard his cell phone ring he jumped and ran as fast as he could back into the living room to answer it. The number on the caller ID was unknown and his heart raced as he pressed the green answer button. He wanted to hear from Special so bad that it was slowly killing him.

"Hello." When he heard the familiar recording from the federal operator telling him that he had a prepaid call from a federal correctional facility he was a little disappointed. *Kingo.* He pressed the number five on his cell phone and accepted the call. "What's good, dread?"

"Weh yuh depon, mon?" asked Kingo.

"What am I doing? I'm sitting here in New York counting a whole lot of fucking money, my nigga."

Kingo smiled and said, "A nuh nuttin, there's plenty more where that come from, mon. You did good, real good. Me brotha and men were very impressed. You will be called again in the future. Proud of you, mon."

"What you mean no big deal? I'm loving this shit, Kingo! For real everything is going better than I even dreamed it would. No problems and plenty of money. Shit, at this rate I'll reach my goal way faster than I thought."

"Everything bless, mon. When you go to Miami?"

"I was just sitting here thinking about that. After I finish up out here I think I'll head that way."

"You t'ink?"

"Yeah, it depends on how I finish up this East Coast trip. It looks as if everything will go nicely for me though. Get at me in a week and I'll let you know the business."

"Will do! Papio. Be careful out there, mon. 'Nuff respect."

"Gotcha," Papio said as he hung up the phone. Just as he pressed the end button his cell started to ring again. This time the caller ID read: PRIVATE. He tried not to get too excited like last time but he couldn't help himself. He got butterflies in his stomach right before he answered, "Hello?"

"I know I'm a fool for making this call but my business moves have been put on hold for a sec, I'm way out here in New York by myself without shit to do, bored out of my fucking mind. And on top of everything I can't seem to get your pretty-ass face off of my fucking mind."

Papio's smile was so bright he felt as if his cheeks would break. "Well, hello to you too, Special."

"*Ugh!* I can see your ass just cheesing like crazy. Don't flatter yourself, pretty nigga. Like I said, I. Am. Bored. With a capital B."

"For real, Special, I don't give a damn what your reason is for getting at me, I'm just glad you did. Do you feel like getting your club on tonight?"

"Anything beats sitting in this boring-ass hotel room. What you got planned?"

"Let's do this, since it's way too early to hit the clubs, let's get together and go somewhere and have a nice meal; and then we can hook up with my mans and go out and see how these New Yorkers get down."

Special liked the sound of that. "I'm with that. Where are you staying?"

"I'm at the Crowne Plaza in Times Square. Get dressed and catch a cab over here. Then we'll make it do what it do. Oh and Special."

"What?"

"Dress fly. I mean really fly."

"Please, nigga, you really think you gotta tell me that?"

CHAPTER FIFTEEN

Papio came downstairs to the lobby of the hotel feeling and looking real good. He knew when Special saw him she would be very impressed. Normally he didn't give a damn what a woman thought about him; the only woman who mattered in his life was Mama Mia. But for reasons he couldn't quite understand he really wanted to impress Special.

As he entered the lobby he had no problem locating Special. She was the finest girl in the lobby. She was looking so beautiful he felt weak in the knees just staring at her from a distance. He continued toward her slowly and was trying his best to absorb every ounce of the energy she was releasing into the lobby by just standing there looking so damn fine. When she turned and saw him headed her way he watched her eyes as she did a quick survey of what he was wearing. She smiled after she finished checking him out and right then he knew that this woman could be the woman Kingo had told him about. She could be the one true love of his life. She could make him change a lot of his wicked ways for real. Her smile did something to his heart that words couldn't begin to explain. When he was standing in front of her he paused before he spoke and gave her a survey of his own. What he saw he definitely liked. She was wearing the hell out of a black lacy dress by Azzedine Alaïa; and if Papio remembered correctly that piece right there cost a nice chunk of change, over $5,000 to be exact. *Impressive,* he thought as he continued to check out her outfit. On her small feet were a pair of black and gold Jimmy Choo pumps. He noticed that she wore a diamond toe ring on the second toe of each foot. Her toenails were painted the same color gold as her pumps and, man, did they look edible! *Calm down, baby, you gots to play this one just right. This ain't the average broad; she got class as well as major game. Don't forget that she's in the business so she has gangster too,* he told himself as he let his eyes meet hers again.

"So what you gawking at, pretty man?" she asked with that damn gorgeous smile of hers.

"I should be asking you the same question, Special."

"I figured from that night at that party you had some style about yourself. Looking at you now confirms it. You're giving Versace its proper respect, pretty man."

He frowned and said, "Kill that 'pretty man' shit, baby. Papio will do just fine."

"Oh, so you a sensitive nigga. Ahh, I'm sorry for hurting your little feelings. It's just that you're sooo pretty," she said as if she were talking to a little child.

Papio ignored her humor and took her by the hand and said, "Come on before you ruin the evening before it even gets started."

Papio gave one of the bellboys a twenty dollar bill to get them a cab. When he saw that the bellboy had secured them one they stepped out of the hotel and walked quickly toward the cab. When they were inside of the cab Papio told the cab driver, "Take us to the 40/40 Club please."

The foreigner gave him a nod and pulled into traffic. It was a little after 8:00 P.M. so Papio figured they could go dine and use this time to get to know one another before they came back to his hotel and hooked up with

Nick for the late-night festivities. He turned in his seat slightly and said, "All right, tell me as much as you're going to tell me about yourself. Like for starters, where are you from?"

She smiled and thought, *Damn, this pretty nigga looks good and he smells good, too.* "What cologne do you have on? I never smelled that one before, pretty man . . . I mean, Papio," she said with a smile.

"DKNY for Men. Now answer me, Special."

With raised eyebrows she asked, "What was your question again?"

"Where are you from?"

"California."

"I know that; where in California? Stop playing."

"Look, I was born up North, moved to the South when my mother was killed. Where doesn't really matter. We're both in the business where too much information could become detrimental to our get down. We're way out here on the East Coast for whatever reasons; leave it at that, Papio. We're not two squares out on a date. Tonight is what it is; hopefully we'll have some fun and enjoy each other's company. All that getting to know one another shit is nothing for real because odds are after tonight we will not see each other again. You do you and I'll do me. So, let's enjoy the moment and kill all that square shit."

Damn, she makes a nigga feel like a sucka. "Check it, Special, I like everything I see in you and a nigga wants to get to know you better. You right, fuck all that square shit because that ain't in me neither. Regardless of what our get down may be I am still feeling you. And I do want to see you again after this East Coast move is over. No lovey-dovey shit, just want to spend some time with you and see what may pop off from that."

She sighed. "That's what I'm trying to tell you, Papio; nothing will pop off because I'm not the wifey-type bitch. That wifey-boo shit ain't for me, it's for Suzy Q or some shit. I love money and I get my own. Don't depend on no one to get it for me either. I do me. Whether you believe it or not I am very good at what I do."

He smiled and thought, *My God this broad is special for real.* "I'm not doubting your paper-getting skills at all, Special. Shit, for real, we have that in common and believe me when I tell you I am one of the best at getting that fucking money. You never know, maybe we can link up and get some paper together."

"Doubt it. I move better solo or with whomever I have in with me on a lick, which most times means a sucker who's not about to get a dime after everything is everything."

"Like that huh?"

"Exactly like that."

"Tell me something then, is there anything you wouldn't do for the money?"

"Nothing. I'll fuck for it if the offer is right and I mean really right."

"What's really right?" he asked with a sly grin. He was hoping to get the pussy for free, but if he had to pay for it he probably would.

She thought about his question for a few seconds and then answered, "Six figures right."

"Damn, that pussy got a gold lining in it or something?"

She smiled at him and said, "You'll never find out."

"I spend six figures shopping, baby."

"Then my price just shot to seven figures."

Before he could respond the cab driver pulled in front of the 40/40 Club. Papio paid the cab driver and they climbed out of the cab and entered the restaurant.

After they were seated and made their order Papio said, "You know you already fucked up a nigga's night right?"

"Why's that, because you thought you might get you some tonight?"

Papio just shrugged his shoulders in response.

"Kill that, pretty man. You never know; I might get drunk enough and give you a little bit." She said this with her index and thumb held inches apart.

Papio held up his hand and jokingly said, "Waiter, can we get a bottle of vodka over here?" They both laughed.

After their meal was finished they sat back and sipped some cognac and enjoyed watching several of Jay-Z's famous friends enter the club/restaurant. "Look at them. All stars are the easiest marks to get at."

"Not really; they're too hard to get close to."

"Not for me. It's easy for my sexy ass to get close to any man," she said confidently.

Papio ignored her comment; he didn't want to start hearing about all the dudes she got with. "So, what kind of move you got cracking out here?"

"A nice little something something, should clear a few tickets if everything goes right. Everything is on hold right now because the marks are out of town. Been trying to get them to let me roll with them but they're still on some secret shit. That has to loosen up soon. I'm wasting a lot of time out here."

"And time is money."

"You fucking right."

"Okay, back to that 'there's nothing you wouldn't do for the money' shit. Would you kill for it?"

She stared at him for a moment and said, "I've killed for free so you best believe I would kill for this money. What about you, are there any restrictions to your money-getting skills?"

He shook his head no. "Absolutely none. Whatever it takes to get it I do it."

"Have you killed for it?"

"Killed for free, for vengeance, for fun, and more than once for the paper."

"So, not only are you one pretty-ass man, you're telling me you're a stone-cold killer?"

He raised his eyebrows and gave a wicked smile.

"That shit turns me on right there, Papio; you might just have upped your chances of getting some later on."

"In that case let me tell you about the time I—"

She cut him off with her laughter and said, "Wait a minute, killer, fall back and let's enjoy the rest of the night first." She checked the time on her expensive diamond watch and asked, "It's already after ten; when are we getting with your peoples so we can hit the club? I'm ready to kick it a little bit."

"My man Nick is sending a limo to pick us up around midnight so yeah, we better get up out of here." He pulled out his wallet and grabbed three hundred dollar bills and left them on the table.

Special noticed that the tab was a little over $200. *At least he ain't a cheap nigga,* she thought. They walked out of the club hand in hand. She couldn't remember the last time she had done some square shit like this. She was actually enjoying herself. When they were inside of another cab heading back to Papio's hotel she leaned next to him and asked, "Are you a Pussy Monster, Papio?"

"A pussy what?"

"A Pussy Monster?"

"Please explain to me what a Pussy Monster is."

"A nigga who can last a long time and make this pussy scream as if it has seen a monster."

He smiled. "In that case, yeah, Special, I'm a Pussy Monster."

She stared into his light brown eyes with a serious expression on her face and said, "You better be."

His eyes almost popped out of their sockets as he stared at her, not believing what he heard her tell him. *Thank you, Virgin Mother, thank you so much,* he said to himself and smiled at Special.

CHAPTER SIXTEEN

Papio and Special were having a drink in the bar of the hotel when Nick called Papio and told him that he was outside of the hotel in the limousine. As they were walking toward the limousine Nick popped his head out of the sunroof of an extra-stretch Cadillac Escalade limousine and yelled, "Damn, son! You didn't tell me you was bringing a friend! Especially someone as fine as this dime! You gon' shut the club down with this piece for reals, B." The driver of the limousine stepped out of the stretch SUV and came around to open the door for them. Once inside of the vehicle Papio shook his head and said, "You are one real classy guy, Nick; I mean truly top of the line all the way."

Ignoring Papio's sarcasm Nick smiled at Special and said, "Hello, lovely lady. I hope you weren't insulted, because my words were meant purely as a compliment. Don't let this sensitive-ass dude give you the wrong impression of me."

"Don't worry, he didn't," she said. In her mind she was thinking, *You fucking jerk.*

As the limousine driver eased the huge vehicle into traffic Papio asked Nick, "Where are we headed?"

"Where else would Harlem Nick take y'all, son? Harlem, baby! It's going down at Club One tonight. My mans and 'em are performing around one or two, so by the time we get there everything should be real live, B."

"Who's your mans and 'em?" asked Special.

"Jim Jones and the Dipset crew, minus Cam'ron right now though."

"That's cool, he's kind of cute. Is that guy going to be there, too; what's his name, umm, Juelz something?"

"Juelz Santana. Yeah, that's family right there, he should be there for sure. Now, sit back and relax, let's pop a bottle, because it's definitely going to be a good night." Nick reached inside of a miniature refrigerator and pulled out a bottle of rosé and popped the cork. The bubbly champagne spilled onto the floor of the SUV and Special noticed how Papio was looking at his man. It was as if they were sharing the exact same thoughts: *No class at all.*

Harlem, Lennox Avenue, the Apollo Theater, Malcolm X, the thought of all that famed history had Special feeling kind of excited as the driver brought the limousine to a stop right in front of Club One. She smiled as Papio stepped out of the limousine and reached back to help her out of the vehicle. *This pretty nigga is being the perfect gentleman this evening. I think I'm going to enjoy him,* she thought with her smile still in place as Nick climbed out of the SUV last and quickly stepped in front of them and led the way past the long line and directly into the club. Nick had a little pull and he made sure that he let it be known.

"These are my peoples, B. No way in hell does a real money-getting Harlem nigga gots to do no waiting, B."

Papio and Special gave each other a look like, "is this fool serious?" They shared grins as they let flossy-ass Harlem Nick lead them inside of the club. Of course Nick took them straight to the VIP area. After ordering a couple of bottles of rosé Nick left them so he could go speak to a few of his friends.

"Man, that's your man for real? You were batting a hundred until you brought that clown into the equation," Special said as she sipped some of her champagne.

"Check it, I've never really kicked it with Nick like that, but we have pulled a few moves with each other. He's solid when it comes to doing what it do. Never knew he was flossy like this though." He shrugged and added, "That's him though; me, I do me and I don't let those around me affect my moves. So don't you let that affect you either."

"Your business is your business, but dealing with a nigga like him can become dangerous sooner or later. He's not only flossy with it, he's careless."

"Careless? What makes you say that?"

She shrugged and said, "It's a feeling I guess. I wouldn't trust that nigga as far as I can throw him, let alone make any moves with his ass. He'd cross you out in a heartbeat. But that's your, B, not mines. Watch your six though."

Papio let her words sink in. He smiled at her and said, "Come on, let's get out there and rep the West. These East Coast clowns can't fade us!"

"You better believe that shit. Come on, let's go!"

They went out onto the dance floor and got to dancing and partying as if it were New Year's Eve. They were enjoying each other's company and having a real good time. The DJ slowed it down and Special started to step off of the dance floor but Papio shook his head no and said, "Uh-uh, I've been waiting for this. You're going to slow dance with me, sexy." He pulled her into his arms and they danced slowly to a Keyshia Cole song.

Special put her head onto his shoulder and enjoyed inhaling his scent as they got their slow groove on. When she felt his erection poking her on her thigh she smiled and eased her left hand between them and gave him a soft squeeze. "Mmmmmmmm. You just might be a Pussy Monster, pretty man," she whispered into his ear.

Papio smiled but chose to continue to enjoy the moment. Not only was Special drop-dead gorgeous, she was gangster with it as well. A quality he never thought he would like in a woman. But right now he was realizing that he was definitely feeling her way more than he ever thought possible. The physical thing was super strong no doubt, but there was much more to this woman and he wanted to get to know as much as he could. *I'm not letting her ass get away from me,* he said to himself as the song came to an end. "Thirsty?"

"Mm-hm," she said as she pulled him back toward the VIP.

Nick had four females sitting with him in the VIP when they returned. "That's the business, son! I saw y'all out there gettin' y'all's Cali groove crackin'. That's what's up! As you can see I've found me a few beauties to join us for the morning because in the NY the party don't stop until the sun comes up!"

"Well, keep popping them bottles, boy, and let's party," Papio said as he sat down next to Special. He refilled her flute with some more rosé and asked, "You good?"

"Fine. I have to go to the bathroom. I'll be right back," she said hurriedly as she stood and left the VIP before he could say anything else.

After she left the table Nick eased next to Papio and said, "Look, those Indian clowns we're going to hit just came into the club, son."

"Where?"

"Check the bar to the right. Those fools standing with that cute bird."

"Is that your bird?"

Nick smiled when he answered, "Yep. Didn't know they would be here though; now I can check them out a little more, na-mean?"

"Yeah, I feel you," Papio said as he stared at the Indians standing by the bar. *Damn, those are the same fools I saw Special with the other night at Caroline's,* he thought as he continued to stare at them. *Fuck! Please don't let those fools be in her line of fire. Damn. How the fuck am I ever going to get this broad if I keep beating her to her licks? Fuck,* he thought as he watched as Special came back and sat down next to him.

The lights dimmed before either of them could speak and the DJ screamed, "Dip! Set! Dip! Set!" Jim Jones led Freeky Zeeky and Juelz Santana out onto the stage and they started performing "Pop Champagne." The crowd went crazy dancing and singing along with their hometown hero. The atmosphere inside of Club One was electric as everyone enjoyed the music. By the time Jim Jones performed "We Fly High" *Baaalllinn!* Everybody went bananas. Nick's drunk ass was standing on top of their table in the VIP, screaming and yelling like a true groupie-type nigga, as Papio stared at him with disdain. *Can't believe I never peeped how this nigga moved before. Straight sucker shit,* he said to himself.

Special noticed how Papio was looking at his man and smiled. *He's waking up,* she thought. She reached out, grabbed his hand, and pulled him out of his seat. They went back onto the dance floor and started dancing without paying any attention to anyone else inside of the club. For the next hour or so it was all about them. By the time they returned to their seats they were both sweaty and tired.

"You tired?" asked Papio

"I'm tired of this club. I'm ready to do something else. What about you?" she asked with a seductive look on her face.

Without answering her he stood and signaled Nick to come go with him. He turned back to Special and said, "I'll be right back. Get ready to bounce; we're out of here when I come back."

"Good," she said with a smile. She watched as Papio and Nick left the VIP. While she waited for Papio to return to the VIP she surveyed the club. She was completely taken by surprise when she saw the Indians out on the dance floor dancing with two females with really bad weave jobs. *Ain't that a bitch. Those punk-ass motherfuckers gots the nerve to be down there getting they club on. Shit! How the fuck am I going to play this one?* she asked herself. Then she smiled, snapped her fingers, and said, "Got it." She stood, smoothed out her dress, and checked to make sure that she was right. She then stepped out of the VIP and went directly toward the dance floor. She stepped up to one of the Indian men and whispered something in his ear. The Indian looked shocked as she strolled away from him with much switch in her sexy-ass hips. She knew that his eyes were glued to her perfect-shaped ass. *Yeah, keep on staring at it, nigga, because I know you want it even more now.* She was correct; he couldn't take his eyes off of her. She made it back to her seat a few minutes before Papio and Nick returned.

Papio stood in front of her and reached out his hand. "Let's shake this spot, baby; time to go make our own music."

"I know that's right." She turned and noticed how Nick had a screwed-up face and said, "It was a pleasure meeting you, Harlem Nick. Take care."

Nick ignored her and told Papio, "I'll hit you in a day or so, son; you know that business will be serious next week."

"Business is always serious, B," Papio said as he turned and left the VIP with Special's hand held firmly in his.

As they were leaving the club Special shot another look toward the Indians and was amused at the expression on their faces. They looked pissed. *Good,* she thought. She also noticed how Nick was looking at them as they were leaving. *That's a grimy nigga if I ever saw one.* She gave Papio's hand a slight squeeze and smiled at him when he turned to make sure she was okay. *Watch your man, Papio; watch that nigga,* she thought.

CHAPTER SEVENTEEN

Papio was glad that Nick let him use the services of the limousine; that would save them a lot of time. As soon as the limousine driver closed the door Special wasted no time. She grabbed Papio by his face and pulled him toward her. They shared a kiss so intense it was damn near primal. Papio was shocked, but he rolled with it and was loving every minute of it. He never had an aggressive woman before and that shit turned him the fuck on. He slid the thin straps of her dress off of her shoulders and cupped one of her perfect grapefruit-sized breasts. He pulled his lips from hers and dropped his head to her chest and began to suck and nibble on her nipples.

She moaned and said, "Don't nibble on me like that, pretty nigga, bite 'em!"

Papio did what she told him to and the moan she gave told him that he did exactly what she wanted the way she wanted, which further excited him. By the time they made it to the hotel they were so fired up that they looked a hot mess as they exited the limousine. Papio slapped three hundred dollar bills in the limousine driver's hand and thanked him as Special pulled him toward the entrance of the hotel. When they stepped into the elevator Special dropped to her knees before Papio even had a chance to press the button for the floor of his suite. An old white couple was approaching the elevator and saw Special kneeling in front of Papio, unfastening his pants just as the elevator doors closed.

When Papio and Special made it inside of his suite their sexing went from wild and crazy to flat-out nasty. They tore through the suite as if they were two tornadoes battling for territory to destroy. He had her bent over the table in the dining area giving it to her real hard from the rear. She in turn was backing all of that ass right back into his dick as hard as she could; her only thoughts were, *This nigga is a Pussy Monster. I love this shit! I love it!* By the time they made it to the bedroom she came so many times she felt as if she would faint.

Papio laid her down and began to suck her pussy as if his life depended on the outcome. *My God, even this woman's pussy is special!*

Since this was a one-time sexapade to Special she wanted to make it very very memorable. No holds barred. She got off of the bed and turned Papio onto his stomach and began to lick his salty body from head to toe. She sucked each of his toes and smiled as they curled inside of her mouth. She got a big kick out of watching him squirm and try to get away from her when her tongue made it to the crack of his ass. She placed her hands firmly on his ass cheeks, opened them and began to toss his salad and man she blew Papio's mind! By the time she turned him onto his back his dick was so hard it had reached its full ten inches. She smacked her lips and smiled as she licked her way down to that beautiful brown super-sized piece of meat. When she had him inside of her mouth she swirled her tongue around his head and drove him crazy. Though he already came twice he felt his third approaching quickly. Not wanting this to end without being back inside of that good, tight pussy, Papio grabbed her by her face and pulled her off of him. She climbed on top and began to ride him slowly, never once taking her eyes off

of his face. Papio's eyes were closed but he could feel
her eyes on him. When he opened his eyes and saw how
she was staring at him he knew for sure that he could
definitely love this woman. *What the fuck?* he thought
as he continued to stare at her as she gave him the best
ride of his life. After a few minutes of this he came and
came and came. It felt as if his third nut was his first he
shot so much sperm into the Magnum condom he had
wrapped tightly around his dick. She slid off of him
and sighed as she laid her head onto his shoulder and
whispered, "That was good, Pussy Monster. Thank you,
I really really really needed that."

"You acted like you ain't had no dick in years! You
tried to work the hell outta nigga."

She smiled but remained silent and continued to
rest. He turned his head and tried to look into her eyes
but she had them firmly shut. He closed his eyes and
slowly drifted off to sleep. The last thing he remembered was that the clock read 8:15 A.M. *Damn, that
means we fucked for over three hours. Wow!*

Papio opened his eyes a little after two P.M. to see that
Special was nowhere to be found. When Papio walked
into the living room he was surprised at the damage
they had done to the suite. Furniture was flipped over,
the little table was broken, pillows were torn open.
Damn, that is one wild-ass woman, he thought as he
went back into the bedroom. He suddenly got nervous
that Special had robbed his ass and rushed to the closet
to make sure that the black duffel bag containing his
money from the bank job was still in place. It was.

She may have been with all that front shit but he
could tell she was feeling him just as much as he was
feeling her sexy ass. *But will she still be feeling me*

when I beat her once again at a nice come up? That's the question, he asked himself as he lay back down. He had wanted to tell her about his plans to take down the Indians but he got distracted by her aggressive nature. He didn't want to fuck off his chances of getting with her but there was no way in hell he was about to pass up a move like this one. It was time to get those punk-ass Cubans their ends so he could have some breathing room. *Fuck it, it is what it is,* he said to himself as he closed his eyes and went back to sleep.

Papio spent the rest of the week shopping and kicking it in Harlem with Nick. The more time he spent with Nick the more he realized that he really didn't like how that nigga got down. He was so caught up with impressing all the hood mothafuckas that he was slipping and didn't even know it. *I got to shake this nigga as soon as possible. He's sitting here flossing to all of these fucking wolves not knowing that the very first chance they got they would do his ass for all of his riches. There is no way in hell I'm going to let that nigga get me caught the fuck up with his so-called homies. This nigga is a readymade lick and he doesn't even realize it. Damn fool. Shit, I might as well get that shit for myself,* he said to himself with a smile on his face.

"Check it, Nick, I'm about to head back to my suite and wait for baby to get here. Let me kick it with her for a few hours and then we can make that move."

"That's the business, son. Hit me when you're ready. I'll get the rental and get shit together, B."

"The weapons?"

"All that."

"What time do you want to head out?"

"We can leave any time after seven. That way when we make it out the way it will be late night and we'll be able to ease on in and get situated."

Papio checked his watch and said, "That's straight, that will give me enough time to kick it with my baby and give her a dose of Papio's finest."

"I hear you, playboy. Tell me, what happened to that bad-ass bird you had last week? Don't tell me you fucked that one off; she was one bad-ass bitch, son."

Hearing Nick speak on Special that way, even though it was supposed to be meant as a compliment, irked the hell out of Papio. He blew it off and said, "All right, playa, I'll holla at ya later."

Papio caught a cab back to the hotel and waited for Brandy to arrive. Even though he was waiting for Brandy his mind wouldn't stop thinking about Special. Brandy was a perfectly nice woman but Special was exactly what her name implied: special. Shit, she was extra special. He started watching television but the television was actually watching him because his mind was elsewhere. Special consumed all of his thoughts. *Damn, why hasn't she gotten at me?* he wondered. *I know she's feeling me.*

He stared at his cell phone as if he could will it to ring. "Come on, tough-ass girl, hit ya boy up." He thought about that wild morning they spent together and the mere thought of her luscious body and gorgeous face got him extremely hard. *Man, a broad has never had me like this,* he said to himself. A knock on the door snapped him back to reality. As soon as he opened the door Brandy dropped the carry-on bag she had been holding and jumped into his arms. They shared a nice long kiss.

"Mmmmm, I guess it's safe to assume you missed me huh, *mami?*"

"You better believe it," Brandy said as she stepped aside so the bellboy could bring in her luggage. After Papio tipped the bellboy he made sure the door was locked. "Why are you smiling like that, daddy?"

He motioned with his head toward his crotch. "Because daddy has really been missing his *mami*. Come here."

Brandy stepped into his arms and they shared another kiss. Though Papio was really feeling Brandy and loved everything about her she was no comparison to Special. Thinking about Special turned him on to the point where he felt as if he was about to come on himself right then and there. He scooped Brandy into his arms and carried her into the bedroom. He sat her on the bed and began to take off his sweatpants. Brandy smiled at him as she began to undress also. When she was naked he was still in awe of how damn good her body looked. *She may be thirty-eight but she is definitely still a bad-ass woman. Firm in all of the right places plus pretty as hell.* Before he knew it he was sucking her pussy and she was moaning and groaning real loud. Somehow they ended up in the 69 position and Papio was in heaven. Tasting her sweet juices while getting his dick sucked felt absolutely divine to him. He kept thinking back to Special licking his asshole and it turned him on even more. When he felt himself start to come he tried to move but Brandy held on to him firmly. She wanted to swallow his juices and when she did he felt as if he died and went to heaven for real. Special may have still been on his mind but right then Brandy had his full attention.

CHAPTER EIGHTEEN

Papio and Brandy were lying in bed, totally spent after sexing each other crazy for a good two hours. Papio was tired and wanted to nap but he knew it was the perfect time to drop the bomb on Brandy to see if she would hold him down with what he had planned for the Niagara Falls move. "Check it, Brandy, I got some business I need to take care of before we really start kicking it on this trip. We're going to Niagara Falls tonight."

"That's so exciting, baby; I can't wait to see the Falls. What kind of business do you have to take care of, daddy?" She stared at him with nothing but love in her eyes.

This is going to be too easy, he thought. "I got a move to make that's going to bring me a major amount of money. But I'm going to need you to do something serious for me." He then went on and explained how he was going to have her drive the money back to their suite.

"You see, the original plan was for you to take the money to my man Nick's people and wait for us to return. But I got a funny feeling that shit going to fall fucked up. So what I want you to do is come back here and get another suite in your name. Once you get here text me and give me the room number."

"But won't your friend get suspicious, daddy?"

"It won't matter. I'll take care of that end. The most important thing to me is keeping you safe. When you hit me and let me know that you're good I'll take care of everything else. Then we'll enjoy our week out here shopping and doing whatever you want to do. Cool?"

"All I have to do is drive back here with the money?"

"I refuse to not keep it one hundred with you, baby; there will most likely be some drugs, too. What kind or how much I'm not really knowing."

She smiled lovingly at him and said, "That means it's going to be a whole lot."

He returned her smile and said, "Right."

She shook her head. "Lord, I done went and let you get me sprung on your sexy ass. To even consider something as dangerous as this is crazy. I'll do it. But you're definitely going to make this trip the best trip of my life."

"I was going to do that anyway, so don't even trip, *mami*. I got you."

"In that case you might as well start showing me right now by giving me some more of that," she said as she pointed toward his dick. With no more words said he scooped her into his arms and gave her a tight hug before he started giving her what she craved.

Nick came and picked Papio and Brandy up a little after seven that evening. They made it to Niagara Falls, New York at 4:15 A.M. They got two rooms at the Seneca Niagara Casino/Hotel. Instead of Brandy being tired from all of the sex and seven-hour drive she wanted to gamble. Papio was kind of pumped himself so he decided to go give the blackjack tables a try. They gambled until nine in the morning and came back to their room and got some much-needed rest. Papio was so tired he didn't have time to trip off the fact that he and Brandy had just fucked off $11,000 gambling.

Nick called and woke Papio at noon and told him that everything was ready; he had received the call from his bird. "So get your ass ready to roll in twenty, son."

"I'll be ready," Papio said as he climbed out of bed and hurried into the bathroom to get dressed.

He woke Brandy and told her, "*Mami,* I need for you to get up, get you something to eat, and get ready. When I come back you gots to be ready to make that ride for me."

"How long will you be, daddy?" she asked groggily.

"I'm not knowing. But it's crucial that you be ready to get on as soon as I call you. I'll hit you from my phone so you can come meet us in front of the hotel. No stops other than gas, *mami.* And remember, as soon as you get back to the hotel get another suite for us. Grab all of our stuff and wait for my call."

"I got it, daddy. You just make sure you be careful okay?"

"Don't sweat it, I'll be fine. Give me a kiss." They shared a kiss and just as Papio pulled away from her there was a knock at the door.

"Got to go get this money, baby. Get ready."

Brandy climbed out of the bed and watched as Papio walked out of the hotel room. Her heart was beating so hard she thought she was having a heart attack. *Calm down, Brandy, he knows what he's doing,* she said to herself as she went into the bathroom to take a shower.

Once they were inside of the van Nick told Papio, "Look, there's a souvenir store about two miles from here. We're going in hard from the gate. Everything is in the back. So we take control of front and hit the back. My bird told me the ends and the work and shit is stacked in boxes in the back so we pile up and get the fuck, B."

"If that's how we're going to play it we might as well park in the back of the store so we won't have to load everything right on front street."

Nick shook his head no and said, "No good, can't get access to the back. We're going to have to one-two that shit. You snatch a box and walk it to the van and as I see you coming back I'll be headed out. We do that shit until the shit's empty, son."

"Let's do this," Papio said seriously. He then reached into the back and grabbed a duffel bag that was full of different weapons. He grabbed two chrome .45 Glocks and made sure that each was loaded with live rounds inside of each chamber. He then pulled out two more 9 mm and repeated the process to make sure they were loaded and ready as well. He gave Nick two of the weapons and asked, "Are we popping anybody in the store?"

Nick gave a shrug of his shoulders and said, "That was my plan. But if you think we can let 'em make it, son, then I'm with that too."

"We'll see."

Less than ten minutes later they pulled into the souvenir store. Papio smiled when he saw that no customers were inside of the store. *Good, don't need no innocent bodies on my fucking conscience,* he thought. He looked at Nick and said, "Come on, fool, let's get this fucking money!" They jumped out of the van with their weapons held down by their sides and entered the store quickly. Nick stepped straight to the counter and pointed his gun at a small, big-nosed Indian woman and smiled.

"Don't make a sound, squaw, and you will live. If you make any unnecessary moves you dead." The Indian woman gave him a nod of her head in understanding. She gave a yelp when he grabbed her by her blouse and snatched her over the counter. Papio was standing at the door, making sure that no one was coming. When he saw that Nick had the woman under control he turned and put the CLOSED sign in the front of the window and locked the door.

When Papio joined them in the back Nick smiled at him and said, "This is it, son, let's load up." He then smacked the Indian woman in the back of her head with his pistol and caught her before she fell to the ground. He carried her to the back door and laid her onto the ground, unconscious. He turned and gave Papio a grin. "At least she's breathing."

They then proceeded to load up box after box inside of the van. Papio checked a few of the boxes before he carried them outside and was so shocked his legs began to tremble. Every box was either full of money or drugs. Ecstasy pills, codeine, and kilos of heroin. *Damn, this is the lick of a fucking lifetime,* he thought as he continued to carry the boxes to the van. They hopped into the van and pulled away from the souvenir store without incident. *That was too damn easy,* Papio said to himself as he wiped sweat off of his face.

He pulled out his cell phone and called Brandy. When she answered the phone he told her, "Okay, *mami,* we're on our way. We'll be there in less than ten minutes. Be out front waiting on us. I'll call you and give you the directions where you have to go once we get up to the room," Papio lied, sticking to the script for Nick to think everything was kosher.

Brandy understood what he was saying and said, "Okay, daddy. I'll be there."

Papio hung up the phone and reached into the back and grabbed the duffel bag and pretended to put both of his guns back inside of the bag. When Nick stopped at a red light Papio held the bag open so Nick could put his guns inside of the bag too. He wanted to smile when Nick deposited his weapons inside of the duffel bag. *Gotcha, nigga,* he said to himself.

Brandy was waiting in front of the hotel when Nick pulled up. They hopped out of the van and went straight into the hotel without turning to watch as she got inside of the van and pulled off. They went straight to Papio's room. "We did that shit, B! We did that shit!" screamed Nick.

"Nigga, will you calm the fuck down. Relax, we can't celebrate until we get the fuck up outta this bitch. Here, give Brandy the address to your people and then we're going to go out and get our gamble on and do some tourist shit," Papio said as he passed Nick his cell phone. Nick gave Brandy the address to his man's brownstone in Harlem.

He gave the phone back to Papio. "You got that, baby?"

"Yes, daddy, I got it."

"Good. If you have any problems call me and Nick will guide you where you need to go."

"I will. Bye, daddy," she said as she hung up the phone so she could concentrate on driving carefully because she was scared shitless.

Papio told Nick to go change so they could go out and be seen around the casino.

Twenty-five minutes later they were on the elevator on their way down into the casino. They went and played some blackjack and Papio couldn't help but smile as he kept winning hand after hand. It was meant for him to get his money back, he thought. Nick on the other hand was making bad bet after bad bet and was losing like crazy. *Might as well enjoy yourself, nigga, because you die today,* Papio said to himself with absolutely no remorse. *The game's cold and only the coldest wins.* Papio knew there weren't any rules to this game; even if there were rules he didn't give a damn, because he don't play fair.

CHAPTER NINETEEN

A couple of hours later Papio and Nick were eating some Indian tacos in a restaurant inside of the casino.

"Aren't you going to get at your bird broad?" asked Papio.

"Nah, I'll wait until she gets at me back in Harlem. She'll be there by the time we get there for her split. At least she thinks she'll be getting her split." Nick laughed.

"Remember, she's your work, son."

"I got her, B."

They went back to their rooms and grabbed their carry bags and left the hotel without checking out. Papio frowned when he saw Special enter the casino/ hotel quickly trying her best to keep up with those same two Indians he saw her with at Caroline's. As they passed each other he raised his right hand to his ear with a serious expression on his face and mouthed the words, "call me." She gave him a slight nod in understanding and continued to follow the Indians inside of the casino/hotel.

They caught a cab to Hertz and Nick rented them a Dodge Intrepid with his fake ID and credit card. Once they were on their way Nick asked, "Did you see your bird come into the hotel as we were leaving?"

"Yeah, I peeped her."

"But did you pay attention to who she was with?"

"Yeah, I peeped that too."

"What's up with that one, son?"

Papio shrugged his shoulders and said, "Not knowing. Who gives a fuck for real? We did us; she can do what the fuck ever as far as I'm concerned."

Nick had a puzzled expression on his face but chose to let the questions running through his mind go. Seeing Special made Nick wonder where Brandy was. He started getting a bad feeling about her. *Too bad she has to get caught up in Papio's shit. Collateral damage, she gots to die right along with this nigga,* he said to himself.

They had been driving close to four hours and Papio figured it was time to make his move. He waited until they were in a nice rural-looking area and told Nick, "Damn, dog, pull this bitch over. I got to take a piss."

"Damn, son, why you didn't do that shit when we gassed up twenty minutes ago?"

Papio frowned and said, "I didn't have to take a piss then. Nigga, pull the fuck over."

Nick did as he was told and Papio got out of the car and stepped to the side and began to relieve himself. Nick was tapping the steering wheel impatiently, waiting for him to get back inside of the car, not paying him any attention. Papio pulled his Glock from the small of his back and held it down by his side as he got back inside of the car. He closed the door and watched as Nick was reaching to put the car in gear. Papio raised his gun and shot Nick three times in his torso. He didn't want to take a chance on a head shot because he didn't want to shoot out a window. Nick fell against the door and faced Papio with a shocked expression on his face. With a cold smirk on his face Papio shot him three more times. He got out of the car and reached back inside and pulled Nick's dead body over to the passenger's side. He closed the door, got into the driver's seat, and eased the car on to the high-way. He did all of this with absolutely no emotion at all; it was strictly business as far as he was concerned. A sound business decision.

Three hours later Papio entered the New York City limits. He stopped at a Shell gas station that had one of those Quick Wash automated carwashes. He pulled out three dollar bills and inserted them into the Quick Wash machine. As soon as the automated carwash began spraying water all over the rental he reached over Nick's lifeless body, opened the door, and pushed him out of the car. He then closed the door and let the Quick Wash finish washing the rental car. He then pulled out his cell phone and called Brandy. He gave a sigh of relief when she answered the phone. "You good, *mami?*"

"Mm-hm. I've been a nervous wreck waiting for your call, daddy. You okay?"

"Yeah, I'm good. Did you do what I told you to?"

"The van is parked across the street at that under-ground parking lot. I paid it up for a week just like you told me to. I got us a suite on the fourth floor and I got all of our stuff here with me."

"That's right. I should be there in about thirty min-utes."

"Good. Can we start having some fun now that your business is over?"

He smiled and said, "You better believe it, *mami.* Whatever you want you get."

"I've always wanted to see a Broadway play, daddy," she said with a smile on her pretty face.

"Well, it's way past time that you get that out of the way then. See you in thirty," he said and hung up. *Mission complete.*

***

Papio and Brandy spent the next five days shopping, sexing, touring New York, sexing, eating at the
finest restaurants, and more sexing. By the time Papio
dropped her off at JFK Brandy was so tired she felt as
if she needed to take another week off just to recuper-
ate from all of the sex and fun she had. Papio gave her
a kiss and told her that he would see her in Oklahoma
City within two to three days. They kissed passionately
in front of the airport for a few minutes and then Papio
gave her a pat on her firm behind and told her, "Now
go on. I gots me one hell of a long drive ahead of me."

She kissed him again and said, "Be careful, daddy."

"I do it no other way, *mami*." He turned and got back
into his freshly rented Lincoln Navigator and pulled
away from the curb without looking back. He was now
focused on getting the hell out of New York.

Though he knew he could make the drive from New
York to Oklahoma in a day and a half he took his time
and made it there in three days. When he pulled into
his driveway he smiled and thought, *Now it's time
to get at those fucking greedy-ass Cubans*. He went
into his house and went straight to the bathroom and
started running some bathwater. While the tub was fill-
ing he grabbed the phone and called Brandy to let her
know that he made it home safely. "Get your sexy ass
over here pronto."

She smiled and happily told him, "I'll be there within
the hour, daddy."

"I'm about to take a bath. I'll have some steaks out
for you so you can make me something to eat. I'm so
fucking tired of fast food that it don't make no sense.
So hurry your pretty ass up."

She laughed and said, "I'm on my way right now."

He went downstairs and took the steaks out of the
freezer, then grabbed one of the boxes that contained

some of the money and carried it upstairs to the bedroom. He emptied the box onto the bed. Stacks and stacks of one hundred dollar bills were all over his bed. "Damn, we'll be up all fucking night counting this shit. I fucking love it!" He was laughing as he grabbed the cordless phone and brought it with him inside of the bathroom. He eased himself into the hot water and relaxed. "Ahhhh," he said as the hot water immediately began to soothe his aching body. That drive had taken more out of him than he realized. Papio let the warm water soak in for a few minutes; then when he was nice and relaxed he made a phone call.

"Let me speak with Mr. Suarez."

"Who is this?" asked one of Mr. Suarez's flunkies.

"Tell him it's his main man, Papio," he said with a smile on his face.

Two minutes later Mr. Suarez's number-one flunky came on the line and said, "Mr. Suarez wants to know where are you?"

"Tell him I'm home and that's all he needs to know for now, Castro. And if he wants this gift I have for him he really needs to be getting on to the phone real quick like." Papio heard the phone being set down.

A minute later Mr. Suarez came on to the line and asked, "Papio, where are you, friend?"

"Where I am right now doesn't matter, Mr. Suarez. What does matter is that I have something for you. I will be in Miami in one week. Please give me the opportunity to meet with you. We have much to discuss."

"Good. I'll see you in a week then." The phone went dead in Papio' s ear and he started laughing.

Mr. Saurez hung up the phone with a smile on his face as he relaxed in his big leather chair. "I was wondering how long it would be before our friend Señor Papio would contact me."

"Our friend? That half-*mayate* half–Puerto Rican pussy gave up the location of our money as well as way too much drugs, Mr. S.; there is no way in hell he is a friend of ours," Castro said with venom in his voice.

"Señor Papio knows that we know what he did. He also realizes that he has to correct his wrongs."

"Even if he gives us back what we lost he still deserves to die."

"Maybe, and then again, maybe not."

"Come on, Mr. S., you can't seriously be thinking about letting that half breed get away with what he basically had taken from us. This is crazy!"

Mr. Suarez gave his number-one man a hard gaze before speaking. "Last time I looked around here I was the one running this ship, and as long as that remains true I will continue to do as I please. Watch yourself, Castro, you are not high enough on this chain to question any decisions I make. Am I understood?"

"Sí. Forgive me, Mr. S, it's just—"

"I understand, and believe me if Señor Papio doesn't have a substantial amount for me when he arrives next week he will be severely punished for the wrongs he committed against us. On the other hand if he comes correct then I don't see why we shouldn't afford him the luxury to continue breathing. Especially since he will still be heavy in our debt," Mr. Suarez said with a smile.

Castro smiled also and said, "Interest right?"

"Heavy interest. Señor Papio is a man who gets money. Don't forget that he made quite a considerable amount for us before that unfortunate turn of events. Really, I understand why he did what he did. It was risky as hell because he put his mother's life in jeopardy, but what other choice did he have? I respect him because he didn't take the coward way out and snitch like most men would have done in the same situation."

"True."

"For that reason alone he deserves a shot at making things right."

"But?"

"But if he fucks up again he dies and so does his loving mother," Mr. Suarez said in a deadly tone.

CHAPTER TWENTY

Brandy outdid herself with another scrumptious meal. After they finished eating Papio took her upstairs to the bedroom and showed her the bed full of money.

"Have you ever seen that much money before, *mami?*"

She looked at him as if he'd lost his mind and said, "Hell to the no! How much money is that?"

He shrugged and said, "I haven't counted it yet; from the looks of it it's probably a little over a million."

"Tha . . . that's what I had in that van?"

"Yep. And there's three more boxes full of money just like this one downstairs in the Navigator. We'll get to that shit later though. I'm too tired to deal with that shit right now. Can I lay you down and make that body feel real good before I crash out for the night?"

"On one condition."

"What's that?"

"Can you make love to me on top of all that money? I want you to fuck me good on top of a million dollars, daddy."

He smiled as he pulled her to the bed and slowly began to take off her clothes. When she was naked he began to make her body tingle all over as he licked and sucked her from head to toe. After they finished making love Papio fell into a peaceful sleep.

The next morning when he opened his eyes Brandy was up getting dressed for work. She smiled at him and said, "I counted that money for you, daddy. You were right, it was over a million dollars. 1.5 million to be exact."

He sat up in the bed, wiped sleep from his eyes, and asked, "You counted all of that damn money? How long did it take you, *mami?*"

She shrugged and said, "A couple of hours. I was so excited about seeing all of that money I couldn't sleep. You were knocked out and I didn't want to disturb you so I pulled all of it off of the bed and set on the floor and counted it for you." She pointed toward the money that she neatly stacked on the floor next to Papio's dresser and said, "If there's three more boxes full of money downstairs then you will have well over $5 million. Isn't that enough for you to go legitimate?"

Papio shook his head from side to side and said, "Nope. That money is owed to someone. Once I take care of a tab I have then I can get really focused on reaching my goal."

"What is your goal?"

He held up the index finger of his right hand and told her, "$100 million. When I have $100 million in my possession the game will be over and I will have won it. A few million wouldn't do shit for a nigga like me, Brandy. My tastes are way above some crumbs like that." He noticed the confused expression on her face and decided to dead the discussion; a square broad like her would never understand. *That's why I need Special in my life,* he said to himself.

"Don't trip, baby; everything is all good, trust that. Now go on and get to work so you can do you. If you can get at Kingo tell him I said to call me."

"Okay, daddy. Do you have any plans later?"

"Other than spending some quality time with you, nope, my evening belongs to you and only you, *mami.*"

That put a bright smile on her face as she stepped to him and gave him a tender kiss. He smiled as he watched as she happily left for work. He climbed out of the bed and went downstairs to the garage. He then brought all of the boxes from the Navigator inside of the house.

It took him hours to finish taking inventory of the goods from the Niagara Falls lick. There were fifty kilos of heroin, 250 bundles of X pills, and a total of 600 ounces of bottled codeine. *Okay, now I got to find a fucking way to dump all of this shit. The heroin alone would make me a grip for real,* he thought. *Shit, a kilo of that shit is like eighty Gs. So all I gots to do is dump each one for like fifty Gs a kilo and I'll be good,* he said to himself as he grabbed the phone and called a number in the 504 area code. When his man Cell answered the phone Papio said, "What it do, my nigga?"

"Papio? Nigga, I know they ain't let your ass out them mothafucking Feds, ya heard me?"

"Yeah, I been out a little over a month now. Check it, I got something for you, fool. A nice something."

"Is that right? Talk to me."

"I need you to get down here to OKC as soon as you can. And, Cell, you will definitely need a way to take this blessing I'm about to drop on you back to New Orleans with you."

"Come on, Papio, you killin' me, ya heard me? Tell me what I'm coming to scoop."

"A whole bunch of that shit y'all get down with your way."

"H?"

"Yep."

"How much?"

"A lot, Cell."

"What's my ticket?"

"Fifty apiece."

"Is it straight?"

"No more talking, you'll see when you get here. And trust me, you won't be disappointed, so bring some money, Cell, enough to make me feel comfortable giving you this blessing. I might just give it all to you if you do right."

Cell smiled into the receiver and said, "I'll hit you as soon as I get into OKC, ya heard me?"

"Bet. I'll be waiting for your call," Papio said as he hung up the phone. He knew that Cell would take the heroin back to New Orleans and make a killing. He would flip those fifty kilos of heroin so many times. As long as he gave Papio his money Papio was cool with it. The next call he made was to a friend of his out in Longview, Texas. When J.S.'s country ass answered Papio said, "What it, boo?"

"Boo, who the fuck is this playing with me?" J.S. asked, agitated.

Papio started laughing and said, "Still a sensitive nigga huh? It's Papio, fool."

"Papio? As in the pretty-boy-ass Papio? What up, fool?"

"Shit, just trying to make it out here in this mothafucking recession."

"Recession? Nigga, you gots to be fucking with me. I know how your ass gets down; you probably sitting on a major fucking grip right now, talking about a damn recession."

Papio laughed again and said, "You know how I do. Check it, I got something for your syrup-sipping ass. But before I get into that I need to check your pockets real quick. You good?"

"That depends on what you talking about."

"I got about six hundred zips of codeine and I'm trying to dump it real quick like."

"Yeah? Shit, what you trying to drop them for?"

"I'll be real with you because I expect for you to be real with me, J.S. I don't know much about this shit. Throw a number at me and let me see if it'll be worth my time."

"You said six hundred zips, okay, so that's like six gallons. A gallon runs like 2200, so if I do the math that's like almost twelve Gs. Yeah, that's about right."

"Bring me ten and you can have this shit."

"You still out in Oklahoma?"

"For the moment. How long will it take you to get here?"

"Let me get my Li'l Mama and I'll be on the highway this evening."

"Cool. Hit me on this number when you touch the city."

"You know it, fool. Tell me something, Papio; when the fuck did you get out? The word my way was that you got hit with thirty or some shit like that."

Papio laughed and said, "Now you know damn well you can't believe all that shit the streets talk. They had me but I wiggled out of that shit the G way."

"If I thought you was a weak nigga I wouldn't believe a word you just said. But I know how you do it and ain't nothing fake about you, my nigga. See you in a li'l while," J.S. said and hung up the phone.

After Papio hung up the phone he thought about the X pills and figured the best thing to do with that was to sit on them until he figured out what those Dallas youngsters were up to. That might help him with the moves he was going to make on they ass. *Everything is going just as I want it to,* he said to himself as he closed his eyes. Just as he was drifting off to sleep his cell phone started ringing. "Hello."

"I can't believe you did that shit to me again, you pretty-ass nigga!" yelled Special. "Do you know how much time and money I've wasted on those fucking Indians? You are one cold motherfucker, nigga!"

Papio was so happy to hear her voice that his palms actually started to get sweaty. "Check it, if your ass wouldn't have pulled that Houdini shit the next morning I would have been able to put you up on everything that was going down. I was going to put you in on it so you could get a piece of that cake with me and my man."

"Hmph. Your man huh? That nigga was found dead with six rounds in his body."

"For real? You bullshitting?" Before she could react to his sarcasm he told her, "I know you are like way salty at me but by the time I pieced all of that shit together it was too late to stop it. So I had to do me. When I saw you as we were shaking the spot I told you to get at me; what took your ass so long?"

"I couldn't just up and shake those crazy-ass Indians. They were on the fucking warpath so I had to bide my time until I could get the fuck out of the East Coast. Those bastards are trying their very best to find out who put that shit down on they ass, so you better hope you dotted all your I's and crossed all your T's."

"Always. Check it, why don't you meet me in Miami next week and let me make up for some of your losses."

Special started laughing and said, "So, you on some Robin Hood type shit now, pretty man?"

"Nah, I just want to see your sexy ass again and I know the only way your ass will agree to it is if some chips are involved," he replied honestly.

"You got that shit right. How much you talking about, pretty nigga?"

"If your ass don't kill that pretty nigga shit it won't be too fucking much."

She smiled into the receiver and said, "Sorry, forgot how sensitive you are about your good looks. So, Papio, how much are we talking about?"

"Five hundred Gs."

"Fuck you! You get away with damn near fifty keys of some top-flight H, a gang of pure codeine, over two hundred bundles of X, plus six million in cash and all your punk ass wants to kick a bitch is five hundred Gs? Nigga, that's fucking insulting!"

$6 million? Damn, I gots to count this shit to make sure that's right, he said to himself. "I was just checking your temperature, baby. I'll throw your sexy ass a ticket. But only because I feel bad about beating you out of both of those licks. Let's meet in the M-I-A and kick it for a few days."

"Everything on you?"

"Everything."

"Shopping too?"

"Yeah, we can tear the malls down."

She paused to think about his offer. "Deal."

"Don't think you're not going to give me some of that good-ass pussy either, Special."

She laughed and said, "For a ticket, plus a few days of kicking it and shopping, nigga, you thought I fucked you good in the NY. I'm really going to put it on your ass in South Beach!"

That put a smile on his face. "I can't wait. Now give me a number so I can get at you and give you the details when I'm ready to bounce."

"Why don't I just get at you in a few days and you can let me know then?"

Shaking his head no as if she were there in front of him he said, "Nah, I want to be able to get in contact with you. Give me the digits or the deals off," he stated firmly.

"Fuck," she whispered. She then gave him her number and said, "Don't be no sweat a bitch type nigga, Papio. I mean that shit."

He started laughing and said, "Don't worry about it, Special. The pussy is good, you're one fine female, you gangster and all of that shit, but ya ass ain't that fucking special for me to become a sweat a bitch type nigga."

CHAPTER TWENTY-ONE

J.S. arrived first from Longview and brought Papio the $10,000 for the codeine. They sat at Papio's bar and had a drink while J.S.'s Li'l Mama and Brandy sat in the living room getting to know one another.

"So, tell me, fool, how in the hell did you get the fuck out of them Feds?" asked J.S.

After Papio told J.S. the move he made against the Cubans he added, "What the fuck else was I supposed to do? Those punk mothafuckas was going to leave me stuck the fuck out."

"All ready. Nigga, you did what had to be done. At least y'all didn't go out like a bitch-ass rat. But I know you know them hoes gon' be looking for your ass when they figure out your ass is home."

"They already know because I called they ass. I'm flying out to Miami next week to give them they money and have a sit down."

"What? You got $4.5 million, fool?"

Papio smiled and said, "I've been kinda busy since I've been home, my nigga."

J.S. checked the time on his platinum Rolex and said, "Well, fool, I gots to hit that highway; it's time to get that paper."

"I know that's right, dog. If I come up with anything else you know I'll holla at you."

"All ready," J.S. said as he went and got his Li'l Mama and left.

Papio gave the $10,000 to Brandy. "That's for you, baby; do what you want with it."

Brandy shook her head from side to side and said, "You never cease to amaze me. You are one hell of a man. Thank you, daddy." She gave him a kiss.

"That's nothing, you earned way more than that shit for real, but I gots to take care of a real big tab. Once I get that situated you will be broken off way more than those crumbs right there," he lied with a straight face.

"You don't have to continue to give me money; I'm good just being with you. I know you will always take care of me. I don't want you to think that it's all about the money."

Warning bells started sounding off inside of Papio's head. *Uh-oh, she done went and got sprung. I don't want to hurt her but I'm just not feeling her like that. Now Special, she's another story,* he thought. He smiled at Brandy and said, "Come on, *mami,* you ain't gone and started catching feelings have you? You know that ain't in my program right about now."

"I know, daddy, and I won't let my feelings ever interfere with you or your business. I fell in love with you and I won't deny that fact. But I also respect you, everything about you. I won't ever become a problem for you, promise. I'm enjoying everything about you and even though I want more, I'll sit back and continue to play my part in your life. That's what you want right?"

"That's right, *mami.* You're a good woman, Brandy, and no matter what, I will make sure that you continue to have whatever you want. Check it, I gots to make another move in a little bit. I'm meeting this dude out of New Orleans; he's good people but not good enough to come to my home. After I hook up with him we can go out and get something to eat. Cool?"

"Whatever you want to do is fine with me, daddy."

Papio pulled out his cell phone and called Cell. "Where are you, fool?" Papio asked.

"I just came through Norman. I should be in the city in the next fifteen minutes."

"All right, check it, I want you to get a room at the Days Inn right off I-35 when you get to the south side. Call me and let me know the room number. I should be there no more than ten minutes after you get there."

"That's what's up," Cell said and hung up the phone.

Brandy watched as Papio went and grabbed the box that contained the heroin and put it into his Range Rover. When Papio came back into the house she told him, "I'm coming with you, daddy. That way we can go on and get something to eat after you've handled your business."

"Nah, I'm good. I have some more business to take care of and in no way am I having you all in this street shit." He stepped up to her and said, "Listen to me, *mami;* your life will not be ruined because of my get down. You don't have to go out of your way to show me you're down for me. I already know that shit. I know you got my back and you will always be there for me and that touches me deeply. But you have a square life that I do not want you to forget about. Do you understand what I'm saying?"

"Yes, bu—"

He cut her off. "No buts, *mami.* I got this. Now go on and chill until I get back." He gave her a quick kiss and left the house.

Everything with Cell went even better than Papio expected. Cell gave him a cool million dollars of the 2.5 he owed him for the heroin. After Cell tested the heroin and saw that it was in fact some high-grade dope he told Papio that there wouldn't be any problem with having his money within a week or two, tops. Papio left the Days Inn with a million dollars cash in his possession feeling real good. As long as everything went well when he met with the Cubans he didn't see why he wouldn't be able to get that $100 million he wanted within a year or two. *But shit, if these easy ass licks keep falling in my lap it won't even take that long,* he thought as he pulled in front of Kammy' s shop.

Kammy saw him parked in front of the shop and quickly came outside.

"Ride with me for a minute."

Kammy climbed inside of the Range Rover. Papio pulled out of the parking lot. "What's up with them Dallas niggas?"

"They're just about ready, baby. The head nigga is sniffing all on this pussy and begging a bitch for some of it. So as soon as you give me the green light we can make the next moves."

"That's what's up. But I don't want just a quick lick; I want everything they got. This is what I want you to do: tell him about me, let him know that I got some good X and I'm willing to have a sit-down if they want to take this shit off me for a nice ticket. I got about twenty bundles that I may be willing to give him for five dollars a pill."

"Shit, for five a pill he will definitely jump on it. I'll get at him when I get back to the shop. So, when are we getting together, Papio?"

He stared at her and smiled. "You ain't playing huh? You really trying to take it there, Kammy?" She leaned over to the driver's side and unbuttoned his pants, pulled out his dick and began to suck it slowly to answer his question. He moaned and said, "I guess you are serious. Damn, don't stop that shit, baby; that shit feels good as fuck!"

***

By the time Papio made it back to his house Brandy was asleep. *Oops. Couldn't help it.* He took Kammy to her house out in the country and fucked the shit out of her fine ass. *That freaky bitch wore me the fuck out,* he said to himself as he went into the bathroom and took a shower.

When he was finished he went downstairs to the media room and began to watch television. He was watching *Menace II Society* on TNT when his cell phone rang. Special didn't press private when she called him, which made him smile. *Looks like she's coming around,* he thought as he answered the phone. "What it do, special lady?"

"Looks like your pretty ass didn't cover all of the bases, Papio," she said seriously.

"What are you talking about? Those Indians don't know shit about me."

"Wrong. They found out that this punk bitch that one of them was fucking with was real tight with your man Nick. Long story short, Nick told her your name and she gave the name to them. So they're having their connections see if they can get a line on your ass. So, it's just a matter of time before they find you. Watch your ass, Papio. I'll be waiting on your call for our Miami trip," she said and hung up the phone.

Papio sat there, stunned from the news Special just gave him. *Damn, maybe I took Nick too damn quick. Should have waited until I could get him and that bird bitch of his together.* "Shit," he mumbled as he started to form a plan. He knew for a fact if those Indians had some solid folks on they team they would find him. He looked around his media room and frowned; it was time to shake the city for a little bit, maybe forever. He didn't want to leave his home; he loved it and had

worked hard to get it the way he wanted it. But if he
wanted to make $100 million and stay alive he was go
ing to have to get ghost.

He made a decision as he cuddled next to Brandy.
*Dallas. I'll go out there and get me a nice spot and
chill. That way when it's time for me to make any
moves out here I'll still be relatively close. Yep, that's
the business, Dallas it is,* he said to himself as he closed
his eyes and fell asleep, comfortable with his decision.

CHAPTER TWENTY-TWO

Papio received a phone call from Kingo as he was on his way to Will Rogers World Airport. After pushing the number five on his cell phone to accept Kingo's call Papio said, "What's good, dread?"

"Everyt'ing kriss, mon; how 'bout you? You good?"

"Everything is everything. I'm on my way to the airport now."

"Where you go?"

"I'm on my way to Miami. I'll be out there for a week, maybe longer if things go as I hope they will."

"Miami? Good! Very good, Papio!" Then in a stern voice he added, "Doah truble truble, 'til truble truble yuh, mon."

"What does that mean, dread?"

"It means avoid mischief. Take care of the business."

"I got this. I already spoke to those fools and everything is good. I already sent that change out there; all I have to do is pick it up from the post office when I hit South Beach. I'm meeting a very special person out there also. So after the business is handled I'm going to kick it a little and see if I can get to know her better."

"Eeeh? When you meet this woman?"

"During a business move a few weeks ago out in L.A. I'm telling you, Kingo, she is really something. Check it, I'll tell you all about her later. Hit me in a day or so and I'll let you know the business. I just pulled into the airport."

"Okay, mon, be safe," Kingo said as he hung up the phone.

Papio pulled his BMW into the extended parking lot of the airport and paid for two weeks in advance. He grabbed his Gucci luggage and strolled into the airport terminal.

To say he was excited would have put it mildly. Not only was he about to relieve some pressure off of his business moves, he was also about to spend some time with a woman he had really started to feel more and more. Special has been a mainstay on his mind ever since she agreed to meet him in Florida. He wanted her in the worst way, and it wasn't all about the sex with him either; it couldn't be if he was actually about to give her a million out of the $6 million he took from the Indians. What was originally thought to be $4.5 million turned out to be an even $6 million. He would give the Cubans $5 million; that would be the $4.5 million he owed them and another half a million as some good faith money to let them know that he always had full intentions to pay them back everything that they had lost. He was seriously banking on Mr. Suarez to show him some love.

He made himself comfortable for the flight. He closed his eyes and smiled. *I'm on my way, Special.*

Papio was all smiles as he deplaned and strolled happily out of Miami International Airport. He was determined to make a lasting impression with Special. He wanted Special to be his exclusively; he didn't know how he was going to make that become a reality. What he did know was that he was willing to do whatever it took to keep her in his wild and crazy life. His smile brightened as he climbed into a cab. He told the cab

158   Clifford Spud Johnson

driver to take him to the Ritz-Carlton, where he had a $2,500-a-night suite reserved for the next seven days.

He tipped the cab driver as he got out of the cab in front of the Ritz-Carlton. A bellboy came and took his luggage. Papio strolled confidently into the luxurious hotel.

While he was soaking in the Jacuzzi bathtub he grabbed the phone that was mounted on the wall next to the tub and called the front desk and asked if anything arrived for him. The manager of the hotel informed him that there was a rather nice-sized box waiting for him. He smiled and asked the manager if he could have the box brought up to his suite. The manager assured him that the box would be brought up to him immediately. Papio thanked him and then made another call. When Special answered her cell phone he said, "What's good? I hope you're in sunny Florida by now."

"Calm down, pretty man, I'm on my way to the hotel right now. I should be there in about ten minutes. What's the room number?"

He answered, "Suite 6590 on the sixth floor. See you in a li'l bit."

"I feel icky, so make sure you have me a nice hot bath ready."

He started laughing and said, "I'm in the bathtub right now; want me to wait for you?"

"If that's how you want this trip to start then stay right where you are, Pussy Monster.

Just know that if you have anything else planned for us it's not going down today. Because when I get a hold of you it's going down in a major way. It won't be shit like the last time we got down. Trust that."

"In that case let me get the fuck outta this tub 'cause I got some business to take care of before we kick this vacation off."

"Business? You got some moves to make out this way?"

"Nah, got to drop something off to some old friends. Don't trip, I give you my word the next seven days will be all about us. See you when you get here," he said and hung up the phone.

All about us? Shit, thought Special with a smile on her face. No matter how much she tried to deny it she was really feeling Papio's pretty ass.

Papio got out of the tub and got dressed quickly in a pair of cream linen pants by Dolce & Gabbana with a white linen shirt and some cream alligator open-toe sandals. There was a knock on the door just as he slipped on his sandals. It was his package from the front desk. He gave the bellboy a hefty tip and closed the door behind him. He opened the box and stared at the neatly stacked money and thought, *God, I hope those fucking Cubans ain't with no bullshit.*

He shook that negative thought out of his head and began to take the money out of the box. He stacked the money on the table in the dining room of the suite. He set the $1 million aside for Special and then quickly put the remaining $5 million into a large black duffel bag that he pulled out of his luggage. Just as he had the money secured there was another knock at the door. When he opened the door Special was standing in front of him looking even more beautiful than he remembered. *Damn, this woman is fine.*

"Hello, Special."

"Hi, pretty man," she said as she stepped by him and entered the suite, followed closely by a bellboy carrying her luggage. Papio stopped him and relieved him of her bags, gave him a tip, and rushed him out the door. He didn't want the bellboy seeing the money he had out for Special. After he closed the door he turned and watched Special with an amused expression on his face as she stared at the million dollars that was stacked on top of the dining room table. He stepped behind her and wrapped his arms around her waist.

"Always remember, Special: Papio is a man of his word."

"I can respect that, Papio, I really can." Before he could see her eyes getting watery she stepped toward the bedroom of the suite. With her back to him she said, "I'm taking me a long, hot bath; how long will you be out?"

He followed her into the bedroom and said, "It should be no longer than a couple of hours."

"Okay, cool. I'll take me a light nap until you return. What's the plan for the rest of the day?"

"I figured since it's too late to get a nice day of shopping in we could go hit the beach and chill. Then we can do dinner or a club or something. Whatever you want to do. So you can make up your mind while I'm gone."

Special turned toward him and asked, "Why are you doing all of this, Papio? You got to know that we're not right for each other."

"That's where you're wrong. I like everything I know about you so far. All I want out of the next seven days is to see if I can learn and like even more about you. The money in there is yours because I feel like shit for beating you out of those two licks. Believe me, that right there is a rare thing for me, because all of my life it has been about nobody but me; for me to do this shows me that you've touched me in a place that is completely foreign. All I ask of you is to give this a chance. If it don't fit I won't force it. But if shit looks and feels right let's roll with it. Cool?"

"Fair enough, just as long as you know going in that I am not making you any promises."

"I can dig that. Now, let me go handle this business." He stepped close to her and gave her a kiss on her forehead and said, "I'll be back in a li'l bit." He left her standing in the bedroom with a schoolgirl grin on her face as she watched him leave the room.

CHAPTER TWENTY-THREE

"Can I rent me a car for the week?" Papio asked the concierge at the hotel.

"What sort of car would you like, sir?" the concierge asked.

Papio smiled and said, "Something convertible and expensive."

"I do think we can accommodate you, sir. One moment please," The concierge was happy to accommodate Papio because he saw a big commission coming his way.

Papio checked the time and saw that he was right on schedule. He wanted to hurry up and get this meeting over with. Special was on his mind and he couldn't wait to get back to her. He inhaled deeply and tried to calm his nerves. The concierge returned five minutes later with a key chain with one key on it in his hand. "Here you are, sir. I do think this should fit what you requested. Shall I charge this to your suite?"

"Yes, that would be fine," Papio said as he accepted the key from the manager.

"I've already arranged for the car to be brought to you in the front of the hotel, sir."

"Thank you," Papio said as he pulled out his wallet and tipped the manager with two crisp one hundred dollar bills.

The manager beamed and thanked him.

Papio picked the duffel bag up and left the hotel. When he made it outside he smiled; the manager's taste was pretty damn good. There was a sky-blue 2009 convertible Bentley Continental GT waiting for him. He tossed the duffel bag onto the passenger's seat of the luxurious vehicle and stepped around to the driver's side. Once he was on his way he pulled out his cell phone and made the call.

Castro answered the phone and Papio said, "I'll be there in twenty minutes." He hung up the phone before Castro could say a word. Papio was hoping that move would piss Castro the fuck off. *Fuck that fat fucker,* Papio thought as he turned on the radio and began singing along with the rapper Rick Ross.

Exactly twenty minutes after he left the hotel Papio pulled into the vast estate of the notorious Mr. Suarez, one of the biggest drug lords in the game. A huge wrought-iron gate opened slowly and Papio eased the Bentley past it and drove up a long, winding driveway. Castro was standing in the doorway of the mansion as Papio came to a stop in front. Papio hopped out of the car, reach inside, grabbed the duffel bag with the money inside of it, and stepped right in front of Castro and said, "Here you go." He dropped the bag in front of Castro's feet and smiled.

Castro had a grin on his heavily tanned face when he told Papio, "It's going to be one glorious day when Mr. Suarez lets me take your life, Papio."

"Castro! I'm shocked at you, what's all of that for? We do good business, *papi;* no need to get your panties in a bunch, hon. I get money, clown; you know it and so does Mr. Suarez. As long as I can continue to do me you'll have to remain on your leash just like a good little puppy dog. Now, can you take me to your master?" Papio said with heavy emphasis on the word "master."

If Castro weren't so tanned one could see that he had turned beet red from Papio's blatant disrespect. "Turn the fuck around. Time to get frisked, motherfucker."

After the pat down Castro pushed Papio into the house.

As soon as Papio entered Mr. Suarez's home he relaxed; he knew if he was going to die it wouldn't be this day. He would never have made it this far. So when he came face to face with Mr. Suarez his swagger was turned on big time. He stepped to the drug lord, smiled, and shook his hand. "Forgive me, Mr. Suarez, making that move against you was the only play I had left. I know it looked like a big sign of disrespect but please believe me that was not the case. I had to get out of that place and you know that there just ain't no snitching in me."

"Though I don't like what you did, I respect it. I have always respected you, Papio, because I know you are loyal only to you. I like that. I like it because I know when it comes to you making money you will do what-ever needs to be done. Spending twenty-six years off of a thirty-year sentence would have killed you. You live for the money and now I expect for us to get plenty more, sí?"

Papio gave him a nod and said, "Sí, Mr. Suarez. That is why I've brought you $5 million of what I owe you. I've been home a little over a month and I have been busy. I will continue to do what I do until I have cleared my debt to you. The extra half million is a gift for you. I know I am still in the red for the weed and the coca; tell me what I owe you and I will get right on it. My word," Papio said sincerely.

Mr. Suarez turned and sat down on a very expensive and comfortable sectional sofa and said, "The money you have brought me shows me that you are still at the top of your game, even after a three-year absence. I ap-plaud you, Papio; you never cease to amaze me. But I'm curious, why hasn't Señor Charlie come up missing?"

I was wondering the same thing, you fat bitch, Papio said to himself. He had a frown on his face and told Mr. Suarez, "To be honest I haven't given that clown a thought since I've been home. Money is the only thing that I've been on. I don't have too much time for those vengeance moves. For real, I thought you would have taken care of that coward, sir."

"I see. This is what I suggest: please take care of that for me and I will squash all penalty as far as interests goes. You take care of him personally and you will only owe me for the drugs and no more."

Papio smiled and said, "No problem. Thank you for your generosity, Mr. Suarez. I will get on top of that as soon as I make it back that way."

"Good. Now, tell me, what are your plans? Are you ready to get back into the business?"

Papio shook his head no and said, "Not exactly. This last month has shown me that that dope boy shit just ain't as profitable as it used to be. Now I do have plans on making some moves in the near future, but right now I have more on my plate. When I do need to purchase anything heavy I will make sure I spend with you."

"Sí. May I ask what have you been into that has gotten you all of this money so swiftly?"

"With all due respect, Mr. Suarez, I have to keep those moves close to my vest. I will tell you that I will have your money, soon, real soon."

Mr. Suarez laughed out loud and said, "See, Castro, I told you. Papio is one serious hombre."

Castro frowned but remained silent. He held a look of contempt on his face as he stared at Papio.

"I may need to call upon you, Señor Papio. I expect for you to respect me and get back with me quickly if and when I do."

"Sí. You know me, sir; if there's money to be made I am with it. But I will not put myself in a position to get caught up ever again. Every move I make has to be calculated. So with much respect, please understand that I don't work for you or anyone. I'm solo and I will remain that way. No one can look out for Papio better than Papio can."

Mr. Suarez was silent for a moment and then he broke out into loud laughter. "You are something else, Papio. I respect your words and I understand them. But you should know that if I ever call you it will be for some serious money. Yes, I know you. I also know that there's not much you won't do for the money. So when something substantial lands in front of me I will give you a call, sí?"

"Sí. Now, if you'll excuse me, sir, I have a very special person waiting for me back at my hotel. I'm officially on vacation for the next seven days and I plan to enjoy me some of this Florida sun."

"Where are you staying?"

"The Ritz," Papio said with a smile.

Mr. Suarez burst into laughter and said, "Nothing but the very best for Señor Papio huh?"

"Always, Mr. Suarez. Always."

"Don't be a stranger, Papio."

"There's no way in the world I could ever be a stranger to you, Mr. Suarez; you have eyes everywhere."

"I'm glad you realize this. Never cross me again, Papio. The only reason why you have been given this opportunity is because I do feel responsible for putting you in that situation. If I wouldn't have insisted that you deal with Charlie you would never have been indicted. I apologize sincerely for that. That's the past now. Never make the mistake of crossing me again. Am I understood?"

"Sí, Mr. Suarez. Thank you for the opportunity for making this right between us. I will not disappoint you."

"I know you won't, Papio. There is one more thing that we need to discuss before you leave me."

"Yes?"

Mr. Suarez stared hard at Papio for a full minute before speaking. The silence and the look on Mr. Suarez's face was making Papio uncomfortable.

"Tell me, have you just given me a part of my own money?"

Papio was confused. "Excuse me, sir?"

"Did you have anything to do with the robbery and murder of Lee in Oklahoma City?"

Without hesitation and with a straight face Papio answered, "No, sir, I did not. I found out about what happened to Lee and my man Hugh while I was away on the East Coast taking care of some major business."

Mr. Suarez gave him a nod of his head and said, "Okay. I have no reason not to believe you Señor Papio, but if I ever find out that you have lied to me this day, this will be considered as crossing me. Sí?"

"Sí, and that means I will be able to do to you what I want to do so badly," Castro interjected.

Papio smiled and let his swagger enter his voice. "With the utmost respect to you, Mr. Suarez, I understand what you have said here today and, like I said, I will not cross you. I will get the money I owe you and I will do good business as I have always done. But you must please explain something to this minion of yours. I am a man and though I may not be in the position to handle a full onslaught from you or your men, if that day comes where we were to have to go against one another, God forbid, I promise you that before I die I will kill your man right here for all of the fruitless threats he's given me over the years. With that said, I must go; like I said I have a gorgeous woman awaiting my company."

Mr. Suarez started laughing so hard a tear came to his eye. After he regained his composure he told Papio, "It is so good to have you back in the thick of things, Señor Papio."

Staring directly at a highly pissed off Castro, Papio smiled and said, "It's nice to be back in the thick of things, sir."

"Charlie?" asked Mr. Suarez.

"As soon as I get back to Oklahoma City and locate him, Charlie will become a dead man," Papio said in a deadly tone.

"Sí," replied Mr. Suarez.

Papio and Mr. Suarez shook hands as Papio exited the house.

He pulled out of the estate with a huge smile on his face. He had one thing on his mind. He pulled out his cell phone and called Special back at the hotel.

"Are you dressed yet?" he asked.

"Mm-hm. Just sitting here looking pretty while I count my money."

"That's cold. What, you don't trust a nigga?"

"Has nothing to do with trust, pretty man . . . I mean, Papio. I was bored that's all. Where are you?"

"I'm on my way back to the hotel now. Get your stuff and meet me in the front of the hotel in about fifteen minutes. And be ready to have a good time; it's time for us to get our vacation on."

As soon as Papio pressed the end button on his cell the phone started ringing. "Hello?"

"Hi, daddy, what you doing?" asked Brandy.

"Taking care of business, *mami*. You good?"

"I guess, just missing you."

"I'm missing you too," he lied. "Don't trip, I'll be back in a week or so and we'll get together and do something real nice."

"That's fine. Okay, I won't hold you. I just needed to hear your voice. Be careful, daddy."

"Always, *mami,* always," he said as he hung up the phone.

Though he was feeling Brandy he knew that if things went the way he wanted them to with Special, Brandy was out of there. He couldn't describe the feelings he felt for Special; he had never experienced these feelings before. All he knew was that he had to see if she was the one. *Has old Papio fallen in love? Wow, that's a trip,* he thought and continued to drive toward the hotel.

Papio pulled in front of the hotel and saw Special standing outside looking fly as ever. She was rocking an orange, black, and gold sundress with a pair of black Givenchy sandals.

Her toenails were painted a bright orange matching her dress and complementing her outfit perfectly. *Damn she's fine,* he thought as he climbed out of the Bentley and opened the door for her.

"Damn, you do know how to do it big huh?" she complimented him.

He shrugged and said, "There's no other way to do it, Special." He drove the luxury vehicle away from the hotel with their long hair blowing in the sunny Florida breeze.

They cruised South Beach and enjoyed the view for a couple of hours before Papio took Special to a restaurant he heard a lot about. "I hope you like steaks because we're about to eat at one of the best steak houses in Miami."

"Good. I could really tear into a fat, juicy T-bone right about now," Special replied.

"That's right. Prime 12 is the best. There's normally a monster line in front of that place but don't trip; we won't have to wait long."

Special smiled and asked, "What, you got it like that way out here in the M-I-A, Papio?"

"You better believe it. Impressed?"

She answered with a smile and reached across the seat and let her hand rest on his lap.

When they pulled in front of Prime 12 the line to enter the restaurant was in fact wrapped around the corner of the restaurant. Papio found a parking space and they climbed out of the Bentley and walked straight to the front door of Prime 12. Papio stepped to the maitre d' and pulled out four one hundred dollar bills, slid them to the maitre d', and said, "Table for two."

Without any hesitation at all the maitre d' smiled and said, "This way, sir."

As they entered the restaurant it was as if all of their senses were attacked with the aroma of the dry-aged prime steaks they were so well known for. The banquettes and lush wood throughout the building gave the restaurant a real relaxed setting. They both ordered T-bones medium rare and sat back and watched as a few celebrities entered the restaurant.

They were sipping some wine when Special slid closer to Papio, grabbed his hand, and whispered, "I don't have any panties on, Papio." To prove this fact she grabbed his hand and placed it under her dress. He felt her shaven pussy lips and instantly became erect. He slid a finger inside of her and started to slowly play with her sex.

He smiled and asked, "You like?"

With her eyes half closed she said, "You damn right. And you better not stop. Mmmmm."

Their waitress came to the table with their salads. When she saw the look on Special's face she knew what was going on and blushed a deep crimson. "Here you go, guys. If you need anything else please let me know."

Without removing his finger from Special's pussy Papio said, "Thank you, we will."

Before the waitress could leave Special smiled at her and asked, "What's your name, pretty?"

The waitress pointed to the nametag pinned to her blouse and said, "Inga."

"You are one beautiful woman, Inga. Where are you from?"

"The Dominican Republic."

Special stared at the waitress's light brown skin. "Are you a natural redhead?"

"Yes," Inga answered and continued to blush.

Special felt as if she was about to come when she asked, "Do you know what we're doing right now?"

"Yes," Inga answered in a hushed tone.

"How does that make you feel?"

Inga stared at the couple for a few seconds then answered honestly. "Horny."

What the fuck is this crazy-ass broad doing? Papio asked himself as he sipped some more of his wine and stared at Special while he continued to finger her and rub on her clit.

Special said seductively, "I thought it did." She then reached under the table and inserted a finger inside of her pussy right next to Papio's and fingered herself quickly. She pulled her finger out of her sex and held it up toward Inga and said, "Here, taste me."

Papio watched totally amazed as Inga smiled shyly, bent, and sucked the pussy juice off of Special's finger. "You taste divine, ma'am."

"Special; call me Special, Inga. What time do you get off?"

"In one hour."

"Okay, my boo here is about to finish making me cum and then we're going to finish our meal. We're staying at the Ritz-Carlton. If you want to taste some more of me as well as my boo here meet us in the lobby of our hotel in two hours. Do you want to do that, Inga?"

Papio stared at the waitress's perfect double Ds and smiled like a kid in a candy store when she answered, "Yes. I would really enjoy that."

"Gooood," Special said as she felt her orgasm begin.

When Special finished Inga said, "I'll be waiting for the both of you at your hotel. Please hurry!"

Papio and Special watched as the sexy waitress strolled back toward the kitchen. Her ass was nice and firm and Papio was having some major freaky thoughts run through his mind as he watched her leave his sight.

"Are you with that, boo?" Special asked with a wicked smile on her face.

"I'm so with that shit that I damn near want to say fuck the food and snatch your ass out of this restaurant so we can go back to the suite and do the damn thing right now."

Special placed her small hand on the right side of his face and said, "No need for all that; she's going to be waiting for us, baby. So let's eat and enjoy our meal. Steak has a lot of protein right?"

Yeah."

"Good. You're going to need all of that shit because it's going to go down tonight, baby. I'm going to make sure that this is one vacation you won't be forgetting for a real long time. It's going to be—"

Papio cut her off, and finished her sentence for her. "Special."

She gave him a sultry look. "Exactly."

CHAPTER TWENTY-FOUR

Papio and Special both had smiles on their faces as they entered the lobby of the Ritz-Carlton hand in hand. Their smiles brightened when they saw Inga sitting in the lounge area of the lobby looking adorable in a pink sundress. Her long red hair was hanging loose past her shoulders and, man, did she look good. She had a mischievous gleam in her eyes as she approached them. Without saying a word she reached out and grabbed Papio's free hand and let him lead the way toward the elevator.

When they made it to the suite Special asked Inga if she wanted to take a shower with her. Inga smiled and said, "Sure."

While the ladies went to get fresh and clean Papio ordered a couple of bottles of wine. Hearing the shower running, he couldn't resist the urge to go into the bathroom to see what those two scrumptious-looking women were doing. When he stepped into the steamy bathroom his grin turned into a gigantic smile when he saw the silhouette of Special and Inga locked in each other's arms, sharing what looked like a very passionate kiss. His erection grew so large he felt like bursting into the shower stall and squeezing in between the two lovely ladies. He shook his head, turned, and left the bathroom thinking, *Be patient, big boy, be patient. Let them do them you will get yours all night long.* He went into the living room and turned on some music. This was definitely going to be one night he would never forget.

By the time the bottles of wine had been delivered the ladies came into the living room; each had on one of Papio's shirts. Special chose one of his wife-beaters while Inga had on one of his Ed Hardy tees. The ladies came and joined him on the soft sofa, one on each side of him.

"So, tell me a little about yourself, Inga?" Papio asked just to start some sort of conversation. Really, all he wanted to do was get straight to the freaky shit, but felt it would be better if he continued to show patience.

"Well, I'm finishing my last year at the U."

"The University of Miami, that's impressive. What's your major?"

"Marketing."

"Cool. How long have you been out here in sunny Florida?"

"I was born here. My mother and father moved here from the Dominican Republic while she was pregnant with me."

"I see."

Special sipped some of her wine then said, "Okay, we've gotten to know Ingy; now let's have some fun shall we?"

"Ingy?" asked Papio.

"Yes, that is my nickname," Inga said shyly.

"Well, come here, Ingy; let me kiss those sexy-ass lips of yours." She leaned forward and Papio kissed her softly. Their kiss went from soft and tender to hard and passionate in a heartbeat. While they were kissing Special set her glass down and pulled Papio's dick out of his pants and began to give him some head. He moaned as he continued to kiss and suck Inga's tongue. Inga began playing with her pussy while they were kissing and the heat index skyrocketed inside of the suite. Before any of them realized it they were each naked. Papio stood and led the way into the bedroom. Once they made it to the bed Inga aggressively climbed on top of Papio and began to ride his dick as if her life depended on it.

Special also climbed on top of him, only she was sitting on top of his face. Papio began eating her out slowly while she faced Inga and began to suck and nibble on each of her firm breasts. They sexed like this until Papio moaned that he was about to come. Inga slid off of him and dropped to his dick and inserted it into her mouth. Not to be outdone Special climbed off of Papio and moved Inga over so she could suck on his nuts. This caused a gigantic eruption from Papio as he came like he never had come before, long and hard. His impressive-sized organ went limp after that monstrous orgasm; both of the ladies wore satisfied smiles on their faces.

"Now, what are we to do while he regains some strength?" Inga asked with a devilish smile on her face. Without answering her question Special pulled Inga into the 69 position and they began to eat each other's pussies. The sight of the ladies eating each other out had Papio back hard instantly. He pulled Inga off of Special and turned her so she could go back to eating Special out. Now that Special was lying on her back getting eaten out by Inga he got behind Inga and slid his dick back inside of her soaking-wet pussy doggie style. He rammed himself as deep as he could inside of her. While he was digging deep inside of Inga he was staring at Special, who had a content smile on her flushed face as Inga brought her to a very satisfying orgasm. Although Papio was enjoying Inga's wetness. He wanted to cum inside of Special. He pulled out of Inga and gently pushed her so she could climb on top of Special's face. He lifted Special's legs onto his shoulders and slid himself inside of her. He paused and took a few deep breaths and regained some control of himself. After a few minutes of this Inga slithered off of Special's face and watched as Papio continued to fuck her nice and good. After they both came she smiled and said, "May I clean you both?"

Both being totally spent from two very nice orgasms, they mumbled their consent thinking that she was going to go to the bathroom and grab a washcloth. But Inga had another way of cleansing them in mind. She went down to Papio's crotch and began sucking his limp dick. He rose slightly and Inga smiled as she continued to suck and lick all over his genitals. After she felt that he was cleansed she slid over to Special and began to lick and eat her pussy again. Special moaned and grabbed Inga by her head and held her right where she wanted her to be. Papio slid down next to Inga and joined her in eating Special's pussy. The feeling of two tongues on her pussy at the same time took Special over the edge and she came again harder than the last two times.

"Oh! My! God!" she screamed as she squirted a combination of her juices and Papio's cum into both Papio and Inga's mouths.

The next morning when Papio opened his eyes he saw Inga standing next to the bed fully dressed. She smiled at him and said, "Thank you for a wonderful time, Papio. I have to go get ready for class. I hope I'll be able to come see the both of you before you leave?"

He returned her smile and said, "If Special doesn't have a problem with it I sure won't. Check it, let me give you a little something, no diss or nothing, just something to show you how much I appreciated what you gave us."

Before she could object he got out of the bed and led her into the living room so they wouldn't disturb Special, who was still knocked out. Papio grabbed his wallet and pulled out ten crisp hundred dollar bills and gave them to Inga. "Take this and go buy yourself something nice."

Inga accepted the money and gave him a tender kiss. "Thank you for this, Papio."

He wrapped his arms around her waist and before he knew what happened she pulled from him and pulled out his dick from the slit of his boxers and began to suck his dick feverishly. *Six A.M. and she has one mean-ass head game,* he thought as he stared down at her as she did her thing. Wanting to feel her one more time he pulled away from her and turned her around. He then flipped up her sundress and moved her pink thong to the side and rammed his dick inside of her as hard as he could. She was already wet so he slid in without any resistance. He humped her fast and hard for five minutes and then erupted inside of her. With weak knees he staggered and pulled himself out of her pussy. She turned around and smiled. "That was a nice quickie, Papio. Thank you."

He mumbled something incoherent and watched as she went into the bathroom to clean herself up. Papio was back in bed when Inga came out of the bathroom ready to leave. She stepped to the side of the bed and gave Special a kiss on her lips and said, "Good-bye, Special." She then finger waved good-bye to Papio and left the bedroom. Papio had a content smile on his face as he drifted back to sleep. *What a mothafucking way to start a seven-day vacation in the M-I-A.*

CHAPTER TWENTY-FIVE

Papio woke up again later to Special singing in the bathroom. He climbed out of the bed and stood in the doorway of the bathroom. He watched while she soaked in the Jacuzzi tub with her eyes closed and a pair of earplug headphones connected to her MP3 player. She must have felt his presence because she opened her eyes and turned her head toward the door. "Good morning, Papio; or should I say good afternoon?"

He stepped to the tub. "Shit, you're lucky I'm even up now. You and Inga worked me something nice last night."

She grinned and said, "If it wasn't last night that did you in it had to be this morning when you got your good-bye fuck on in the living room."

Papio shrugged sheepishly and chose to remain silent; he didn't know if she was teasing or mad at him so he didn't want to stick his foot in his mouth.

Special started laughing and said, "As long as you enjoyed yourself, baby, I'm good."

He sighed with relief because the last thing he wanted was for her to be upset with him. "So, what you want to get into today?"

She smiled brightly and said, "Shopping, baby! I want to go do plenty of shopping. Let's go spend some of that hard-earned money of yours!"

"Hard earned huh? Whatever. Go on and finish your bath. I got some calls to make and then I'll get dressed and we'll go tear a few malls down."

"That's the business, baby. Do me a favor and go pick me something to wear. Something chill so I can be comfortable while we're shopping."

He bent forward and gave her a kiss and said, "I got you." He didn't know why he kissed her but it felt really good when she responded. *This woman is really special,* he thought as he turned and left the bathroom. He went into the bedroom and grabbed her bags and picked her outfit for the day. He chose a pair of white cotton shorts by Baby Phat with a pink Baby Phat baby tee. He grabbed her other Gucci bag and found what he was looking for: a pair of pink and white low-top Nike Air Force Ones. He set her clothes on the bed and grabbed the phone. He called Brandy to check in with her to make sure she was good. After speaking with her for a few minutes he called Twirl out in L.A. "What it do, my nigga?"

"It's all gravy in the West right now, dog. I got at my man E.T. and he has a nice maneuver for us in like a week."

"What the figures looking like?"

"One to two tickets easy, three-way split. Jacking some Mexicans that he fucks with. There might be some work there too, either bud or the yayo."

"All right, check it out. I got to hit Dallas and take care of a few things; then I'm sliding back to Oklahoma, so I should be back in the West no later than Thursday. Cool?"

"That's straight. Get at me when you know for sure when you'll be touching so I can get at my nigga."

"That's what's up. How you doing on that other thang?"

"'JLovely.' I'll have a nice stack for you when you get this way."

"Cool. I'll holla at you next week then."

After Papio hung up the phone he called Kammy out in Oklahoma City and smiled when she told him that she had everything ready for them with the Dallas youngsters. "Like that huh?" asked Papio.

"What, you thought a bitch was faking or some shit? I don't play when it comes to that paper, Papio. Especially after you done gave me some of that good-ass dick, you got a bitch damn near sprung."

He started laughing and said, "Come on, ma, let's keep to the BI. Ain't no time for that square shit. Check it, I'll be there by Monday morning and we'll put everything together."

"That's cool. The nigga Chico's paper is way longer than I expected. Do you know he actually showed me like three million dollars? I was like damn, I didn't know you could really make that kind of money out here in the city. That nigga and his boys ain't playing, Papio."

"Good. That means we'll be able to knock they ass off and get paid properly. Continue to get as much information as you can for me, baby; when I touch everything will be everything."

"I will. Let me go. I got a shop full. Bye."

"Later," he said as he hung up the phone and thought about that move he was going to make back in Oklahoma City. *Just what the doctor ordered,* he thought as he stood and went and chose what he was going to wear for the day. He picked a pair of white True Religion jean shorts with a fresh wife-beater and a pair of brand new white Nike Air Force Ones. He went into the closet and opened the small safe that was inside of it and pulled out several stacks of one hundred dollar bills. *Hmm, yeah, that should be enough,* he said to himself as he closed the safe and put a little over $200,000 inside of the waistband of his jean shorts. Special came into the bedroom looking damn good wrapped in a big, fluffy white towel. Papio smiled at her as he said, "Your clothes are right there." He pointed toward the bed. "Give me twenty minutes and I'll be ready to bounce."

With her lips stuck out she asked, "Why didn't you come join me in the bathtub, Papio?"

"Because we would have ended up getting it cracking and your day shopping would have had to be put off for another day," he said as he left the bathroom.

Special dropped the towel she was wrapped in and yelled, "In that case, hurry your pretty ass up!"

"What I tell your ass about that pretty shit, Special!" he yelled back.

"Sorry!"

Five and a half hours later Papio and Special returned to their suite totally shopped out. Papio spent every penny of the $200,000 he brought with him. He bought Special everything from designer clothes, expensive shoes, purses by Chanel and Gucci, perfumes, even some expensive-ass hats. The only thing she didn't ask him for was jewelry and that shocked him.

Though he was tired he felt real good and wanted to do more. He watched Special as she got onto the bed and kicked off her Nikes.

"Come on, baby, we're done shopping but we ain't done vacationing."

"I'm tired, Papio; let's relax and chill for a little while," she whined.

"That's exactly what I had in mind. Come on." He grabbed her by the hand and gently pulled her off of the bed. They left the suite and went downstairs by the pool bar. They took off their shoes and put their feet in the shallow end of the pool and watched the activities of the youngsters playing around the pool area. A waitress came from the pool bar and asked them if they needed anything. Papio ordered some strawberry margaritas for the both of them. After receiving their drinks Papio and Special walked down to the beach to watch the sunset.

"This is some real romantic shit, Papio. I didn't know you had this type of flavor in you," teased Special.

"For real, neither did I. You bring out a different side of me, baby."

She remained silent for a moment and then said, "We can't let this turn into something it's not, Papio. We're not made for any of this square shit. Don't let your feelings get in the way of us having a good time."

"Why won't you at least give this shit a chance? I know what we do, but that shit shouldn't stop us from seeing if we can become closer. I'm not saying I'm in love and shit, believe me. I have never been known as a loving type of nigga. But I do know that I'm feeling you more than I have ever felt a female before."

"You're feeling me and all you know about me is that I'm in the life? That's some sucka shit and you know it. I could be setting you up to get got right now, look at your ass wide open straight slipping like a mark."

"I've robbed and set plenty of mothafuckas up and I know damn well when shit is real and not fake. Not only have I given you money, we've spent the day together enjoying each other's company, you know it as well as I do. Don't fight it, Special, that's all I ask. Roll with it and let's see what it can do."

This nigga has spent a nice chunk on me as well as fucked me right; why not give him a chance? she asked herself. *Because you know damn well you will end up fucked up no matter what,* she said to herself. She sighed and said, "You got that, Papio."

"That's what's up! Now, tell me something."

With raised eyebrows she asked, "Tell you what?"

"Tell me something about you."

She shook her head and said, "Straight square shit."

"Special," he said in a chastising tone.

"Okay, corny-ass nigga," she said. "Like I told you before I was raised up North in Oakland. Me and my mother had it hard for years but we remained close until the day she died. After I lost her I moved to the South and started making moves. I've been a loner for as long as I can remember, Papio; that's why it's so hard for me to give us a try. I can't afford to get caught up with emotional shit. I don't need love. I need money. Period."

"Who don't?"

"You are not hearing me, baby. I lost the only person in my life I have ever loved; that shit hurts me every time I think about it, which is every fucking day. I cry no more though. I've shed too many tears over the years. So I have to do what I have to to get that fucking money. No patience for that school and job shit; whatever it takes to get that paper I'm down to do it. Now how could you be with a woman who has absolutely no morals at all? Because I will fuck and suck twenty niggas if the price was right. And that's if I was with or without you. I am loyal to money and money only, Papio. I can't get hurt that way. The suckas I be working are the ones who gets to cry now. It's their turn as far as I'm concerned and nothing will ever stop me from getting my fucking money. I know they say everybody needs love, Papio, but for real, baby, I don't."

During her explanation they had stopped and watched as the sun slid out of sight.

Papio's thoughts were running crazy inside of his brain; he couldn't believe that he had met a woman

with so many of the same characteristics that he possessed. He turned toward her and smiled. "We're so
much alike, baby, that it's scary. The only woman in
this world I have ever loved is my mother, Mama Mia.
We had it rough for years after my father was killed.
During those hard times I swore to myself that we
would never want for nothing. I did everything up under the sun for this money and I'm not done yet, Special. Whatever it takes to get that money I'm 'bout it.
Check it, you gon' do you regardless and I respect that
shit, believe me I do. I'm going to do me too. There's no
reason why we can't kick it though. We were brought
together for a reason, baby, I honestly feel that shit.
Love is love and all of that and neither of us may need
it, but for real we deserve it. If it comes that means that
it was meant. I don't believe in all of that lovey-dovey
shit but damn, baby, I am feeling you in ways that I
never thought possible. I'm a fucking pirate, baby, and
I move best solo. Anyone with me or on my team is
temporary, pawns used for me to win the game, baby.
I'm in it to win it with everything I involve myself in.
Believe that, Special. I would never interfere with your
paper; if anything I would continue to assist you."

"See, that's what I don't want or need. I got me,
Papio. I don't need no one to give me a damn thang.
The only reason why I accepted what you gave me is
because I felt it was owed to me. You fucked me out a
grip, not once but twice. Other than that I would never
have came out here to fuck with you. I have the power
to do me at all times. I have to keep this power, baby.
I'm a bitch who's all about making moves, either by
manipulating or forcefully taking what I want; whatever I have to do I will do. Power is important to me,
Papio. I have to keep hold of that. Keep the power you
keep the money, period. I don't give a damn about respect as long as I got my money right."

Changing the subject he asked, "What happened to your mom?"

Tears swelled up in her eyes quickly. "Don't."

Papio kissed her eyes just as a tear slid out and said, "Talk to me."

She sighed and stared at his handsome features and wondered what the fuck she was doing. She got on her tiptoes and gave him a kiss and said, "My mother was killed by her lover. I watched as the life left my mother's body from one gunshot to the chest."

"Damn. What made him do that punk shit?"

Special grinned when she said, "It wasn't a him, it was a her."

That's where she gets that pussy-licking shit from, Papio said to himself. But to her he simply said, "Oh."

"She shot my mother because she was jealous, jealous of me. That dyke bitch hated the fact that my mother loved me more than she did her. Which for real was some straight bullshit because my mother told me plenty of times that she loved Deb more than anyone in the world. She also told me that the love she had for Deb was totally different from the love she had for me. She told that to that dumb bitch over and over also. And the bitch still killed her. That day changed my life forever. Not only did I watch my mother die that day, I committed my first murder."

"Huh?"

"You heard me. When Deb shot my mother she dropped her gun and ran to my mother and held her in her arms as she died. The bitch had the nerve to tell my mother as she was dying that she had to do it; she couldn't live if she didn't love her and only her. When I saw my mother breathe her last breath something snapped inside of me. I calmly stepped past them and picked up Deb's gun. I turned and faced Deb and told her that she could now join my mama. I shot that dyke bitch three times in her head, Papio. She killed my mama and I killed her skank ass."

"Damn. And I thought my shit was hard."

"What do you mean?"

Papio stared at her for a moment and without any emotion he told her, "I killed my father."

"What?"

"My first body was my father. I killed his punk ass because he kept putting his hands on Mama Mia. He used to be in the life but he didn't have what it took to get rich. Too tricky with it, that nigga didn't have any dick control. He was a straight sucka for a big, firm ass and a pretty face. He had the nerve to come home and put his hands on my mother when shit didn't go right for him out in them streets. The day I killed his ass was the day I chose the life. I had to because I didn't see any other way to be able to take care of Mama Mia. Like I said it was rough for a minute until I got lucky and hit some nice licks. Since then I have kept Mama Mia living in luxury. Fuck being comfortable; she has to have nothing but the very best as far as I'm concerned. I will continue to get this fucking money until I have enough to make sure that we both will have the very best of everything that this crazy world has to offer."

"How much is enough for you, Papio?"

He stared at her and smiled. "$100 million should do it."

"A hundred million? Are you serious?"

"I've never been more serious about anything in my life, Special."

She stared at him admiringly but all she could think to say was, "Damn."

CHAPTER TWENTY-SIX

The last five days of their vacation together was spent eating at the finest restaurants Miami had to offer, clubbing at the hottest spots in South Beach, shopping at the most expensive stores in Florida, and some of the most exciting sex Papio had ever encountered in his life. Papio was thinking about all of this as he waited in the parking lot of the post office while Special mailed the million dollars in cash to herself somewhere out in California. He gave her the game so she would be able to get her money back home safely. Now that their week together was over he was saddened because Special still hadn't told him whether they would be able to spend some more time together. Since he was about to take her to Miami International Airport for her two o'clock flight to LAX he knew that this was his last opportunity to get her to at least think about spending more time with him. He didn't want to let her get away from him for nothing in this world. Especially after realizing how much their lives mirrored one another, it was like they were meant to be. Corny thoughts like this had never been a part of Papio's MO, but they were there now and he didn't give a damn; he was feeling Special and he wanted her in his life more than he ever thought possible.

Special slid inside of the Bentley and said, "You better be right about this crazy shit, Papio. I'm not trying to trick off a million behind this move of yours."

"Don't panic, baby, I get down like this all the time. It's safe and you won't have a thing to stress. Tomorrow morning when you get up you will have your ends. Check it, you let me spend a nice chunk of change on you this past week on everything from purses, clothes, and shit but you never once mentioned anything about jewels. Why?" he asked as he pulled the car into traffic, headed toward the airport.

Special smiled. "Because when it comes to jewelry my taste is even more expensive than my taste for clothes and everything else. A bitch like me gots to have Oprah diamonds."

"Oprah diamonds? What the hell are Oprah diamonds, Special?"

"Big ones, Papio. Real big, expensive ones, baby. Look, you gave me the time of my life the past seven days. You are the first man I have ever let get this close to me. You gave me a million dollars cash! That's crazy for real. But at the same time it shows me that you are truly one of the last real niggas in the life. I respect you, I respect your get down, and on top of everything else you're a Pussy Monster. That right there has put you in the top spot in my life. I can't believe I'm actually saying this shit, but I refuse to fight how I feel. I like you, Papio. I like you a lot and I plan on spending as much time with you as I can. Just do me one favor okay?"

"Anything."

"Don't let your feelings fuck up how we get down. I won't stop doing me, Papio. Don't try to change my get down; if you do you'll never hear from me again," she said as she reached inside of her purse and pulled out a card and gave it to him. "These are all of my numbers so you'll be able to get in contact with me whenever you want to. If I tell you that I'm busy when you hit me, respect that and get back at me later. When you make

L.A. make sure you get at me and we can make it do
what it do. Let's take this nice and slow and see what
we can make of this." With a wry grin on her face she
said, "Never know, I might just end up being your Bonnie. You with that, Clyde?"

He laughed and said, "Damn, I give you seven days of
some good dick and you done went and got all mushy
on a nigga huh?" Special punched him on the arm and
laughed. "Nah, for real, Special, I'm with it and I feel
you. Thank you, baby, thank you for the chance to see
if we're meant to be." He stopped the car in front of
the American Airlines terminal, cut off the car, leaned
over, and gave Special a tender kiss.

After they finished kissing Special flashed that pretty
smile of hers. "Okay, Pussy Monster, I gots to get back
to work. I'll give you a call when I touch the West."

"That's what's up. I got to hit Dallas to take care of
some thangs, and then I'll be out in Oklahoma for a day
or so, and then I'll be headed westward bound. I do
plan on doing dinner with you so make sure you keep a
slot open for your Clyde," he said with a grin.

She shook her head from side to side and climbed
out of the car. Papio lugged all of Special's luggage to
the outside check-in counter and tipped a young porter
fifty dollars for taking all of Special's stuff.

"I'm so not good with this square shit, so don't get all
soft on me, Clyde."

He stared at her and was once again amazed at how
much that smile had captured his heart. That slight
gap in her teeth made her seem as if she was the most
perfect woman in the world for him. That imperfection
completed her as far as he was concerned. He gave her
his tough guy look and said, "Yeah, I ain't with that
goody-goody shit either." He gave her a kiss and said,
"Get at me, Bonnie." Without another word he turned

and strolled back to the Bentley. As much as he wanted to he didn't look back. *Keep it gangster, nigga, keep it gangster,* he said to himself as he pulled away from the curb and tried to get his mind back on his money. It was time to get back on his grind.

Papio made it to Dallas and got in contact with the Realtor he looked up before he left for Miami. He knew Dallas well but this particular area was new to him and he didn't have any time to be wasting; he wanted to get his new home situated so he could make the neces- sary moves out of Oklahoma City. It was time to switch some things up; too many people knew how to get at him. With that thought he wondered if it was time to move Mama Mia. *Maybe I could bring her out here,* he thought as he turned on to I-75 headed north to the city of Plano.

Twenty-five minutes later Papio pulled into the driveway of a 4,550-square-foot Florida-style home that looked just perfect to him from the outside. He jumped out of the SUV and stepped quickly toward the real estate agent, who was standing by the front door of the very expensive home.

Papio reached out his hand and said, "Hello, my name is Preston, Preston Ortiz."

"Hello, Mr. Ortiz. My name is Sharron Mosley. Come, let me show you this exquisite home. I'm sure you're going to fall in love with it," the real estate agent said as she led the way inside of the house. As soon as they were inside of the house the agent went right into her spiel describing every expensive feature the home possessed. "This house is ideal for entertaining, offering a twenty-two-foot-high foyer and great room. There's two fireplaces, five bedrooms, five and a half baths, main floor master and in-law suites, a gourmet kitchen, office overlooking a landscaped yard with a heated in-ground pool, finished basement, and a two-car garage. Twenty minutes tops from downtown Dallas so it's very convenient for you if you work in that area." She finished with a smile.

Papio liked everything he saw and knew that he was going to get it. He had to play the game to see how much this bad-ass pad was going to cost him. "How much?"

"The asking price is $2.5 million. But I'm sure a substantial offer could bring the price down somewhat. Are you financing, sir?"

Papio gave the agent a grin and said, "No. If I choose to get it I'll be paying cash."

"I see." *Thank you, Jesus!* the agent said to herself, thinking about the huge commission she would get with the sale of the home. "What would you like to offer, Mr. Ortiz?"

"Call me Preston, please."

The agent smiled and somewhat flirtatiously said, "Sure, Preston." *With your cute, rich ass,* she thought.

"Do you think I could get it for 1.5?"

With an ill-advised moment of honesty the agent said, "I doubt it. You'd have a better chance offering two."

Papio smiled and gave her a nod. "Are there many offers on this home?"

"No, Preston, none at all actually. But I am showing two other families the home later this week."

"Okay. Sharron, this is what I want you to do for me. I like what I see and I want this house. I'm used to getting what I want. So it's very important that you make this happen for me." He stared directly at her as he said this; he noticed how she was blushing and knew instantly that she was feeling him. Normally he would get his flirt on and line it up for a future fucking. *The cute little agent looks like she could go,* he thought as he admired her thickness and pretty face. Special had him in more ways than one because fucking the real estate agent was something that he hadn't even thought about. *Damn.* "I want you to offer the 1.5; if they don't go for it raise it to 1.75. You can go to two but see if they'll bite for the lower number first. You got me, Sharron?"

With the kind of money you about to spend, hell yeah, I got you, you sexy specimen you, she said to herself. "Yes, Preston, I got you."

"Good. Excuse me for a minute. I have to make a call so we can get everything put in motion." He pulled out his cell phone and called Quentin out in Los Angeles. When Quentin answered the phone Papio said, "Check it, Q, here in Dallas. I'm trying to get this spot out the agent. I'm giving Sharron Mosley your information so you can get at her and handle everything for me."

"Now, please tell me what the hell do you need with another expensive-ass house, Papio?" asked Q.

Papio started laughing and asked, "How do you know it's expensive?"

"Are you fucking kidding me, dude? You do it no other way. How much is it?"

"They're asking $2.5 million but I'm offering 1.5. I gave the agent the green light to go all the way to the two but I want to see if they'll bite for the lower ticket."

"That's smart. Okay, give her what she needs and I'll take care of everything."

"Thanks, Q. What's up out that way?"

Quentin started laughing and said, "Sude, you won't believe who's right back doing him and still slipping hard as ever."

"Our boy Nicoli still acting huh?"

"Yep."

"Got him?"

"Exactly."

"I'll be out there in a couple of days. I'll hit you up then."

"Talk to ya later, dude," Quentin said as he hung up the phone. He loved fucking with Papio; there was nothing he wouldn't do for money. And Quentin always got to keep his hands clean while Papio did all of the dirty work. *Life is good when Papio is in the game,* he thought as he went back to sorting some files out in his office.

Papio hung up the phone. "This is my personal assistant; give him a call when you have all of the paperwork ready. He'll take care of all of the finances and particulars."

"I'll need a way to get in contact with you also, Preston. Especially once I've received the confirmation of your offer."

Papio added his number to the card he gave her. "Call me when everything is ready."

"I will. You have a nice day, Preston."

"I always do, Sharron, I always do."

CHAPTER TWENTY-SEVEN

Papio left the city of Plano feeling confident that he would soon be an off-and-on-again resident. As he got on to the highway he was undecided if he should go on and make the two-and-a-half-hour drive on into Oklahoma City or get a room for the night and get some rest. Since he didn't really feel tired he chose to go on and make the trek. He stopped and got himself a bottled water and a bag of chips to munch on and hit I-35, headed north to Oklahoma. He set the SUV on cruise control at seventy-five miles per hour and started thinking about everything that was about to go down when he got into town.

He had to get with Brandy and let her know that he most likely wouldn't be returning to the city because of business reasons. He didn't want to spook her by telling her about the situation with the Indians from Niagara Falls. He would miss Brandy, but if things went as he hoped he would be caught up with Special anyway. That thought put a smile on his face.

His mind went back to the matters at hand. *Get with Kammy and put that thing with those Dallas youngsters to bed and get that money. Then the most important part of the trip will be getting with that bitch snitch-ass nigga Charlie. That will be fun for me. I'm going to kill that nigga nice and slow. Nah, fuck all that Hollywood shit; smoke that nigga and keep it moving. I ain't got time for the bullshit. I got a hundred million to get,* he said to himself as he reached and grabbed his cell phone off of the center console. He dialed Brandy's number and waited for her to answer.

"What's good, *mami?*"

"Everything is good now that I'm talking to you, daddy. How are you doing?"

"I'm good, on my way to the city now."

"Really? Ooh, can I see you tonight, daddy?" She sounded overly excited about being able to spend some time with him.

"Of course. We got some things to discuss because shit done got thick for me, *mami.*"

With sincere concern in her voice she asked, "What's wrong?"

"We'll chop it up when I get in town. I'm on the highway now. I should be there in a couple of hours. When you get off work meet me at the house."

"Okay, daddy. Is there anything you need me to take care of for you?"

"Nah. I'm good. I'll see you in a li'l bit," he said as he hung up the phone.

He called Kammy's shop and told her that he would meet her at her house sometime after eleven that evening so they could put everything together for the Dallas youngsters. She was with the program and that put a smile on his face as he thought about how that freaky old broad was going to try her best to fuck him when he went over her house later. The mere thought of sex put Special on his mind. He pulled out his wallet and grabbed the card Special gave him. He dialed the first number and gave a sigh of relief when she answered the phone on the first ring.

"I see you made it back safely, Bonnie. Thanks for calling and giving me that bit of information," he said playfully.

"See, there you go already catching feelings and getting all sprung and shit," she teased right back. "How you, Clyde?"

"I'm good. On my way to Oklahoma to handle some BI and then I should be headed west."

"When?"

"Three days tops.".

"That's cool. We should be able to hook up. I don't have any moves for the next week or so. That is, if you're good?"

"I got a couple of moves to make but that won't stop nothing. I'll let you know what's what when I get in town."

"All right. Tell me something, Clyde; do you miss me?"

"I was missing you as soon as I pulled away from the curb at the airport."

She smiled into the receiver and said, "Talk to you later, Clyde."

"Bye, Bonnie."

Time to get to work.

Brandy was already at Papio's home when he arrived. He went into the house and let his nose lead him into the kitchen to see what was smelling so divine. He was surprised to see Brandy standing in front of the stove frying something, dressed only in one of his wife-beaters. Her firm ass was poking out of the bottom of his shirt and he instantly got an erection.

"Damn, *mami,* like that?"

She turned off the stove, stepped to him, and gave him a tender kiss that turned passionate immediately. "Hi, daddy. Are you hungry?"

"Yeah, I want to eat you. Come on, we can come back after we finish handling our business." He didn't wait for a response; he just scooped her up into his arms and kissed her as he carried her all the way upstairs to the bedroom.

Forty-five minutes later they were both tired and sweaty from their sexing. Brandy was one bad-ass woman and he hated that he had to let her go, but he had to handle shit and get gone.

"Check it, *mami,* I'm about to be gone for a good minute and I'm not really knowing for real when I'll be back. I got a lot of moves to make and I'm going to need you to hold me down for real."

"You already know whatever you need from me, daddy, I got you."

"I want you to move in here so you can take care of my spot for me. You can keep the cars and everything. The ends I gave you should be enough for you to maintain the place. If by some chance something happens to me the place is yours. I'll get at my man Q in the West and let him know of my wishes. I'll leave you with his numbers so you can check with him if need be."

With tears sliding down her pretty face she asked, "Why? Why are you leaving, daddy? Are you in some kind of trouble?"

He wiped her eyes and said, "Nah, I'm good. I got a lot on my plate though and none of it concerns Oklahoma. I don't have a timetable for my moves but I do know it will be a good minute before I return. I just wanted to do you righteous and bless you with my most prized possession. You deserve that."

"Will I ever get to come spend some time with you, daddy?"

"Uh-uh. I don't want to give you any bullshit, baby, because you already know that's not how I get down. But I will be in contact with you. You got the numbers; they ain't gon' change. I don't expect for you to put your life on hold either, *mami.* If you meet someone, live your life. I won't be mad at you."

"Is that what you're doing, daddy? Have you found someone else?"

With his poker face intact Papio told her, "Money is what I live and breathe for, *mami*. I told you that and I meant it, ain't shit changed."

"I understand. But you have to know that I would never disrespect you and bring another man into this house. I fell in love with you when I first saw you, Papio. But I also knew that it would never be because of how you do your thing. I have tried my best to prepare myself for this day because I knew eventually it would come. Now that it's here I'm scared. I'm scared, daddy."

"What are you scared of?"

"I'm scared I'm going to be lost without you in my life."

"Baby, you won't be lost, you're one strong-ass black woman and you will do what needs to be done. So kill that noise."

Before she could continue with all of this emotional drama Papio changed the subject. "Check it, I need you to go on back to the kitchen and get that food ready. I need to eat something before I go out and make some moves tonight."

"Okay, daddy. How long will you be in town?"

"Two, maybe three days. It depends on how some shit falls for me. I should know for sure when I get back later on. Go on now; daddy is starving." He watched as she climbed out of the bed and went into the bathroom to clean herself up before she went downstairs to prepare his food. When she left the bedroom he called his man Cheese and said, "What's good, li'l nigga?"

"Papio?"

"Yeah, what's the business?"

"Shit, just maintaining. I guess you getting at me for a line on ya man huh?"

"You know it."

"I'm still at the same spot in the North Highlands; come get at me and we'll talk."

Papio checked the time and saw that it was a little after eight P.M. and said, "I'll be through in a hour."

"How much will you be bringing?"

"Enough," Papio said as he hung up the phone just as Brandy came into the bedroom with a steaming plate of food.

Papio arrived in the neighborhood called the North Highlands and frowned as he saw a bunch of young-sters hanging on the block looking zoned out. *What the fuck is wrong with those fools?* he wondered as he pulled into Cheese's driveway. He jumped out of the Range and went to the door.

Cheese answered the door. "My nigga, come on in."

"Damn, yellow nigga, you can't gain no weight or some shit? Looks like you need to get on some weight gainer or something." Before Cheese had a chance to respond to him Papio asked another question. "Man, what's the fuck wrong with them young fools out there? They look like they some zombies or some shit.'"

"Since you been gone, dog, shit done changed. Them fools are just Xed out. It's like niggas in the city don't be getting no serious money no more. Especially over here. It's some Dallas niggas out here that got shit on lock. None of the real Gs are around no more; either they locked up, squared up, Xed out, or dead. The few real niggas left just don't have the tools necessary to keep up with those fools."

"What's your business then, Cheese? You gave up too, nigga?"

"I'm gon' always eat, Papio, you know how I do it. But for real, them Dallas fools makes it hard for a nigga to do bigger thangs."

Papio shook his head from side to side and said, "Looks like I got to come and save the day again huh?"

"What you mean?"

"Check it, give me what I came for," Papio said as he reached inside of his baggy jeans and pulled a stack of one hundred dollar bills, $20,000 to be exact. He tossed the stack of money to Cheese and said, "That's a dub for you, nigga. In a day or so I'm going to come and drop you a blessing. You will know what's what when you get it. I expect for you to handle your business and get shit right around the way. I'll leave you with a number so you will have a plug to maintain shit. Make sure you use it, Cheese. If you don't I'll know and then I'll come back and take back my blessing. You feel me?"

Cheese smiled. "Do I!" He then went on and gave Papio the information he came for. When he finished telling Papio where his first cousin Charlie lived and worked he asked a question he already knew the answer to. "Are you going to kill him, Papio?"

Papio stared at Cheese for a moment and said, "Make sure you have your black suit dry-cleaned, li'l nigga."

CHAPTER TWENTY-EIGHT

Papio drove directly from Cheese to the address where Charlie lived. He drove by the house slowly to get a lay of the land. *This nigga think he layin' low 'cause he way out here.* Satisfied that this was going to be an easy hit Papio headed to Kammy's.

"What's the business, sexy?" He stepped by her into the house.

"Everything is how it should be, Papio. That young nigga is sprung and feeling a bitch something terrible."

"That's what's up. So when you gon' get at him again? We need to go on and handle this shit."

"We're supposed to hook up tomorrow at his place out in Edmond."

"Edmond? Damn."

"What's wrong, baby?"

"A nigga really don't like fucking around in Edmond; you know with all them crackers around and shit."

"It's cool out his way though; he stays back that way behind Frontier City. You remember that guy Greg Sutton?"

"The fool who played pro basketball?"

"Yeah. Chico stays like around the corner from him."

"Okay, I remember that neighborhood because that nigga Greg used to throw them swim parties out there back in the days all the time. That's a real quiet neighborhood though."

"We shouldn't have to make too much noise, baby; in and out real smooth like right?" Papio looked at her as if she'd lost her mind. "Do you really understand this business, Kam? I mean for real, I got to smoke that nigga. You do understand this right?"

She sighed. "I was thinking about that, baby; why can't we just tie the nigga up and get the money and dope?"

"Sure! We can do that. Then after we split that loot and work up I'll go on about my business and then them Dallas niggas will come to your shop, scoop you up, and take your life slowly. That's just fine with me if it's cool with you," he said sarcastically.

With a stupid look on her face she said, "Oh."

"Don't trip, I got this. I'll handle everything nice and quiet like. Just give me that nigga's exact address. Hit me up when you know what the business is and what time you'll be there. After that go on and do you. I'll already be posted on deck ready to make everything pop off. Leave the nigga's door unlocked for me. Are you sure everything is there with him?"

"Mm-hm. That nigga don't even trust his own people for reals. He keeps all of that dope in his fucking pool house in the back. The money is in the closet locked in one of those big-ass safes."

"Safe? That nigga is lame for real; niggas don't waste money on shit like that no more."

"He's a youngster who came up too fast; he don't really know what he's doing. A straight rookie."

"I see. What's up with his people? How deep is his crew?"

"There's seven of them. His team mostly stays on the other side and over in the Highlands. They got shit locked on the north and the south from what I heard. The X, the Purp, and the yayo."

"How much money do you think he has in that place?"

She shrugged her slim shoulders and said, "From what he showed me I'd say at least a few million. He was so caught up flossing to me that I don't even think he realized he was telling me all of his business. Then again he's so cocky with it he probably did and just didn't give a fuck. He said he makes at least three million a trip. And since he's been back for a few weeks now he should have at least three million or better, baby."

"Good. Check it. After I handle the business we'll be out of that spot. Make sure that that nigga picks you up so your shit won't have to be seen at his tilt. We'll come back here and split shit up. We split the ends only, Kammy. I get all the work. Cool?"

"Hell yeah! I don't have no way to be moving that shit anyway." She smiled and continued, "Damn, a bitch is about to have some serious money."

"You better fucking believe it."

Papio woke up the next morning just as Brandy was leaving for work. *Damn, I'm going to miss this classy-ass woman,* he said to himself as he got out of bed. He stepped to her and gave her a hug. "What are you doing when you get off, *mami?*"

"I'm going to go by my house and start packing some stuff to bring over here. You aren't leaving today are you, daddy?"

He shook his head. "Nah, I got some BI to take care of later. Most likely it will be tomorrow or the day after. When you get off we'll go out and have dinner. Cool?"

"That's fine."

"Do me a favor and tell Kingo I said to call me. I need to holla at him."

"Okay. Talk to you later," Brandy gave him a kiss good-bye.

After she left the bedroom Papio sat on the edge of the bed and thought about how he was going to do Charlie. *I should go blast that nigga tonight after I hit that nigga Chico; nah, that's doing way too much. You can live one more day, Charlie. I'll get your ass tomorrow,* he thought as he slipped on his pants and went downstairs to the garage, He went behind the 600 and grabbed a medium-sized box and carried it into the media room. He set the box down in front of him and opened it up. He pulled out two MP-5 submachine guns and two silencers and set them on the table.

Should I or shouldn't I let Kammy live? Fuck, that's some cold shit for real. I can't leave no loose ends like that. Them niggas will definitely come and get at her when they find out that they man is dead. She won't hesitate to give my ass up when they start getting rough with her ass. Fuck it, it ain't like she will be able to tell them niggas where I'm at. Let her live, Papio, let her live, he said to himself as he stood and went back upstairs.

Papio and Brandy were enjoying their dinner at an expensive restaurant downtown by the Ford Center when Papio got a call from Kingo. He excused himself and stepped outside of the restaurant so he could speak with his man in private.

"What it do, dread? You good?" he asked after pressing the number five button on his phone to accept Kingo's call.

"Me just fine, Papio. What about you, mon?"

"Everything is everything on this side of the fence. I'm handling my business and making all the right moves."

"Good. Miami?"

"That's straight too. Took care of them as far as the cash is concerned. Got to get back with that other issue though."

"They good with that?"

"Yep."

"Mmmrrunm. Okay, tell me, what you do to your girl, mon?"

"What are you talking about?"

"Don't make me talk when you know I can't do that. Me can tell she not the same; she sound different."

"Everything must come to an end, dread, you know that. Don't trip, she's good. I'm leaving her my pad out here."

"Where you go?"

"Time to shake this town, at least for a minute."

"What's wrong, mon?" Kingo sounded concerned.

"Nothing serious. I got some heavy moves to make in the West and I'll be out that way for a while that's all. I'm in the process of getting a spot in Texas so I won't be too far. It's time for me to move on, dread; trust me I'm good."

Recognizing the lies as he heard them Kingo chose to ignore them for the moment and said, "Make sure you use those numbers I gave you, Papio. The 619 number will come in handy if things gets too wild for you, mon."

"I got you. I'll be getting at them once I get every-thing situated out West." Changing the subject Papio asked, "You good on that other thing or do you need to be touched up?"

That put a smile on the old Jamaican's face. "Now, you always know I can be touched up with that, mon. I haven't been too bad but me do need to get right ya know?"

"Got you. Let me go; I was in the middle of dinner. Hit me in a few days or so."

"Be careful out there, Papio."

"Don't worry, old dread, there's only one way up and believe me I'm on my way up!"

With a serious tone Kingo said, "Understood. You just make sure that you understand this: what goes up gots to come down, mon."

Papio hung up the phone and went back inside of the restaurant thinking about Kingo's words. Before he could get back to his seat Kammy called.

"Chico is picking me up after I close the shop."

"What time will that be?" he asked as he made his way back to his seat.

"In about a hour or so."

"I need an exact time."

Kammy paused and checked the time on her watch and said, "I should be through around ten, so I'll call him and tell him to come get me at ten-thirty."

"All right. I'll be there before y'all."

"You sure? You remember where he stays right?" She sounded nervous.

"Don't panic, baby. I'll be right where I need to be. I don't got a bad memory. Go on and handle your BI and I'll see you when it's time to get this fucking money."

"All right, bye, Papio."

"Later," he said as he closed his phone. When he looked up Brandy was staring at him with a frown on her face. *Oops,* he thought.

"I know you deal with a lot of different women, daddy. I have tried my very best to not let those thoughts mess with my head. But for the life of me I can't help being jealous."

Papio smiled confidently at her and said, "*Mami, when I deal with the ladies it's business and business only, believe that. You know who owns my heart.*"

"Yes, I know who owns your heart, daddy. Money," she said in a sarcastic tone.

Papio sipped some of his wine, smiled, and said, "Exactly."

CHAPTER TWENTY-NINE

Papio grabbed the two silenced MP-5 machine guns and gave Brandy a kiss. "I should be back late so don't wait up."

"You come in here and grab some very serious-looking weapons and tell me not to wait up. Come on, daddy, that's crazy."

"Don't sweat this shit; it's for protection that's all. I'll call you when I'm done handling my business so you can get some rest, cool?" he tried to reassure her.

She shook her head yes. "Give me another kiss, daddy."

He gave her a kiss that was meant to be a quickie but turned into a very passionate and intense one.

After a full minute he pulled from her embrace. "Let me go get this money, *mami*. Don't worry about me, I'm good."

He didn't wait for a response; he just walked out of the front door. *Yeah, shit is about to go real smooth,* he thought as he pulled out of the driveway.

Papio was parked four houses down from where Chico stayed in a well-kept home in the city of Edmond. Papio was relaxed and focused as he waited patiently. He smiled as he watched Chico pull into his driveway right on time. He watched as Kammy went to the front door, unlocked it, and then stepped quickly back toward Chico, who was waiting inside his car. She leaned inside of the car, gave him his keys and a kiss, then went inside of the house. Papio smiled at that because never did she even try to look and see where he was parked. *That's my girl; keep ya game face on, baby,* he said to himself as he watched Chico pull out of his driveway. *This shit is going to be easier than I expected.*

His cell phone started ringing. "What's good, Kam?" he answered the phone.

"That fool said he had to go make a run and for me to get ready because he has some kind of surprise for me."

"That's what's up. That makes things that much easier for us."

"What you mean?"

"Open the door and I'll tell you when I get inside," he said and hung up the phone. Papio grabbed both the machine guns and held them down by his side as he stepped quickly to the front door of Chico's home.

Kammy had the door open just as he made it there. When she saw the two machine guns in Papio's hands she asked, "Damn, nigga, what you gon' do with them mean-looking-ass guns?"

He ignored her stupid-ass question and said, "Show me where the fucking pool house is."

He followed her outside to the backyard. When they made it to the pool house he said, "Check it. Go on back inside and wait for that clown-ass nigga. I'll be there in a minute."

"What are you going to do, take the safe with you?"

He shook his head no and said, "Nah, I ain't got time to be cracking no damn safe. That nigga gon' open this bitch up before he dies."

"What if he refuses to open it, then what?"

"Trust me, he will open this mothafucking safe. Now go on inside before that nigga comes back."

Kammy went back inside of the house more nervous than she already was. *God, I hope this nigga knows what the fuck he's doing,* she said to herself as she went back inside of the house.

Papio smiled when he saw a dolly propped against the far wall of the pool house. He grabbed the dolly and slid the lip under the huge safe, then rolled it toward the back door of the house. With more strength than he thought he would have to use Papio pulled the safe up the two steps of the back porch.

I hope this mothafucka is this heavy because of its contents.

Papio left the safe in the kitchen, then went back out-side, grabbed his guns, and quickly came back inside of the house. He stepped into the living room and told Kammy, "Check it, this is how it's going to go down. When that fool comes back I'm going to pop him in his knees right off the bat so he will know that this busi-ness is serious and there's no room for any bullshitting. Once he opens the safe I want you to start grabbing ev-erything inside and bag it up. You did bring those bags like I told you to right?"

She grabbed her medium-sized Dooney & Burke bag and pulled out four Hefty trash bags and held them up for him to see. "What, you think I'm on some dumb shit, Papio?"

"Kill that noise, baby. I'm just making sure every-thing is good. Anyway, after you bag up all of the good-ies I want you to go out and pull my truck behind that fool's load. I'll handle the business and be right out with everything and we'll be on our way."

Before Kammy could say a word they heard Chico's loud music bumping from his expensive car stereo. Kammy inhaled deeply and said, "Oh, shit! Here he comes, Papio!"

"Relax, *mami;* it's all about the business now. Be cool," he said as he checked and made sure that both machine guns were loaded and ready to fire. Kammy went to the window and saw that Chico wasn't alone. "Oh, shit! We got a serious problem, Papio. Chico ain't by himself."

"Huh? Who the fuck is with that nigga?"

Kammy turned around with a smirk on her face and said, "Mani."

"Great. Fucking great."

"So what now, you gon' kill her too?"

With a determined look on his face and a deadly tone in his voice Papio told her, "You fucking right."

Chico put his key into the lock and opened the front door. He took a step back and let Mani enter his home first. When Mani saw Papio standing in the middle of the living room holding two machine guns in his hands, she stopped dead in her tracks and put her hands over her mouth. Chico stepped inside behind her and locked the front door without paying any attention to why she had stopped.

"What the fuck?" Chico exclaimed when he finally saw Papio.

"Hi, Chico. You're about to be got for all of your ends, fool." With precision, he fired a three-round burst from one of the MP-5s. Chico fell to the ground, screaming and holding his shattered right knee.

"That's to let you know that this business is real. Don't play no games and you will live through this night, nigga. Try me and you will die. Understood?"

"Man, I don't know what you think I got, but ain't no money here! You trippin', dog!"

Papio smiled and said, "So, you mean to tell me that big-ass safe I hauled into the kitchen from your pool house is empty? That's cool, then you won't have a problem giving me the combination so I can see for myself right?" The look Chico gave Kammy was priceless.

Papio said, "Damn, Kam, that nigga looks like he wants to do you something real bad."

"Fuck that li'l-dick nigga. Get the combination, baby, so we can get the fuck outta here," Kammy said to Papio, then smiled at Mani. "What the fuck are you doing here, Mani? You done made a stupid move, girl. You straight caught the fuck up in a cold mix now."

"Chico said he was going to break me off real good if I came over here and had a three-way with him and another girl."

"A three-way? Ain't that a bitch! Even if this wasn't a jack move your ass wasn't getting no shit like that from me, nigga! I'm strictly dickly!"

"Bitch, after this shit is over your ass will be strictly dead!" yelled Chico.

Kammy smiled and shook her head sadly at him.

"Damn, Mani, you getting down like that now huh? Should've kept your sorry ass around huh?" asked Papio.

"Don't do that to me, Papio; you know damn well the only reason I would fuck with that type of shit is to eat. You left me so fucked up what other choice do I got?"

Papio didn't believe her. He had left her with plenty.

"Fuck you, nigga. I'm ready to die before I give you shit!" Chico blurted out.

Papio gave him a nod of his head and said, "Tough nigga huh? That's cool too. I was prepared for you to go out like that." Papio stepped over to where Chico was lying and put the barrel of one of his machine guns point blank to Chico's left knee and pulled the trigger. Another three-round burst tore his kneecap to pieces.

Chico screamed so loud Papio got spooked. He put the hot barrel of the machine gun on Chico's lips and said, "Shut the fuck up or die now, nigga! I'm not asking your ass again; what's the fucking combo?"

Chico gritted his teeth and said, "Come on hustla; you don't got to do me dirty like this, dog."

"Fuck it. I guess you don't want to live," Papio said casually as he aimed his guns at Chico's head.

"No! Wait! It's 01-16-97!"

Papio smiled. "See, that wasn't that hard now was it?"

He knelt in front of the safe and quickly dialed the combination. The safe popped open and he saw stacks and stacks of money, plus what looked like a ton of X pills and at least ten kilos of cocaine. "Kammy!" he called out.

Kammy came into the kitchen with the Hefty trash bags in her hand and a huge smile on her pretty face. "We did it, baby! We did it!"

"That's right. Now put all of this in them bags and go sit in my truck while I finish this shit up." He stood and then went back into the living room.

When Chico saw Papio come back into the room he said, "Man, you got yours, now please just leave so I can go to the fucking hospital."

Papio shook his head at the youngster and said, "Dog, you really are a rookie in this game huh?"

"Gots to be if he thinks you're going to let him live," Mani said, defeated, already knowing her fate.

"That's right, baby. Since you know that you do know that I gots to do you too right?"

With a defiant look on her face Mani said, "I don't think you're that cold, Papio."

He stepped over to Chico and without saying a word he shot him three times in his face. Bits of brain joined the already growing pool of blood from Chico's knees.

Papio stepped back and said, "Baby, you just don't know how cold federal prison made me."

Mani shook her head as she stared at Chico's lifeless body lying there on the floor in front of her. She couldn't believe this shit was happening to her. Here she was ready to get paid by degrading herself to the lowest level and now shit done got even worse. The one man she loved more than anything in this world was about to take her life. *Hell to the nah,* she thought. *I ain't going out like that shit.* "You have ruined my life, nigga! So you might as well be the one to end it!" With tears sliding down her face she continued, "You gon' kill me, Papio? Huh? You really that cold a nigga now? Do it. Do it then! I'm ready to die, Papio!"

Kammy burst into the room at that very moment pointing a chrome pistol directly at Papio's head and said, "That nigga ain't gon' kill you, Mani. How can a dead man kill somebody?"

Papio turned toward her just as she pulled the trigger to her gun twice. Her first shot grazed his neck and her second shot hit Papio in his right shoulder and knocked him to the floor. He rolled with the momentum and turned the machine gun he had in his left hand and fired multiple rounds in Kammy's direction. Seven out of the ten bullets that left his MP-5 hit their mark. Kammy was dead before her body hit the floor. He slowly got to his feet and stared at Kammy's dead body. He shook it off and got back in money mode. With his brain racing he was trying to figure out if he should go on and add a third murder to his body count. Mani was staring at him with that same defiant look on her face.

"Go into the kitchen and grab those trash bags with all of that work and money, Mani."

"Why? Why should I assist your ass, Papio? You still gon' kill me right?"

"Go get that shit now, Mani! If you don't hurry the fuck up you damn right I'm going to kill your ass!"

Realizing that she had pushed him as far as she could she reluctantly did as she was told. She went into the kitchen and grabbed the four trash bags filled with Chico's money and drugs and brought everything into the living room.

She set the bags next to Papio. "Now what?"

He reached into one of the trash bags and pulled out two thick stacks of one hundred dollar bills and said, "Here, take this." He tossed her the money. "Come on, I need you to bring those bags out to my truck."

She stared at the money. "You're not going to kill me, Papio?"

The combination of the pain from his shoulder and neck caused him to flinch when he tried to move. "If I was going to kill you, you'd already be dead. Now come the fuck on!"

Once they were inside of the truck Papio told her, "You have your life and from the looks of those two stacks you got there you got at least a hundred Gs. My advice to you, Mani, is to get the fuck outta the city and try to go find some happiness."

"What about you, Papio; what are you going to do?"

He smiled at her through his pain and said, "What I always do, Mani: get money."

CHAPTER THIRTY

Papio could tell he had lost a lot of blood because he was feeling lightheaded as he drove toward his home. After he dropped Mani off at her aunt's house he called a doctor friend of his that he kept on deck for special situations like this. He knew that his movements were going to be limited for a minute so he had to get everything in order because, no matter what, he was out of here within a day or two. He had already been in Oklahoma City way longer than he originally intended. Though he was in pain he still was focused on the moves that had to be made once he made it back to Los Angeles. As long as he was breathing he was going to continue to get his money. Nothing was going to stop him.

He pulled the Range into the garage, slid from behind the driver's seat, and stepped wearily into the kitchen just as Brandy entered. When she saw his blood soaked T-shirt she screamed.

Papio held up his good arm and said, "Calm down, *mami*. Please calm the fuck down. I'm good. Help me to the bedroom."

She did as she was told without a question asked. As soon as she had him onto the bed she went into the bathroom and grabbed some towels, peroxide, and alcohol so she could help him with his wounds.

She helped Papio out of his T-shirt. "Here, daddy, let me try to clean your wound." She began to gently wipe his neck where one of the bullets had hit him. She figured that if he was hit in the neck it could be fatal and that she needed to tend to it immediately. With the blood cleared she saw that it was just a graze and began paying more attention to the bullet hole in his shoulder. Papio winced in pain as soon as she touched him. She jumped back and said, "Sorry, daddy."

"It's all good, *mami,* but look, hit me with some of that peroxide. I need you to check my back. I think the bullet went straight through. If that's the case then I should be good."

"Don't you think we need to take you to the hospital? I mean you may have some serious damage inside of there."

Papio was annoyed by her question. "Check my back, Brandy, and tell me what you see."

The tone in his voice shut her up and she did as she was told. She turned him around and saw a smaller hole on the right side of his back. "There is a hole back here too, daddy."

"Okay, cool. Clean that up for me as best you can. Doc-Tee should be here in about fifteen minutes to do me righteous."

Brandy tried to clean him up but the blood kept flowing. Papio was annoyed that she couldn't stop the blood. He didn't understand that until the hole was sewn shut it would keep bleeding.

"Patch that shit up," Papio demanded.

"The blood won't stop, daddy." She tried her best to stop the blood flow by applying pressure to the hole.

"Goddamn, stop touching me. I'll just wait for Doc to get here." Papio pushed her away from him.

Brandy didn't let his anger stop her. She wanted to help her man and knew he was just acting like this because he had lost so much blood. "Do you have any painkillers, daddy? I didn't see any in the medicine cabinet."

"Nah. I'll be good until the doc gets here. Check it, I need you to go down to the Range and grab those trash bags and bring them up here for me."

"Okay, daddy. I'll be right back."

Papio wearily said, "Cool, *mami*. I ain't going nowhere."

By the time Brandy came back into the bedroom Papio was asleep. She stepped to him quickly and slapped him on his face real hard. "Wake up, daddy! Wake up!"

Papio opened his eyes and stared at her as if she'd lost her motherfucking mind. "What the hell you hit me that damn hard for?"

She gave a sigh of relief. "I heard somewhere before that if a gunshot victim loses consciousness that he can go into shock. I . . . I'm sorry, daddy, it's just that I'm so scared right now."

He grabbed her hand and gave it a squeeze. "Don't be scared, *mami*. I'm good."

She stared into his eyes. "What happened? Who did this to you, daddy?"

Before he could answer the doorbell rang.

"I'll put you up on everything after Doc leaves, *mami*. Go on and let him in huh?"

"I'll be right back," she said as she hurried downstairs to go get the doctor.

"Here he is, Doctor." She quickly entered the room with the doctor following close behind.

Doc-Tee, or Doc as he was known by most hood niggas with money in Oklahoma City, shook his head when he saw Papio. "Looks like you finally got the wrong end of the gun huh, Papio?"

"Yeah, Doc, I got hit this time. Come fix me up before we talk though huh?"

Doc stepped to the bed with his black leather medicine bag in his hand and said, "Okay, let's see how much damage has been done." He then began to methodically check Papio out. After a few minutes he said, "Okay, here, this is what we have. You took a bullet in the right shoulder that went straight through; by the way the blood has slowed I'd say that no internal damage has been done. But I can't be one hundred percent positive without taking some X-rays. So you'll have to come to my office tomorrow for me to check that out. The graze on your neck is deep but not deep enough for any stitches. I'm going to give you a shot for the pain as well as a healthy dose of these painkillers for your discomfort."

"So . . . I'm good?" Papio asked hopefully.

"Looks like it to me. But tell me, how long ago did this happen?"

Papio lifted his left arm and checked the time. "I'd say about forty-five minutes ago."

"Hmmmmm. That means you've lost quite a lot of blood. I figured it was serious when you called, so luckily I came prepared for this." Doc reached inside of his bag and pulled a small bag of plasma out and said, "I'm going to hook you up so we can give you some more blood. This should be enough until I can get you to the office tomorrow."

Brandy's eyes grew wide as saucers when she said, "But you don't even know if that blood you have is the correct blood type, Doc!"

Doc and Papio smiled at each other knowingly. "Check it, *mami,* me and Doc been dealing with each other for a real long time. He knows everything there is to know about me medically. Don't worry. I'm in Doc's very capable hands," Papio said confidently.

Brandy pursed her lips. "I should have known, daddy; you are always on top of things."

Papio smiled through his discomfort. "You know this."

"Did you clean this wound, ma'am?" asked Doc.

"Yes, I did," Brandy said proudly.

"Good job. That makes my job easier." Doc began to hook up a line to the bag of plasma so he could inject an IV inside of Papio's arm. Once he had that situated he gave Papio a shot and told him, "Now you should be able to sleep in peace." He set a bottle of painkillers onto the nightstand and continued, "Take these every three hours for the pain. You will be stiff as hell when you wake up but you'll be fine in a few days. I expect to see you at my office at seven A.M. sharp, Papio. And I mean that. You will have to come before hours so I can get you in and out of there before my nurses and other patients arrive. Am I understood?" Doc asked sternly.

"Gotcha, Doc."

Doc shook his head again and smiled. "You are something else, Papio. Make sure you bring everything needed to take care of this house call too!"

"You know I got you, Doc."

"Yes, I know you do. Now get some rest."

Brandy took Doc back downstairs and thanked him repeatedly as she led him toward the door. When she made it back to the bedroom she was surprised to see Papio talking to someone on the telephone.

"Like I told you earlier, if you want to get back on top of the game this is how you're going to be able to do it. But you're going to have to lay in the cut for a minute. I'll explain it more in detail when we hook up tomorrow."

"But I thought you wanted me to come through tonight?" asked Cheese.

"Nah, I'm too tired for that shit. We'll hook up tomorrow. Keep your ears to the streets and your fucking mouth closed. When you hear some shit you'll know the business. Keep it close to your chest and when we hook up you will be back in the game, li'l nigga. Ya feel me?"

Cheese smiled into the receiver and said, "Yeah, I feel you, big homey. Later."

"Yeah, later." Papio hung up the phone. He saw the frown on Brandy's face and said, "Come on, *mami*, don't be mad at me. I gots to stay up on everything. A few little scrapes can't shut me down."

"I just don't understand you, Papio. You could have lost your life tonight and here you are talking as if all of this is nothing. I mean I'm so damn scared it all feels as if I was the one who was shot."

He reached his good arm out toward her and said, "Come here, *mami*." Once she was on the bed lying beside him he gave her a tender kiss and said, "See, that's another reason why I'm shaking this town. I couldn't bear to ever hurt you, Brandy. You're too good of a person to be involved with a man like me. You will never be able to understand my moves or the way I get down. It's just too much for you."

"It should be too much for you too! Daddy, all the money in the world isn't worth your life! You have enough now that if you invested it properly you could live comfortably for the rest of your life. Why don't you—"

He put his index finger to her lips and said, "Stop. Stop, and listen very good. The only way I can live comfortable is when I have $100 million. That's it and that's all. I won't stop until I have that. And nothing you can say to me will ever change how I feel. So do me a favor, baby, and chill out. Lie next to me and comfort me as I close my eyes. I need you to do that for me right now, *mami*. You got me?"

Brandy sighed heavily. "You know I got you, daddy. I love you so damn much."

Papio smiled at her. "I know you do, baby, I know you do."

He relaxed comfortably in Brandy's arms and drifted off to sleep. Even though Brandy had stepped up and taken care of him in his time of need his thoughts were of one person: Special.

CHAPTER THIRTY-ONE

The next morning Papio woke up groaning. His shoulder was killing him. He took a look at the IV that Doc had inserted in his arm and saw that the bag of plasma was empty. He removed the IV from his arm, took two pain pills, then started to get ready. It took him much longer than he expected but thirty-five minutes later he was showered, dressed, and ready to go take care of business.

Brandy finally stirred and opened her eyes. When she saw that Papio was up and dressed she sat up in the bed and asked, "Where do you think you're going, daddy?" She looked at the clock on the nightstand and saw that it was a little after five A.M. and continued, "You need to be in bed getting some rest, daddy."

With a grin on his face Papio stepped to her and gave her a kiss. "I'm good, *mami*. I got shit to take care of so I can get out of here. I got too many moves waiting to be made for me to be lying up."

With a determined expression on her face she told him, "I know you don't think I'm letting you leave this house without me. You can't be driving around taking care of your business while on that medication. You'll overdo it and hurt yourself. I'll drive you wherever you need to go. I won't be in your way one bit," she stated firmly.

Papio checked the time on his watch and said, "Check it, you got less than twenty minutes to get dressed then, 'cause I gots to get going. If you can't make it by then I'm outta here."

She flashed that gorgeous smile of hers, gave him a quick peck on his cheek, and said, "I'll be ready in fifteen!"

She jumped out of bed and ran into the bathroom to get herself together. Papio stared at the trash bags that were full of money and drugs and shook his head as he once again thought about Kammy. "Crazy bitch," he muttered as he grabbed one of the bags and pulled out a few stacks of money. He held the money in his right hand and grabbed the other bags with his good arm and took them downstairs to the 600. When he came back inside he was starting to feel a little dizzy. *Damn, Brandy was right; there's no way in hell I would be able to handle the shit I need to do today, Fuck. I got to get at that nigga Charlie so I can shake the spot and get my ass back West,* he said to himself as he sat down in the living room and waited for Brandy.

When Brandy pulled Papio's Mercedes into Cheese's driveway Papio told her that there was no way she would be able to come inside while he was getting at Cheese. She frowned but didn't argue. "I'm a little hungry, baby; why don't you go to Mickey D's and grab me a couple sausage-egg McMuffins and some orange juice. I won't be too long in here with my man. Then we'll go see Doc and get back to the pad so I can get some rest."

"All right, daddy. It won't take me that long so hurry up, 'kay?"

He reached into the back seat and grabbed the two trash bags of drugs and closed the door.

Cheese was standing in the doorway by the time Papio made it to the front. "What up, big homey? What the fuck happened to your ass?" Cheese stepped aside and let Papio enter his home.

Papio went inside and sat down immediately on Cheese's couch. He was feeling dizzy again and that bothered him. *Damn, this shit is going to throw a monkey wrench in all of my shit,* he thought as he grimaced from the pain in his shoulder.

"Had a good and fucked-up night all at once, my nigga." He then went on and explained what had taken place at Chico's house.

"Yeah? So that was your work huh?" Cheese asked excitedly. "Dog, I heard some shit had happened to one of those Dallas niggas. The word on the street is he got got by that bitch Kammy who runs that beauty shop on the east side."

"Is that right? What else is the streets talking about?"

"Nothing really; oh yeah, word is he supposed to have popped that bitch though. So I guess they both got it huh?"

"Something like that. Check it, this is the play and how it's going to go down, so pay close attention. I'm about to put you on so you can get the North Highlands back like it's supposed to be. You got to get a solid team together so you can make the moves necessary to handle up when the time arises. Because when you start to blow them Dallas niggas gon' start to wonder how you got it like that all of a sudden." Papio gave a nod toward the trash bags that he had set by his feet and said, "I got a gang of X pills, several pounds of Purp, plus a few keys of yayo for you. This is your come up, Cheese; don't fuck it up. I want a ticket for all of this shit. I know you should clear that easily with the yayo and Purp alone. There's no rush for the ends, my nigga, please take your time. But when you got my money I want you to get at my money man and then he'll keep you righteous."

Cheese was stunned as he listened to Papio. He shook his head and asked, "Dog, I ain't never dealt with no weight like this. Are you sure you want to get down like this with me?"

"Damn, nigga, you sound like straight pussy. What the fuck is wrong with you? Here I am laying a true blessing in your lap and you acting straight bitchy with it. You ain't got shit to worry about; just handle your BI and get me my money, Once that is done you will have more X, yayo, or Purp sent to you. Whatever you want will be blasted your way. My money man will make sure that you are righteous from this point on. You're in the game, nigga; no time to be scared now. Either you with it or you ain't. My man fucks with the X heavy but there is nothing he can't get for you. So you make that call."

"Nah, I'll be good just fucking with the X for real. With all of these niggas around the hood I'll have shit on lock."

"All right then, that will make shit run even better. My man Q will be getting at you in a few weeks to touch base with you so don't be spooked when you get a call from a white boy."

"A white boy. Dog, don't tell me your man is a cracka!"

"You stupid. That cracka has been on my team for years. He's solid as a rock. Trust that. Listen, there's much more to this shit. You got to make sure you check those Dallas niggas' temperature; they might try to get at you."

"Fuck them fools. I've been waiting for the chance to get at them niggas for real. With this type of work I can get the shit I need to fade them fools real proper like. When I get at my niggas and let them know we're about to eat good for real they'll be with me all the way."

Papio smiled and said, "Now that's the Cheese I remember. Cool. There's one last thing though."

I knew it; something fucked up had to come behind all of this blessing shit, thought Cheese. "What's good, big homey?"

"I need you to help me take care of that other thang. With my arm fucked up I won't be able to put it down without some help."

"You want me to help you smoke my own blood? That's some cold shit right there, Papio."

"Nigga, what are you talking about? You already gave me his information, clown, so you basically already helped me smoke his punk snitch ass."

"Giving you that info and actually helping you handle the business is entirely different, dog; that's my first cousin!"

"Calm down, it's not like I'm asking you to pull the fucking trigger, nigga. All I need you to do is help me get to his ass. I'm the one who's taking his bitch ass out. Now can you do that for me or what?"

Cheese stared at the drugs in the trash bags and then into Papio's intense brown eyes and knew that there was no way in hell he was about to let this opportunity pass him by.

He sighed. "Yeah, I'm with it. What you want me to do?"

"Good." Papio then told Cheese what he needed done. He finished just as Brandy pulled back into Cheese's driveway. "All right, make sure you get at me as soon as you're ready. And remember, if it can't be tonight it gots to be no later than tomorrow. I got to shake the city like immediately."

"I got you. I'll handle this, Papio, all of it. I've been waiting for my shot at the title for too damn long, and now that I got it I'm gon' get my paper right."

"That's the business, my nigga, that's the business," Papio said as he stood and shook hands with Cheese.

CHAPTER THIRTY-TWO

By the time Brandy and Papio made it back to the house Papio was totally exhausted. He wearily climbed the stairs and went straight to bed. Five hours later he woke up to the ringing of his cell phone. He grabbed it off of the nightstand and answered it. "Yeah?"

"Hey, you," said Special.

Papio was instantly awake. "What's good with you, lady?"

"I hate to stroke your already oversized ego, but a girl just can't help it. I'm missing you something terrible. When are you coming to town?"

"If everything goes like I expect it to I should be out there no later than the day after tomorrow. I'll know for sure soon."

"Make sure you get at me because I want you here for my birthday."

"And when is that?"

"Saturday. I want you, Papio, I want you bad."

"I'll be there, Special; even if shit don't pop off like it should, I will be there. My word."

"Good. Now tell me, what have you been up to since we last spoke? You sound tired, baby."

"Doing me, you know the business. Shit got kinda wicked the other night. I'll explain all of that when we hook up."

She understood that he wasn't trying to speak on the telephone about his illegal activities so she changed the subject. "All right then. You do know that I have to be treated real nice for my birthday right?"

He started laughing and said, "Damn, girl, you really trying to stay in my pockets huh?"

Before she could answer his question, Cheese was calling him on the other line. "Check it, Special, this is the call I've been waiting for. Let me get back at you later."

"Go on and do you. Make sure you get here, Pussy Monster. It's not your money I've been missing, pretty man." She hung up the phone before he could reply.

Papio answered the other line. "Tell me you're ready for me, Cheese."

"Yeah, I'm ready. I'm going out to his house to talk some business in like a hour."

"All right, you know the business: get inside and I'll come and handle the rest."

"That's what's up," Cheese said and hung up the phone.

Papio closed his phone, reached for the lamp on top of the nightstand, and turned it on. He tried to hide his surprise when he saw Brandy staring at him from the doorway of the bathroom. The hurt expression on her face told him that she heard the conversation he had had with Special.

"Damn. What's up, *mami?* Why you standing there looking all salty and shit?"

With her arms folded across her chest Brandy asked, "Who is Special, daddy?"

"My people on the West Coast. Don't do this, Brandy; don't make yourself hurt behind something that neither of us can control."

"Is she why you're leaving me, Papio? Tell me the truth. I'm a big girl; I can deal."

"We have business to take care of when I get out to the West, baby, that's it and that's all. Before you ask I'll give it to you raw as I always have. Yeah, we've kicked it and odds are we will kick it again. But my business comes before anything and anybody. My moves are never determined by a woman. When I'm with you, *mami*, I'm with you. Period. It's all about you when we're together so don't you ever think you don't hold a major part of my heart. But just like I told you from the start my money is what I need most, not a woman."

He saw the pain on her face and it bothered him that he really gave a fuck. No way was Brandy supposed to affect him like she was doing. *I gots to be getting soft or some shit,* he thought as he stared at her and tried to come up with something to ease her pain. His thoughts drifted to Kammy and how he was going to let her make it and then the bitch tried to kill his ass. *Uh-uh, fuck the soft shit; that just ain't me.* He sighed and reached out for the bottle of pain pills that Doc gave him and took two.

"My business will be handled tonight so most likely I'll be on a flight to the West tomorrow. You need to go and get the rest of your stuff moved over here. I'll be out of your way and you can go on with your life and be happy, *mami*."

"Is that what you want me to do, daddy? Go on with my life without you? If it is then you are so blinded by the money that you are just plain stupid. I want you! I want you to be safe and happy! I want you to be here with me! Can't you see that I'm in love with you?"

"Yeah, I can see that shit. And you are too fucked up in the head to understand that I'm not Joe Square! I'm a money-getting nigga who don't give a damn about nothing but my fucking money! If shit is meant for us when I'm where I need to be we'll see what it do then.

But until then please accept my home as my gift to you. A gift that you deserve."

"I deserve your home but not your love? Wow, why don't I feel special?" she said sarcastically.

"This conversation is over, Brandy." Papio climbed out of the bed and stepped past her on his way to the bathroom. His thoughts were on killing Charlie now. *Later for Brandy,* he thought as he started lathering himself. A few minutes later he heard Brandy come into the bathroom. He smiled as he watched her get into the shower stall with him. He saw the tears slide down her face and kissed her cheeks, then her lips.

"Everything is going to be all good, *mami.* I'm a man who plays the game the only way I know how. I play to win and I don't play fair; that's why I know I'm going to win. When I win, you win too. Believe that for me okay?"

She shook her head yes and said, "I'm a fool, daddy, but I don't care. I love you and no matter what I will be here taking damn good care of your home, so when you come back to me everything will be just right."

He didn't respond; instead, he kissed her again and held her tightly with his good arm while the hot water sprayed them both.

Papio pulled his Range Rover in front of the house right next to Charlie's car. He sat and checked to make sure that his silenced 9 mm pistol was loaded and ready. "In and out, Papio, real easy. Dead this bitch-ass nigga and get the fuck." He slid out of the truck.

He stepped quickly to the front door and gave it a soft knock. Just as they had planned Papio heard Cheese tell his cousin, "I got it, Charlie. You expecting somebody, fool?"

Charlie was inside of the kitchen grabbing them both a cold beer when Cheese called out to him. "Nah, probably some kids trying to sell some shit!"

When he stepped back into the living room his jaw dropped when he saw Papio standing in his house, pointing a big-ass pistol with a silencer on it directly at him. He dropped the beers he had in his hands and said, "P . . . please, Papio, man, don't kill me. That shit was crazy, dog. I had no other choice; they were going to give me thirty years, dog!"

Papio shook his head from side to side and told him, "You bitch-ass nigga, they gave me thirty years! I didn't do no fucking snitching! I took that shit like a man, you weak-ass nigga. So don't stand there and give me that bitch shit, fool, 'cause I just ain't feeling that shit." He turned toward Cheese and said, "Bounce, nigga, ain't no need for you to see this shit."

With his head bowed in shame Cheese mumbled, "All right, dog."

"That's how you do family, nigga? You ain't shit, Cheese! You better believe this, li'l nigga, fucking with this nigga you will either be dead or in jail real quick like. He's poison, Cheese! I hope you can't sleep for the rest of your motherfucking life, nigga. You crossed your family out for a motherfucking snake!"

Cheese stopped in his tracks, turned, faced his cousin, and said, "Fuck you, Charlie! You snitch-ass nigga. If you would have stayed down you would have been able to hold on to the respect you once had. Nigga, every real nigga in them streets know you are a wackass hot nigga. You deserve to die, family or not. Don't worry about me, clown, 'cause I'm about to eat real good! Rest in pieces, bitch!"

He didn't look back as he turned and walked out of the door, not giving a damn about what was about to happen to his cousin.

Charlie stared at Papio and was about to beg for his life some more but Papio shook his head no and said, "Enough of this movie shit." He then fired his pistol twice and shot Charlie in both of his knees. Charlie fell to the floor, screaming in pain. Papio pulled out his cell phone with his good hand while he still had his weapon aimed at Charlie writhing on the floor in pain.

He punched in ten digits from memory and hit the send button. When Castro answered the phone Papio told him, "Let me speak to Mr. Suarez."

"Is that business handled yet?"

"Castro, you are a boy, a worker. I don't report shit to you, fool. Now put Mr. Suarez on the fucking phone."

Castro smiled into the receiver and said,"God, I can't wait until the day I take your life."

Papio just laughed.

Two minutes later Mr. Suarez said, "Señor Papio, is everything okay?"

"Sí, sir. I'm staring at that person right now."

"Very good, Papio. Finish that nasty business so we can move forward, sí?"

"Sí. I just wanted to let you know that this was a wrap. I'll be out of the way for a few months, but when I get at you again I will have something nice for you."

Mr. Suarez smiled. "I'll be waiting to hear from you, my friend. So until then, good-bye, Papio."

Papio stared at Charlie for a few seconds after he closed his phone and then shot him two more times; this time both bullets ripped through his face. "Closed casket, bitch," he said aloud as he turned and left Charlie's home without looking back. In and out and real easy, just liked he planned.

CHAPTER THIRTY-THREE

The next morning Papio received a call from his Realtor in Dallas informing him that his offer for the home in Plano, Texas had been accepted. *Perfect,* he thought as he listened to her give him the details on the closing of the home. He told her that he would be in town within a couple of weeks because he had business he had to attend to in Los Angeles. When he finished the call he decided that Brandy would be needed a little bit longer in his life. He smiled at her while she was getting dressed for work and said, "Check it, *mami,* I'm going to need you to do me a favor in a couple of weeks."

She fastened her bra. "What's that, daddy?"

"I want you to bring me the Range down to Dallas. Since you love the six and the Beamer you can keep them out here for the time being. I just bought a spot down there and I'm going to need some wheels. I'm also going to need you to furnish it for me. You know, give it that classy look for me. You can look around here and pretty much figure what I like. Can you do me that, baby?"

She smiled. "Dallas. You're going to be that close to me, daddy?"

"What, you thought I was going to shake you like that? Of course I'm going to be that close. I just can't be out here; shit done got kind of wicked for me. Time for a change for a minute. We'll still do us, I just won't be out this way. So, like I said, can you do me that?"

She stepped to him, gave him a kiss, and said, "I'll do whatever it takes to remain a part of your life, daddy, you know that."

"That's what I'm talking about. Now, go on and get to work. Tell my man Kingo I said to get at me. By the time you get off I'll be gone. I'll hit you when I touch down in L.A. You got the number if you need to holla at me."

"I'm really going to miss you, daddy," she told him with tears in her eyes. "Please be careful out there."

"Don't worry about me, *mami;* daddy is going to be all right. Now go on and handle your business. I'm not taking any clothes so I'm going to need you to pack my stuff up for me and bring that to me when you bring the Range."

"No problem, daddy."

"Good," he said as he slapped her on her ass. "Man, I'm going to miss all that booty right there."

She looked over her shoulder at him. "Then you better hurry up and come back and get some of all this." She switched those sexy hips from side to side out of the bedroom.

Papio's flight landed in LAX on time. He had a smile on his face as he deplaned and strolled out of the crowded airport. Though his arm was still sore he chose not to wear his sling. He was too excited; all he could think about was seeing Special. Once he was inside of his Aston Martin and pulled out of the parking lot, he instantly went into business mode. He pulled out his cell phone and called Q. "What it do, my favorite white boy?"

"I take it you're back in town, Papio?"

"That's right. Time to get some money. Is it still on with that sucker Nicoli?"

"Definitely. That joker just doesn't give a fuck, dude. I mean he still has no fucking security! Crazy dude!"

"It's all good then. Put it together and get at me with the details," Papio said as he turned on to Century Boulevard and told Q about the arrangement he made with Cheese back in Oklahoma City.

"Okay, that's cool. What do you make off of this gesture?"

"Thirty percent of what he spends. After he takes carc of me I'm positive he's going to be at you like serious. So thirty percent is cool. You can put that with the rest of chips in the offshore account."

"Got you. Any news from those Cubans?"

"They good. Dumped them a few stacks and everything is cool; you know those greedy bastards know I'm a money-making machine. They don't want to lose old Papio."

Q shook his head. "You got nine lives for real, dude. I don't know how you do this shit but I'm glad you've made it this far. Don't take those guys for granted though, Papio."

"Underestimating anyone is too dangerous in our line of work, baby boy; that could get a man dead. I don't plan on dying anytime soon. I got this. But believe me, if they ever think they're going to move on me, I'm moving the fastest and the hardest."

"Hopefully it won't come to any of that."

"Yeah, hopefully it won't. Check it, I'm going to be out of the way for the weekend so if any moves need to be made make sure it's after that. Going to spend some time with Mama Mia and catch up on some rest."

"Got you. If you see Twirl tell him I said get at me. I got something extra for him."

"Everything is everything with you and my nigga I see."

"He's doing quite well for the both of us. He took care of you also. I used what he gave me for that purchase out in Dallas for you."

"Cool. If my calculations are correct my small fortune is close to a dub right?"

"More like $26 million. We've made some pretty sound investments this past year."

"Good. All right, baby, gotta go. Hit me if you need me."

"Later, dude." Q hung up the phone.

Papio's thoughts were of his money as he got on to the freeway headed to his home. *$26 million dollars; just seventy-four more to go and I can get out of this game and live like a king for real. I got money coming in from a few different angles but I need that one monster lick. That way I can pay Mr. Suarez off and get righteous. 2009 is going to end up being my final year in this fucking game,* he said to himself as he picked his cell back up and called Special. When she answered the phone he asked her, "Are you ready to have the best birthday you've ever had, baby?"

"I hope that means you're back on Pacific Time, Papio, 'cause a girl is really really horny!"

He started laughing. "Yeah, I just got in. I'm on my way out to Riverside now. After I get settled and spend some time with Mama Mia we can hook up."

"Riverside, that's where you rest at?"

He hesitated for a moment and then thought, *fuck it.* "Yeah, I got a little spot out that way."

Though she noticed his hesitation she ignored it and said, "That's convenient because I'm in Rialto."

"Perfect. We can hook up and do dinner and get this weekend cracking. I'll make sure this will be one birthday you'll never forget."

"That's what's up. Just make sure you put that dick on me in a way that I'll never forget that you're a Pussy Monster."

He started to get erect hearing her words. "No doubt! Tell me, how old will you be tomorrow?"

"Never ask a woman her age, Papio, that's not polite."

"I never said I was a polite dude. Come on with it, *mami,* how old will you be?"

"I'll tell you when I see you. Call me after you get yourself together." She hung up the phone.

The conversation with Special kept a smile on his face as he made his next call.

When Twirl answered the phone Papio said, "You ready to get some more money, my nigga?"

"My man! You better fucking believe it! You back huh?"

"Yeah, I just got in. About to go to the pad and chill. Q will have some shit lined up for us next week. Oh, and he wants you to get at him, said he has something extra for you. Right now I gots to get me some rest. Caught a scrape while handling some BI out in Oklahoma so I'm going to pass on that move with your man. Unless he can put it back for a week or two."

"That's cool 'cause that nigga E.T. hasn't been returning my calls anyway. When he does get at me I'll see what the business is. Did Q tell you I got at him with your chips?"

"Yeah, good looking out, dog."

"If I don't stand on no nigga it will always be you I stand on, fool; you keep a nigga living good," Twirl said sincerely.

"That's right. All right then, hit me if you need to holla; if not I'll get at you next week.

I'm going to be recuperating with someone real nice for the next forty-eight to seventy-two hours."

"I thought you was going to get some rest from your scrape OT?"

With a smile on his face Papio said, "I am. Me and Mama Mia will chill and for a bit. You already know how she's going to act when she sees my li'l scratch."

"What exactly happened out there, dog?"

"Caught one in the shoulder; went straight though but I'm sore as fuck. Plus got a graze on the neck."

"Tell me, did you come up off this move?"

"You know I did," Papio boasted.

"I guess it's safe to say that the other side of this move didn't get so lucky with just a shoulder blast huh?"

"Exactly."

"Good. Now, who are you going to be kicking it with other than Mama Mia? Curious minds wants to know," Twirl joked.

Papio's smile grew wide. "Someone special, my nigga. Someone real special. I'll holla!"

CHAPTER THIRTY-FOUR

Papio pulled into the long, circular driveway of his home. Mama Mia was standing in her flower garden in front of the house, fussing with the gardener, like she was doing when Papio last saw her. He jumped out of the car and stepped to his mother and gave her a hug and a kiss.

"Calm down, *Madre*. Give the man a break huh?"

Mama Mia lovingly held the face of her only child, happy to see him back home safely.

Her smile quickly turned into a frown when she noticed something wasn't right with her child.

She turned and faced the gardener and told him, "We speak about this more when you return. Please don't cut my flowers again such fashion; you do you no come here more. Understand?"

"Yes, ma'am," said the gardener as he quickly made his escape to his truck.

Mama Mia grabbed Papio by his hand and pulled him inside of the house. Once they were seated in the vast living room she asked, "What happened to you, Preston? You no look good, *mijo*."

He shrugged and said, "Nothing serious, *Madre*. Had a little run-in with some guys who didn't like the way I do me is all," he lied with a straight face.

The lie he told his mother went right through one ear and out the other; she knew her son and she knew that he was into serious illegal activities. She never asked any questions because she knew he would never tell her the truth anyway. But the thought of losing him made her go against the norm.

She shook her head. "No, you tell me the truth, Preston. I mean this, what happened to you?"

He sighed and gave in because he didn't want this to linger longer than necessary. "I got into it with some dudes in Oklahoma City and they shot me in the shoulder. I caught a nick on my neck also. I'm good though, *Madre,* so please don't make more out of this than what it is okay?"

"Don't you think it's time to stop the way you are living, *mijo?* You have plenty money now; why do you continue to live so dangerously?"

Not once in his life had he ever disrespected his mother; he loved her too much for that. For that reason alone he checked himself and made sure that he was calm before answering her question.

After taking a deep breath he said, "When I reach the goal I've set, *Madre,* I will gladly leave the game alone. Until then I have to continue to do what I do. You won't ever understand this so don't even try. All I ask of you is to please trust me. Nothing is going to happen to me out there. I got this well under control."

"Under control? You call getting shot being in control? You are loco just like your father was. I can't stand the thought of having to bury my only child, Preston, so please, please think about changing your ways before it is too late. You need to find you a good woman and make babies and be happy."

He thought about Special. "Make babies huh? Wow, that's what this is all about *Madre?* You want some grandkids?"

"Don't you try to change the subject on me; you know it's about you and your safety that all I care for. I love you, *mijo*. I couldn't bear it if something happened to you."

"I understand and please believe me I won't let anything happen. I got this. Now, as for me meeting a woman, I think I already have. She's beautiful, *Madre*. I mean I love everything about her."

Mama Mia noticed the gleam in her son's eyes as he spoke of this woman and she knew that he had fallen for her in a serious way. She was happy to see this. "When can I meet her?"

"Soon. Tomorrow is her birthday and I'm spending the weekend with her. I'll let her know that you want to meet her and see if we can set something up before I leave."

"Leave? But you just got here, *mijo*. Why you leave so soon?"

"I'll be here at least for a couple of weeks, *Madre*. It's not like I'm leaving tomorrow or anything. I have to go to Dallas to take care of some business. After that is finished I'm coming back home for at least a month or so. Maybe we can go on a vacation somewhere nice and relax for a few weeks."

"I'd like that, *mijo*. Tell me, what is your lady friend's name?"

"Special."

"Special? That is her real name?"

"Sí. And believe me when I tell you this, *Madre,* she is special. Very special."

"Mmmmm. Where is she from?" She was skeptical.

"She was born up North but she moved to the South after she lost her mother. We have so much in common that it's kind of scary."

"What makes you think that she's the woman for you, *mijo?*"

Papio thought about her question for a minute before answering, then pointed to his heart and told his mother, "Because I've never felt anything this strong inside of my heart, *Madre*. I think about her all of the time and all I want to do whenever I'm near her is hold on to her real tight and make sure that she is safe."

Mama Mia gave him a nod of her head in understanding. "Sunday Dinner. Here. Five P.M., Preston. And don't be late. Understand?"

He smiled. "Sí."

"Now, go upstairs and take a shower and get some rest. I'll wake you when dinner is ready."

"I don't have time for that. I'm meeting Special and taking her out to dinner. I'll be spending the night down in L.A. because I'm going to make sure that Special's birthday will be one for her to remember. But since it's still kind of early why don't we go catch a movie?"

"Sí, that will be nice. I have a movie I want to go see."

Papio rolled his eyes and said, "Uh-oh." He never agreed with his mother's movie choices.

Mama Mia popped him on top of his head and said, "This is a good movie, *mijo*. Beyoncé's new movie. My friend tell me at the grocery store the other day that it is very good. She say Beyoncé act better than she ever saw before. So we go see Beyoncé, sí?"

Papio gave his mother a kiss on her cheek and said, "Sí, *Madre*. Go on and call and find out what time the next show starts and we'll go see what Beyoncé is talking about. I'm going to go shower and change these bandages so I'll be ready in a little bit."

With concern she asked, "Do you need any help, *mijo?*"

"I'm good. I'll be ready in no time," he said as he stood and went upstairs to his bedroom.

After taking a nice long shower Papio felt even better. *Maybe because I'm so excited to see Special,* he thought.

When Mama Mia saw him she smiled and said, "Look at my *mijo* looking nice. I like when you dress nice like this."

He was dressed casually in a pair of slacks and a crisp white dress shirt with a pair of Italian loafers on his feet.

He smiled. "This is nothing, *Madre*. You know I can get way cleaner than this. Wait until you see what I'm wearing later on when I go get Special."

"You have me really curious about this lady. I never thought I'd see the day that you would be in love with a woman like this. She has to be special." Then she changed her tone. "The movie starts in twenty minutes, *mijo*. You don't have any business to take care of do you?"

"Nope. I'm ready if you are, *Madre*."

"Good. Let's go!" she said with relief.

A little over two hours later Papio and his mother were back inside of his car headed home. Mama Mia was busy giving Beyoncé praise for doing such a good job in the movie *Obsessed*. "See, I told you, *mijo*. Beyoncé did good job. You see how she beat up that white woman! Pow! Ha! I love that movie! I may come back and watch that again soon."

"Sí, it was a good movie, *Madre*. But give me a few days maybe I can find it on DVD for you. That way you won't have to go spend fourteen dollars to come see it again; you can watch it as many times as you want at home."

"That would be nice, *mijo;* please do that for me. What time are you going to get Special?"

"I was about to call her now," he said as he grabbed his phone. "Hey, lady, what's good?" he said as Special answered.

"Nothing much, baby; sitting here letting my toes dry, thinking about how I'm going to get me some of that Arab money. What you doing?"

"Just came from the movies with Mama Mia. I'm on my way home to get dressed; then we can get this weekend kicked off. You want to meet me or do you want me to come scoop you?"

"Call me when you're walking out of the door and I'll give you my address."

Mmmmm, went from not wanting to give me the digits to giving up the address; definitely a good sign, Papio, he thought. "That's what's up. Make sure you pack a light bag. We're spending the night in L.A."

"Oh, I thought I was going to have the pleasure of freaking you real crazy in my California king-sized bed."

"Not this time, baby. I got other things planned for the next two days. Then Sunday we have an invitation to dinner that we absolutely can't miss."

"Where and with whom?"

Papio stared at his beautiful mother, smiled, and said, "At my home with my mother. Mama Mia wants to meet you and she said saying no isn't an option."

"So you're taking me home to meet your mother? Wow!" *This nigga went from hesitating to tell me where he rests to bringing me home to meet his moms; impressive,* she thought. "Please tell your mother I happily accept her invite and that I can't wait to meet her."

"That's cool. Be ready for a few surprises this weekend, Special. Like I said, you will not forget this birthday. Make sure the bag you pack is small; we're doing some shopping in the morning."

"Oooh. I love your style, you pretty man you."

"Special," he said in that tone that she'd grown to love.

"Listen, when I call you pretty it's no longer meant as being sarcastic. It's purely a compliment, baby."

"Babies and women are pretty. Men are handsome."

She laughed. "Fuck what you talking about, you are pretty! Call me when you're on your way. Byeeeeeee."

He closed his cell phone. Mama Mia stared at him for a few seconds and then asked, "Did she call you pretty, *mijo?*"

"Sí, *Madre*. That's her little joke for me."

Mama Mia smiled at her son and said, "I do think I'm going to like Special."

"Why is that?"

"Two reasons. One, she has excellent taste in men."

"And two?"

"She's right, *mijo,* you are pretty!" She laughed.

CHAPTER THIRTY-FIVE

Papio was definitely dressed to impress; he chose his outfit carefully and made sure he didn't miss a thing, from his tailor-made Versace suit to his expensive dress shoes. The only jewelry he wore was his Cartier watch and a pair of solid gold cuff links. He was feeling quite giddy as he pulled out of his driveway. It was intoxicating just to think about Special. She was the one; he knew it and he was going to make her realize the same thing this weekend. Somehow, someway she was going to be his.

Special answered the phone by asking, "Tell me you're on your way to come and make me one happy woman, Papio?"

"As soon as you give me the directions to you I'll be there to do just that, baby," he said.

She told him where she stayed in the city of Rialto.

"I should be there in twenty minutes tops. You good?"

"I packed a light bag: makeup and necessities only. And for real, baby, I'm looking so damn good you're going to want to eat me up as soon as your sexy brown eyes see me."

He laughed. "You don't lack in the confidence department huh?"

"Nope. I'm a bad bitch and you know it too. Now hurry your ass up!"

After he hung up the phone with her he called Brandy in Oklahoma City. "Hey, *mami*, you good out there?"

"Good as can be without you holding me in your arms, daddy. How is your shoulder feeling?"

"I'm straight, Check it, I'm going to be caught up doing me but as soon as I know exactly when I'm hitting Dallas I'll get at you so you can meet me out there. We'll spend some time kicking it and getting the house together. I don't know how much right now but I should know more when I finish up out here in a week or two. Cool?"

"That's fine, daddy. Have you seen Special yet?"

"Stop that, *mami*. Don't go there all right? Let me go get this money. I'll hit you tomorrow or something."

"Okay, daddy. I love you."

"That is definitely a good thing, *mami*. Bye for now." He hung up the phone. *Damn, I done went and got that broad sprung for real, shit,* he said to himself as he drove toward Rialto and Special.

Special was standing in the doorway of her home wearing a dress by Angel Sanchez with a pair of Givenchy pumps on her small feet, looking like a billion dollars. Papio became instantly mesmerized by her beauty. *She wasn't lying, she is dressed to kill!*

He stepped to her and gave her a kiss on the cheek. "Damn, baby, you wasn't faking. I do want to eat your fine ass up right about now."

She smiled at his compliment and pointed toward the bag that she had next to her feet. "Don't worry, baby; you got all weekend to do you. Let's go."

She locked her door and stepped daintily toward his car. He grabbed her bag and happily followed her with his eyes locked on all of that ass she was packing in that little dress. *Damn! Whatever I did to receive this blessing, Father, thank you, thank you so very much,* he prayed silently as he opened the door for her and quickly went around to the other side of the car.

"I have us a suite reserved at the W out in Santa Monica. But first we have a dinner reservation at the Vibrato Grill. I thought a nice French meal would be appropriate to start off the weekend. Afterward I thought it would be cool to hit a club and get our groove on."

"That should be fun. I'm with whatever you got planned for us, baby."

"Cool. After that you know what the business is. I'm taking you to the suite to make that body tingle and feel good all over."

"Mmmmmmm, I like that. Can you do me a favor and take me on the beach and give me some of that big old dick?"

"You got that, baby. Whatever you want and however you want it."

She relaxed in the comfortable leather seats of the Aston Martin. "How's things been going for you since we last saw each other?"

"Well, other than getting shot I guess you can say it's been pretty good. Hit a mean lick for a nice chunk and came up with a lot of work, too."

"Work. So you dabble in the dope boy business, too?"

"From time to time, but that's not my get down for real. If it drops in my lap I know how to get rid of it quick like."

She stared at him for a moment and then said, "Did you say besides getting shot?"

"Yep."

"Where?"

He pointed toward his right shoulder and said, "Right here. Got a little graze on my neck, too." He pulled the top of his collar down so she could see the Band-Aid on his neck.

"Slippin' huh?"

"Yep. Went against my first mind and it almost cost me."

"Ain't no room for slipping in our profession, baby. You got to keep shit in your favor. You know what they say, 'Most times you make it; one time you won't.'"

"Real talk. What about you? How's things been on your hustle?"

"Slow for real, but a bitch got a million in the vault now so I can afford to get my chill on for a minute."

He shook his head. "Ain't no time for chilling for me. Money has to be made at all times as far as I'm concerned."

"Is that right?"

"Yep."

"So since you're going to be with me the entire weekend how are you going to be making any money?"

He smiled and said, "I got money being made for me right now as we speak, Special. My hustle reaches a few different states and nothing stops my grind. Not even when I'm getting my playtime on. So I can afford to chill and be with your sexy, fine ass all at the same time."

"I wish I had it like that."

"You can, baby."

"Please explain to me how."

He took a deep breath as he set the car cruise control. "Be with me, Special. Be my woman and we can do some real live Bonnie and Clyde shit. I mean get some serious money and be one hell of a team. I've never been a nigga who thought I wanted or needed a woman in my life. That is until I laid my eyes on you. I know I only know a little about you but what I do know I like. You got everything I need to be one happy-ass man. We can complement each other in every way. My paper is good and it's only going to get better, *mami*. Once I get that $100 mil I'm out the game and it's on to bigger and better shit in this crazy life. I know you're doing you and got your own thang. I respect that as I respect your get down. But check it, if we hook up and combine our resources we won't be able to be stopped. We can clock a grip and then go wherever the fuck we want to and—"

"What, live happy ever after? Come on, Papio, do you honestly think we can make some shit work like that? You on some gangster-fairy-tale time, boo. True, we got a little chemistry going here," she said with her index finger and thumb held an inch apart. "But what makes you so certain that everything will be so perfect with me and you? Like I said, you know very little about me. I'm not a trustworthy woman, Papio. The hustle is my life, deception is my get down."

He reached across the seat and grabbed her hand. "The heart never lies, Special. And my heart has been telling me over and over that you are the one for me. Enough of that shit; it's time to make your birthday weekend one to remember. I wanted to get that out before we got started. I expect an answer when the weekend ends. Deal?"

"Depends."

"On what?"

She gave him that sexy smile she owned and said, "On how memorable this weekend really is."

He returned her smile with one of his own and said, "It's on!"

CHAPTER THIRTY-SIX

The perfect French meal with some perfect sex was how Papio and Special spent their Friday evening.

Papio woke her up a little after eleven A.M. "I've ordered breakfast. After we eat we're going shopping. Time for you to start enjoying your birthday, baby." He gave her a kiss. "Oh, and by the way, happy birthday." He pressed a small jewelry box in her hand.

She had a grin on her face when she asked him, "What did you get me, Papio?"

"What you told me you liked." He went to the bathroom to let her open the box alone.

She sat up in the huge bed and opened the small box. When she saw the very large diamond ring inside of it she gasped and whispered, "Oprah diamonds. Damn." She slid the ring on her ring finger and the flawless ten-carat diamond mounted in a platinum setting shined so bright it looked as if it had been touched by the sun.

She wiggled the fingers of her left hand and yelled, "Your sexy ass better get ready, Papio! You got some bomb-ass head coming for this one right here, pretty man!" She jumped up and ran inside of the bathroom where Papio was showering. The head he received was definitely the bomb.

They were walking hand in hand in the Beverly Center looking like the perfect couple. Both were dressed down in jeans and tees with Nikes on their feet. Special had her hair pulled into a tight ponytail and so did he.

When they stepped into an exclusive store that Special loved she told him, "Baby, you might wanna go do something. I'm going to be in here a minute."

He shook his head no. "Nope. This is your day, baby, and I'm going to make sure that I watch you enjoy every minute of it. Do you, *mami*."

She smiled and kissed him on the cheek and whispered in his ear, "You're making a very strong case for that relationship shit you want."

"I know." He then slapped her on her ass lightly. "Let's go spend some of this money. Shall we?"

"Yes, we shall."

After four hours and almost $50,000 spent Special was finally ready to have lunch. They went and enjoyed some expensive seafood at the Water Grill. Afterward they went to the Santa Monica pier and enjoyed the sunny California afternoon, riding rides at the amusement park and strolling on the beach. They sat on the beach and watched as the sun began to set. Papio had his head on her lap and was thinking about how good things could be if Special decided to be his woman. *With her looks we can make more moves and get this money even faster together. It wouldn't take but about another year or so to get that $100 million and then we'll be good,* Papio thought.

Special's thoughts were exactly the same. *Damn, I can be with this nigga; ain't nothing plastic about him and his money is right. Pushing a brand new Aston Martin, dropping damn near fifty-plus on me at the mall, spending God knows what for this bad-ass Oprah diamond . . . Shit, a bitch would be a fool to let this pretty-ass nigga get away. Damn, what am I going to do?* she asked herself.

Papio interrupted her thoughts by saying, "Since we didn't do the club thing last night how about we get our clown on tonight?"

"I'm with that. I want to get my party on all damn night."

"It's your day so that's exactly what we're going to do."

"And after that?" she asked with a devilish smile on her face.

"After that I'm going to take you back to the suite and give you the best birthday sex you've ever had."

"I know that's right! I bet your ass I won't tap out either."

"How much?"

"A stack."

He smiled at her and shook his head. "Nah, ten stacks."

"Bet!" She bent forward and gave him a tender kiss. Just as she was pulling her lips away from his she bit his bottom lip kind of hard and said, "Let's go, pretty man. I'm going to need some time to get pretty for you tonight."

His light brown eyes stared at her light brown eyes and Papio knew that he was in love. "You're already pretty enough for me, Special. You're absolutely beautiful, baby." He was hooked.

While Special was taking her sweet time getting dressed Papio decided to make some calls and see what was what with Q.

When Q answered the phone he told Papio, "Dude, I'm glad you got at me. I have been wanting to call you since early this morning."

"What's up?"

"We're going to have to move sooner than I thought on that jerk Nicoli."

"Why?"

"Word is he's about to shake the town for a while. My sources say he's become bored with Los Angeles and is about to set up shop somewhere east."

"Fuck!"

"Exactly. The good news is he's having an all-out party tonight at that club called Kaboom."

"Is that right?"

"That's right. Can you make it happen?"

Papio stared at the bathroom door where Special was getting dressed. "Yeah, I think I can make it happen. Let me call you back in a minute. Special! Come here for a minute, baby!"

Special came out of the bathroom with a towel wrapped around her luscious body. "What up?"

"Change of plans: that fool Nicoli is primed and ready to get got tonight. You with it?"

She smiled. "You fucking right!"

"Good. Now this is how we'll run this move." Special listened to Papio's plan.

When he finished he grabbed the phone and called Twirl. "If you got any plans for tonight change them; we're about to get at that Italian clown again. Do you know where that club Kaboom is?"

"Yeah, that's that nigga who's in the Feds spot. Downtown not too far from the Staples Center right?"

"Yeah, that's it. Check it, meet me in the parking lot in two hours. Since that fool might make us we're going to let a very special friend of mines help lead us to that golden pot."

"Why not just sit on the fool's spot out in the valley and get at him like that?"

"Do you really think he still rests at the same spot?"

"I don't see why not; the clown mothafucka still is flossy with it walking around this bitch like he owns the world without any damn security. Shit he might just be that fucking stupid," said Twirl.

"True, but why chance it when I know we can hit a homerun this way?"

"That's right. I'll be there."

Papio checked his watch. "Let me get dressed. See you in two hours."

"What will you be in?"

"White on white Aston Martin."

Twirl smiled. "Did I ever tell you that you're my fucking hero?"

Papio laughed. "Nah, but after tonight when we get this fucking money you can tell me over and over. Two hours, fool." He hung up the phone. Once again it was time to get that fucking money. This was going to be even sweeter because it would hopefully be the first money-getting move he would make with Special. *Hopefully this lick will impress her enough to join the team full time. And then I'll have my very own real live Bonnie. That's what's up,* he said to himself as he got up to get dressed.

CHAPTER THIRTY-SEVEN

Two hours later Papio and Special arrived at Club Kaboom. Papio pulled his car into the parking space right next to Twirl's cherry-red Cadillac Escalade.

He rolled his window down and told him, "All right, baby is about to go in and do the work. When she comes outside we'll make our move."

"That's the business." Twirl stared at Special; he recognized her immediately from the mansion party. "I like this shit, dog. You gots to tell me how you got that fine-ass female on the team."

Papio smiled, faced Special, and gave her a deep tongue kiss. When he finished he faced Twirl again. "Does that answer your question?"

"Like I said, my nigga, you're my hero!"

"Okay, baby, time to get this money, you ready?" Papio said to Special.

"When that fool sees me it won't take long at all to get his ass out of the club. You just be ready to do you. I want to hurry up and wrap this shit so we can get back to celebrating my birthday."

"Don't worry about a thang, *mami*. After we get this money we're going to find another spot and do us until the sun comes up. Check it, go on and do you. Remember, lead the fool to the car and we'll handle the rest."

After checking to make sure she was together Special smiled at Papio and got out of the car. Papio did the same and tossed her the keys to the Aston Martin, then climbed into Twirl's SUV. They watched Special as she strutted toward the entrance of the club, looking like a big-assed model chick for real.

"You gots to tell me how in the hell did you crack that bad-ass broad, my nigga."

"Long story, dog; just know that she's a bad bitch in way more ways than one. Got a nigga thinking about straight wifin' her ass."

"What? You, with a wifey? She must have that fire for real!"

"It's more than that, dog; she's gangster, she got mad game, and she is one of the realest broads I've ever met in my life. Can't let her get away from me, dog, I gots to have her," Papio said seriously as he watched as Special entered the club. "She's in, let the game begin."

As soon as Special was inside of the club she headed toward the bar while surveying the club without appearing as if she was looking for anyone in particular. By the time she made it to the bar she spotted Nicoli holding court in the VIP area. *Got your ass,* she thought as she ordered an apple martini. After the bartender gave her her drink she took a sip and smiled. *Time to get busy.* She seductively strolled toward Nicoli; her game face was on and it was time for her to make it do what it do.

Nicoli saw Special as she entered the VIP and thanked God for blessing him to be able to set his eyes on her beautiful face again. *You will not get away from me this time, lovely lady,* he thought as he stood and stepped to her quickly.

"Please wake me, gorgeous, because I must be dreaming. Is it really you, my Bella?"

Special smiled. "I'm so happy to see you again, Nicoli. I thought those guys did something terrible to you. I didn't know if I would ever see you again."

Full of himself Nicoli smiled confidently. "Oh, that, that was nothing. Some bums who wanted some crumbs off of my plate. Me, I'm built to last in this life, Bella; nothing or no one will take me off the top of the pile."

"I see you haven't lost your swagger. What about your friend, is he ready to pick up where we left off?" Special pointed toward his crotch.

Nicoli sighed. "Yes, Bella, he wants very much to pick up where we left off. Later for sure, but now we party, yes? Tonight is sort of a going away party for Nicoli."

"Going away party? Where are you going?"

"L.A. bores me. I'm going to the East Coast to see what New York is like. I need constant excitement in my life and this city shuts down too early for Nicoli. If you're nice to me maybe you can come spend time with Nicoli in the Big Apple, yes?"

"I'd love to. Since you're going to be partying hard tonight why don't you let me take you outside to my car and give you a taste of what you're going to get before you head to the East Coast. I think I'm representing the West Coast rather well; wanna come and see?"

Nicoli was intrigued. "Lead the way, Bella."

Special reached out and grabbed him by his hand and led him out of the club. *Too damn easy,* she thought with a confident smile on her face.

Twirl was telling Papio how good he had been doing selling X pills when Papio saw Special come out of the club holding Nicoli's hand.

"There she go, dog. She got that nigga!"

"Damn, she ain't been in that bitch a good thirty minutes yet; she is good." Twirl pulled out his 9 mm and racked a live round in its chamber.

Papio pulled out his Glock. "Let's get this fucking money."

When Special was standing in front of the Aston Martin she turned and faced Nicoli and dropped to her knees to unzip his tailor-made trousers. Once she had his limp dick in her hand she quickly put it inside of her mouth. He hardened instantly and she began to give him some of the best head he ever had in his life. Nicoli moaned loud as he held on to the back of her head. "Yes, Bella, yes! You make Nicoli feel so damn good." He closed his eyes and enjoyed her hot mouth on his manhood.

"I'm glad you're feeling good; that way when you come off that money we can feel even better," Papio said as he tapped Nicoli on the top of his head lightly with his Glock.

Nicoli's hard-on went soft instantly inside of Special's mouth. She stood and gave him a shrug of her elegant shoulders and said, "Sorry, baby, but we have to relieve you of all of that loot before you relocate to the East."

Nicoli was about to say something slick until he saw Twirl shaking his head no at him. Twirl's menacing six-foot frame and mean brown eyes scared the living shit out of him.

"Don't waste your breath, Nicoli. You know how I get down. Let's go, fool; we got your money to go get. Right?" asked Twirl.

With a defeated look on his face Nicoli answered, "Right."

Twirl grabbed Nicoli and helped him into the front seat of the Escalade. Papio turned toward Special and smiled. "Follow us, baby." He got into the back seat of Twirl's truck directly behind the passenger's seat.

As they were pulling out of the club's parking lot Twirl asked Nicoli, "So, where are we headed to this time, old friend?"

"Don't tell me you forgot where we went the last time?"

"You mean to tell me that we're headed to the exact same spot? You didn't think to move? You're a stupid mothafucka," Twirl said and laughed. "I told you we could have just gone and hit that spot up, dog."

Papio stared at the back of Nicoli's head, thinking that something just wasn't kosher.

He pulled out his cell phone and called Special. "Baby, listen, we're headed out to the Valley. I want you to reach under the seat and grab my other Glock. When we get there I'm going to need you to go knock on the door and see if everything is everything inside there. I think this bitch nigga here thinks he's fucking with some amateurs. If someone answers the door, blast they ass. That Glock has a silencer on it so you won't have to worry about making any noise if you have to put anything down. You got me?"

"You fucking right I got you."

"Good," he said and hung up the phone.

Nicoli turned in his seat with a shocked expression on his face. "What makes you think I have someone at my home? I don't want to die. I will not upset you guys; it's only money. That's nothing to me."

Though he was already suspecting some fishy shit Nicoli's nervousness confirmed that he was up to something. Papio smacked him on the side of his head and told Twirl, "Pull over, dog, this bitch is leading us into a trap." Twirl did as he was told.

When the SUV was parked Papio said, "Now, either you tell us exactly who's waiting for us at your spot or I'm going to say fuck the money, and kill your ass right now. You have five seconds to start talking, Nicoli. Five, four, three, two—"

"Okay, okay! Please don't kill me! I have my cousins at my home! Please don't kill me please!"

Papio smiled. "Drive, dog." To Nicoli he said, "This is what we're going to do. When we pull into your driveway you're going to call your cousins and tell them to come outside and help you because you've had too much to drink. If you try to tip them off in any way you will die right there on the spot. You understand?"

"Yes."

"How many of your cousins are inside of the house?"

"Just two."

Papio stared at Twirl and laughed. "And your wild ass wanted to just hit the spot huh? This Italian sucker may be weak but he ain't no damn fool."

Twirl conceded that Papio was right with a shrug of his broad shoulders and a sheepish smile. "That's why you're my hero!"

They both started laughing while Nicoli had his head held down, wondering how in the hell he got caught slipping again.

When Twirl pulled into the driveway of Nicoli's home Nicoli did as Papio told him to. As soon as Nicoli's cousins came outside of the house Special and Twirl had their guns aimed directly at their heads. Papio was still inside of the SUV with his gun aimed at the back of Nicoli's head.

"Tell them not to resist or you get it first."

"Sergio, Benito, do as they say. They will kill us all if you don't."

Both of the cousins put their hands in the air and Twirl was on them immediately while Special watched his back. When Papio saw that his man had them under control he jumped out of the truck and led Nicoli inside the house. What he saw when he stepped inside made his jaw drop. Stacked on top of one another were four medium-sized boxes full of money. Three more boxes that were side by side were full of X pills. He turned toward Special and Twirl and said, "Bingo."

***

A $10 million lick! And that wasn't counting all of the X pills that Q would get. Papio was still tripping off of that shit after they'd finished counting the money. He pushed the large stacks of money toward Twirl. $4 million for himself and $3 million for Special and Twirl.

"Good looking out, my nigga; once again we win, dog." Twirl shook his head as he stared at all of the money that was in front of him. "Dog, we gon' win every time you get down. You a bad money-getting mothafucka for real!"

"I know; that's why I'm your hero!" They started laughing.

"Umm, excuse me, guys, but it's still rather early and today is a bitch's birthday. I am trying to enjoy it." Special smiled.

"You just came up three tickets and you're squawking about enjoying your day? Baby, if this don't make you have a happy birthday then nothing will," Twirl said.

Special's response to his statement was her pretty manicured fingers pointed toward the door of their suite. "Bye, Twirl."

Twirl ignored her attitude and packed his money up. "Break her off good, dog; she needs to relax." He gave Papio some dap.

"You know it. I'll hit you later in the week." Papio closed the door behind his man. When he turned around he watched as Special slipped out of her form-fitting dress. With a quizzical look on his face he asked, "Why are you getting undressed? I thought you wanted to go get your party on."

"Fuck that. I want to get fucked and I mean fucked real good, Pussy Monster. Do you understand me? Come here, Papio. Now!"

He followed her into the bedroom with a smile on his face because he was indeed ready to give her exactly what she wanted. He watched her as she climbed onto the bed and spread her legs wide for his viewing pleasure.

"Damn, that is a beautiful sight."

"Stop looking at it then and come fuck me. Come give me some of that good birthday sex you promised me. I've never been fucked on my birthday, Papio, so make this first time very special for me, baby."

"Technically it's after midnight so it's no longer your birthday."

"You know what I mean, pretty nigga! Come fuck me!"

He took his time taking off his clothes. He turned on the CD player and dimmed the lights. He hit the play button on the remote control and Jeremih's hit single, "Birthday Sex," started playing. She wanted some birthday sex for the very first time and that's exactly what he was about to give her sexy ass: some bomb-ass birthday sex!

After two and half hours of sexing Special, Papio won their bet: he made her fine ass tap out. Just before Special passed out her last thought was, *Damn, I just lost ten stacks!*

Two weeks of Special every single day had Papio feeling as if he were in heaven.

They shopped, dined at the best restaurants, went for long walks on the beach, and spent lots of time with Mama Mia going to the movies and helping her with the garden work.

Everything was perfect as far as Papio was concerned. What made it even more perfect was Mama Mia absolutely adored Special. That confirmed it for him: Special was definitely the one for him. He hated for things to come to an end but he had to get back to his grind. As if Q had read his mind he called Papio.

"When are you going to Dallas to move into that house you bought?" Q asked.

"Since shit is slow I was thinking about bouncing out there this weekend."

"I got something for you out there. Make that move and hit me when you make it to your new home. I'll have more details for you by then."

"What the figures look like, Q?"

"One, maybe two mil. You like or should I pass you on this one?"

Papio laughed. "You know better than that shit, my favorite white person. I'll give you a holla Saturday."

"I figured you would. Later, dude."

Papio hung up the phone and slapped his forehead. "Shit!" He realized that he hadn't spoken to Brandy since when he first got back to L.A. He dialed her cell number and waited patiently for her to answer. "What's good, *mami?* Miss me?"

"Should I miss you? It doesn't seem like you've been missing me," Brandy said with much attitude.

"I deserve that, but you know how I am when it comes to this money. Check it, I'll be in Dallas Saturday and I still need you to bring me the Range. If you do me that favor I promise I'll make sure you have a real nice weekend."

Even though she was really mad at him she couldn't stop herself from smiling; she loved that man too damn much. "Damn you, daddy. I can't even stay mad at your fine ass. Of course I can do that for you. What time will you be getting in?"

"I don't know yet. I'll hit you up and let you know to give you enough time to get everything together. Most likely I'll catch a red-eye out and be there early in the morning."

"That's fine, let me know. Your friend got himself into trouble the other day."

"What did that old fool do?"

"He got smart with the new captain over something trivial and got his butt locked up. He should be out of the hole sometime next week, that is if the captain doesn't make him stay in there longer to prove a point."

"Can you get a message to him for me?"

"I doubt it. It would look really strange if I went to Special Housing and tried to deliver a message to him, don't you think?"

"Yeah, you right. I'm tripping. All right, *mami,* let me get back to the business. I'll see you Saturday."

"Make sure you give me a call and let me know what time you'll arrive, daddy. I want to get there as soon as I can. That way I will be able to spend as much time as I can with you. God only knows when I'll have another chance to see you again, you busy man."

"I got you, baby, and you better believe we're going to make the best of this weekend. Talk to you later," He hung up the phone.

Though Special had him he still couldn't fully let go of Brandy, not yet anyway. *Never know what purpose she can serve later in the game,* he thought as he went downstairs to see what his mother was doing. Mama Mia was walking out the door when Papio came downstairs.

"Hey, sleepy. You're up now. Special is taking me to spa to get a massage and body treatment. She say it feels real nice to body."

"Massage? Body treatment? Since when did you become interested in all of that type of stuff, *Madre?*"

"When my future daughter-in-law asked me to join
her, that's when. She says it will be fun so we make a
day out of it. You go on and handle business and me
and Special will go play," she told him with a smile.

He grinned. "Okay, enjoy your day, *Madre.* You really do like Special, huh?"

"Sí. She is the one for you, Preston. Don't let her get
away from you, *mijo.*"

"I won't."

Special pulled into the driveway and blew the horn
to let Mama Mia know that she had arrived. Papio accompanied Mama Mia outside to Special's 2008 blue
BMW 135CIC convertible.

"Hey, baby, I thought you were still asleep."

"I got up just in time to catch my mother here sneak-
ing out of the house to go on this massage excursion of
yours. What's up with this; you'd rather spend the day
with my mother than me?"

"Wow. If I didn't know better I'd say you were jealous."

"I am. I want all of your time and to see that I have
to share you with anyone, even my dear mother here,
gets me real salty," he teased. "Nah, on the real that's a
good look. I have some business I need to take care of
anyway. You two have fun; when you get back dinner's
on me."

"Where are you taking us?"

"Wherever you want to go. I'm in the mood for a
juicy steak, but whatever you two come up with is fine
with me."

"Steak sounds good; what you say, *Madre?*"

Papio smiled when he heard Special address his
mother in the same fashion that he did.

"Steak is good, *mija*. We can go to the Sizzler, sí?"

Both Special and Papio started laughing. "I think we can come up with a better steakhouse than the Sizzler, *Madre*," said Papio.

"Baby, don't make any plans for us for the weekend. I have some work to do. I'm flying out of town for a couple of weeks."

"That's cool 'cause I was about to let you know that I'm flying to Dallas most likely Friday night."

"Okay. How long will you be out there?"

He smiled at her and said, "A couple of weeks."

"Texas, huh?"

"Yep."

"They say there's big things in Texas."

"I'll let you know when I find out. What's up with your end?"

"Hopefully something nice. I'm flying out to Kansas City to check on some things. When everything is good I'll let you know the business."

"Same here. All right you two, have fun. I'll see you when you get back. Love you, *Madre*."

"Hey! What about me? I don't get any love?" Special teased.

"You can have all of my love if you want it, baby."

With a smirk on her face she said, "I want everything you got to give me, baby."

"Even my heart?"

"Yes, Papio, even your heart." Before he could reply she put the Beamer in reverse and pulled out of the driveway.

Papio stood there with a goofy grin on his face as he watched them leave. "You didn't have to back out of the driveway, baby; that's why it's called a circular drive-way," he said aloud as he turned and went back inside of the house.

CHAPTER THIRTY-EIGHT

Papio caught a red-eye flight on American Airlines. Those two weeks spent with Mama Mia and Special gave him the proper rest and relaxation he needed. The day before his flight he gave his cute little real estate agent a call and informed her that he would be in town the following morning. They agreed to meet at the house so she could give him the keys. Since Q had taken care of all of the necessary paperwork the only thing left was for him to start shopping so he could furnish his new home properly. His smiled widened when he thought back to how the real estate agent flirted with him throughout the entire phone conversation. He decided he would take her to breakfast when they hooked up. *Might as well.*

Sharron Mosely, the real estate agent, was looking casually stunning when Papio's cab pulled into the driveway of his new home. She had on a snug skirt with a matching waist-length jacket. No stockings on her smooth legs only added to how sexy she was looking. *Hmm, I may just have to keep in contact with this sexy little piece,* Papio said to himself as he paid the cab driver.

Sharron smiled at him, putting her cute dimples on full display and said, "Good morning, Mr. Ortiz. How was your flight?"

"Uneventful, thank God. I slept right through it."

"That's good; you should be well rested and full of energy then."

"I'm always full of energy, Ms. Mosely."

"That's even better."

"Well, do you have the keys for me or are we going to stand out here and continue to get our flirt on with one another?" He grinned.

She blushed. "Flirting? Is that what we're doing?" She pulled the keys to the house out of her purse.

"You know the business. Let's go have a nice breakfast and use that time to get to know one another better; that way we'll know what's going to go down with us in the very near future."

"What makes you think something will go down with us in the future, Mr. Ortiz?" She gave him the keys to the house.

"Papio. Call me Papio, and you know just like I do that you're feeling me."

"You don't lack in confidence do you, Papio?"

"Nope. Now, are we going to eat or not? I'm kind of hungry."

She answered his question by turning and walking toward her car. The way her sexy hips swayed back and forth when she walked made Papio become instantly horny. He checked his watch to see if he would have enough time for a quickie with this sexy real estate agent before Brandy arrived.

When he was inside of her car he asked, "I've been to Dallas several times over the years but I've never had to do any furniture shopping. Can you help me out here?"

"Sure. I can take you to a few places if you like."

"I have a friend coming out to help me with that, but if you could give me a few places to check out I'd be very grateful."

She wasn't happy to hear about Papio's friend and the tone in her voice made it evident. "No problem."

"Don't get cold on me like that, lovely; it's all good. My friend is bringing me my Range Rover so I can have a vehicle on deck. She'll only be here for the weekend. When she leaves I'll make sure to give you a call. Cool?"

"What makes you think I would want you to call me, Papio? I mean you obviously don't need any of my attention." She pulled her car into a IHOP parking lot.

Papio laughed and said, "'Cause I'm feeling you just as bad as you're feeling me, *mami*. Now kill that noise and let's go enjoy a breakfast on me."

She raised her eyebrows. "I see I'm going to have my hands full dealing with you."

"That you will. I am a handful. Now come on, let's go eat!"

By the time Sharron brought Papio back to his home Brandy was parked in the driveway waiting inside of his Range Rover.

"Check it, I'll give you a call Monday afternoon okay?" Papio said to Sharron.

"That's fine," she said with a frown on her face.

"Don't be like that, *mami*. What's the name of those furniture spots you told me about again?"

"The more expensive nice stuff is at Cantoni's Furniture right off Interstate 635, the Midway exit. You can't miss it. Right down the street from there is another furniture store called Room Store; they're less expensive than Cantoni's."

"Thanks."

"You're welcome. You know I'm disappointed that I can't even get a kiss from those sexy-looking lips of yours."

He sighed. "Hold up. I'll be right back."

He got out of the car and stepped quickly toward the Range. Brandy stepped out of the SUV just as he made it there. "Here, *mami,* go on inside and take a look around while I sign these last few papers with this Realtor."

"Okay, daddy. Wow, this house is really nice."

"Wait until you check out the inside. I'll be right in." He went back to Sharron's car.

After he was back inside of the car he watched as Brandy went inside of the house. Once she was out of sight he said, "I see you're spoiled huh?"

Sharron smiled. "Blame it on my mama."

She leaned toward him and they shared a nice long kiss. "Whew! If the rest of your package is as good as that kiss was I think I'm going to enjoy spending time with you, Papio," she said.

"Bye, girl. I'll give you a call Monday afternoon."

"Byeeee." She pulled out of the driveway so wet that the only thought on her mind was to hurry home so she could go self-pleasure herself. Papio had that type of effect on her. She damn sure couldn't wait to see his fine ass again.

Papio went inside of the house and called out for Brandy. "I'm upstairs, daddy!"

He climbed the stairs and met her in the bedroom. "So, how do you like it?"

"It's nice. Not as nice as your house in the city but it's definitely you."

"Yeah, I know. Check it, this is the plan for the day. We're about to go hit some furniture spots so I can get this place together. After that we'll hit Walmart and Target to get utensils and whatnot. Plus, we have to go get some groceries. After that we'll come back so you can do all of the wicked things you want to my body.

It's going to be a long weekend so we might as well get started."

"Okay, daddy. But why not give me a quickie before we leave? After all it's been two and a half long weeks," she said as she pulled off the T-shirt she was wearing, revealing those perfect pair of chi chi's.

Papio felt himself getting hard as he stared at that pretty pair of titties. "Yeah, I'm with a quickie." He unbuckled his pants and pulled out his manhood. "You missed him huh?"

She licked her lips seductively. "Come here so I can show you how much I've missed him."

He did as she asked him to and she showed him exactly how much she missed his dick.

CHAPTER THIRTY-NINE

After a weekend full of sexing Brandy and getting his home in order Papio was happy as hell to put Brandy on a flight back to Oklahoma City. All thoughts of calling his young, sexy real estate agent for some loving was lost as he headed back to his home to get some much-needed rest. *Maybe tomorrow,* he thought as he pulled into the driveway. The bed was calling him and he was ready to sleep the day away. As soon as he stepped inside of the house his cell phone rang.

"What's good, baby?" he asked Special when he answered the phone.

"Missing you like crazy. What are you doing, busy?"

"Nah, just tired for real. Been getting this spot I got out here together all weekend."

"I thought you were working."

"Not yet. I'm waiting on my man to get at me with the details of the move. Until then I'm on chill status. What about you; how did things go in Kansas?"

"A couple of hundred Gs has been added to the kitty. My flight back home leaves in a couple of hours. Thought I'd give you a holla to see if you wanted some company."

"Why not. See if you can hop a flight to Love Field in Dallas and you can come kick it with me and make this next move with me too."

"That's what I'm talking about; a bitch going to get rich real quick fucking with you. I'll call you and let you know what time my flight will get in."

"I'm way too tired to come scoop you so just catch a cab to my spot." He gave her the address to his house.

"Go on and get some rest; you're going to need it. I'll text you the time I'll get in. See you later, baby."

"For sure." He hung up the phone and went upstairs to get some sleep.

After a three-and-a-half-hour nap Papio woke up feeling much better than he had earlier. He grabbed his phone and saw that he had three messages, one from Brandy letting him know that she made it back home safely and for him to give her a call.

One was from Sharron asking him why hadn't she heard from him yet. And one was from Special informing him that she would be arriving in Dallas at six P.M. He checked his watch and saw that it was a little after noon. *Good, that will give me some time to get showered and fresh for my baby,* he said to himself as he climbed out of the bed and took a shower. He dressed and called Sharron. He told her that he had to go out of town and that he would be back in a few days. She was disappointed but when he promised he would make it up to her she seemed cool with it. He then called Q to check in with him to see what was up with the move he was supposed to make in Dallas.

"What's the business, my favorite white-boy?"

"I was just about to give you a call. Everything is still being put together. I should have it all in order in a day or so. So make sure you're prepared to go at all times."

"No problem. Can you give me an idea of what this move is about?"

"Jewelry store with a whole bunch of diamonds. Inside job so it will be very easy; in and out just like that." Q snapped his fingers for emphasis.

"That's what's up. Get at me when you're ready."

"You don't need anything do you? I mean you do have weapons right?"

"I thought you said it was a inside move; why do I need heat?"

"Nothing is fool proof, Papio; you of all people know that."

"That's right. Don't trip; you know I got heat."

"Good. Be expecting my call no later than two days." Q hung up the phone.

Papio called Kango out on the East Coast. "What's good, my man?"

"Papio, that you?"

"Yeah, it's me. Just wanted to holla at you to see what the business is. You good?"

"I'm great, man. Everything is lovely; been putting some things together too. You ready for another ride?"

"Always."

"Great. I'll give you a call in a few weeks then."

"You do that. Have you heard from your brother?"

"Yes, he's in the hole for fussing with the captain. He asked about you and told me to ask you why haven't you made that call you were supposed to make."

"If you talk to him before I get a chance to, tell him I said I haven't been sitting still long enough to get at that. Let him know I'm good and I will make that call soon."

"Okay, I'll do that; talk to you soon." Kango hung up the phone.

Papio sat back on the couch and thought about his finances. After this jewelry move he would be over $30 million. Fucking with Kango would definitely put him close to thirty-five. Everything was moving along better than he thought it would. *Charlie's dead, I have some breathing room from those fucking Cubans, Special is feeling me . . . Shit, I can't lose!* he said to himself as he turned on his brand-new sixty-inch HDTV. While he watched the TV he fell back to sleep.

A knock at the front door woke Papio out of a co-matose-like sleep. He wiped sleep from his eyes as he stood and went to the front door. When he saw Special standing on the other side he opened the door with a smile on his face. "What's good, *mami?*"

She stepped inside and set her carry-all bag down and gave him a tight hug. "Hey, baby!"

They shared a kiss and Papio felt as if everything was right in the world. Special was his and he wasn't going to let her get away from him.

She pulled from his embrace. "I'm hungry. I know you got something to eat in this place."

She didn't wait for him to answer; she turned and started walking around the house until she located the kitchen. Papio followed and watched as she raided his refrigerator. She made herself a sandwich, and she grabbed a bottled water and sat down in the dining room.

In between bites she asked, "So, what you got cracking out here?"

"A inside lick on a jewelry store. I got at my man and it's supposed to go down in a day or two. After I blast him the jewels he'll add a nice chunk of change to my vault."

"How much?"

"One, maybe two tickets."

"That's what's up." She finished her sandwich. "That hit the spot. Now, let's go to your bedroom so I can fuck your socks off, Pussy Monster."

"You missed me that much, huh?"

"Take me to your bedroom and I'll show you." He took her upstairs and she showed him exactly how much she missed him.

First Brandy and now Special. Damn, I'm one lucky man, he thought as he drifted off to sleep.

CHAPTER FORTY

"Papio! Wake up, baby! Wake up!" Special said in a serious tone.

When Papio opened his eyes he just knew he had to be having a fucking nightmare. There was no way in the world he could be seeing who he was staring at. He rubbed his eyes so he could focus. When he opened his eyes again he knew that the game was over and so was his life. Standing in front of his bed were the two Indians he and Nick robbed back in Niagara Falls. In their hands were two silenced 9 mms. The wicked smiles on their faces confirmed what he already knew: he was about to die.

Special was standing to the right by the bedroom door behind the two Indians with a smirk on her face. She shrugged and said, "Told you we could never live no gangster-fairy-tale life, pretty man. You know there ain't no room for love in the type of life we live."

Papio stared at her and couldn't believe what he was hearing. *That bitch played me like that? Me! Now ain't that a bitch! All my life I've been the coldest nigga, the nigga who didn't give a damn about no one but Mama Mia and myself. All the years of playing the game the way I wanted to just to go out like this. I get crossed by the first bitch I ever truly loved; this is really some fucked up shit,* he thought as he stared with contempt in his eyes at Special. *I didn't play the game fair so I can't even be mad. Fuck it. At least Mama Mia will be taken care of for the rest of her days,* he thought. He looked at his pistol that was on the nightstand next to the bed.

One of the Indians shook his head no and said, "Don't. You are going to die, but not before you return our money and drugs."

Papio started laughing. "Do you honestly think you're going to get a penny out of me? Go fuck yourself, bitch! I may be a dead nigga but you won't get your ends back, that's for damn sure!"

"That's sad. We'll have to go visit your mother in Riverside, California and see if she can help us locate what we're looking for," said the other Indian with a deadly smile on his face.

Papio stared at Special. "I know the game is a cold one, but I can't believe you would let them do that to Mama Mia. Tell me you ain't that fucked up, Special. Please tell me that."

"Give them what they want, Papio, and nothing will happen to her."

He sighed, defeated. There was no way he could even take the chance of them harming his mother, no way. "I don't have the work but I can give you all of your money back. If you give me an account number I can have the money transferred to you within the hour. That's the best I can do."

The Indians stepped back from the bed and began speaking in low tones with one another. The first one who spoke told him, "That will be fine. Get a pen."

Papio reached into the nightstand drawer and pulled out a pen and a pad. The Indian then gave him an account number to one of their many accounts in some offshore banks. After he wrote the number down he grabbed his cell phone and called Q.

"Q, I need you to write this account number down for me." He then gave him the account number. "I need you to transfer six million to that account for me."

The Indian shook his head no and said, "Not enough, Papio," then he held up both of his palms indicating ten.

Papio sighed. "Scratch that, Q; send ten mil for me. Do it like right now."

"Is something wrong, Papio? Talk to me, dude. Do you really want me to do this?"

"Everything is straight; take care of this for me and hit me right back when it's done." He hung up the phone. "It should be done in about ten to fifteen minutes."

The Indians smiled. "Very good. I give you my word when we go visit your mother I'll make sure she dies quickly."

"What? Come on, man, there's no need for that shit! You're about to get your fucking money; leave my mother the fuck alone!"

The Indian who spoke so menacingly said, "That can't happen. We've been looking for you for the last six months. You cost us more than you will ever know, Papio. We owe our people and we lost honor because of what you did to us. For that you have to die as well as your mother."

Tears slid down Papio's face as he thought back to how he did Chico. How he played the game by his rules and didn't give a damn about no one but himself. He didn't play fair and now all of that had come back to bite him in his ass. *Karma is a bitch,* he thought as he stared at Special with hatred in his eyes.

She shook her head no. "Uh-uh, hold up. You guys said all you were going to do was get your ends back and then take him out. You didn't say shit about hurting his mother. Let her be. You're about to get your money back," Special pleaded.

"Shut up! You've got your money for doing your part. Now you should leave us. Our business is complete," said the other Indian.

"Fuck you talking to like that, Paul?" she screamed.

She turned toward the other Indian and said, "Come on, Jon, don't do this. Get your money, kill him, and be done with this shit. Please. His mother doesn't deserve to die because of his fuckup. Let her make it, Jon, please?"

Though Jon had a soft spot for Special there was no way he could go against his brother for her. He shook his head sadly at her. "I can't do that, Special. You should do as my brother said and leave now. Our business is complete." Jon turned back toward Papio and checked his watch. "Your people need to hurry up so we can get this over with. You should have never fucked with our drugs and money, Papio; that was the worst mistake of your life."

"Fuck you! And fuck your brother! And especially fuck you, bitch!" he screamed at Special. "How much money did they pay your cold-hearted ass anyway?"

Special held up four fingers and said, "Four million, baby. That four million plus the four million I got from fucking with you has made a bitch damn near ten million strong. I'm sorry, baby, but I play this game to win and I never play fair. Good-bye Papio." She turned to leave the bedroom.

"Fuck you, bitch!" he yelled as she left the bedroom.

The Indian named Paul pointed his gun at Papio. "You need to call your people back and see what the holdup is."

Papio grabbed his cell and called Q. "Have you made that transfer for me yet, Q?"

"No fucking way, dude! Not until you tell me what the fuck is going on, Papio!"

Papio took a deep breath. "Good. Don't do shit. I'm about to die, baby boy; you know what to do." He hung up the phone.

He smiled at the two brothers. "Do you really think I'll give you my fucking money knowing you're going to kill me and my mother anyway? Fuck you two bitch-ass pussies! Me and my *madre* can die but you still won't get your fucking money back!" He then started laughing hysterically. "This is some wild-ass shit! The game loves no one and neither does Papio, you sucker-ass bitches!"

Both of the Indians raised their guns and aimed them at Papio, who was still laughing. Papio's eyes grew wide in surprise. Not because of the two guns aimed at him, knowing that he was about to die, but because he watched as Special eased back into the bedroom with two silenced pistols of her own in each of her small hands. She shot Paul first twice in the back of his head; just as Jon turned toward her she shot him twice in his face. Both of the brothers were dead before their bodies hit the floor of Papio's bedroom.

Special aimed one of the silenced weapons at Papio and asked him, "If I let you live will you come after me? Tell me the truth, Papio." Tears were sliding down her face.

"Only if you can answer me one question honestly."

"What?"

"Was all of this really you playing me for those fools, or did you really love me?"

She shook her head sadly. "I did all of this for the money, nigga; you know the business. I told you from the start! You was so caught up that you just couldn't see it. But yes, yes, Papio, I really do love you. Shit just couldn't be avoided. Now tell me the truth; will you let me be if I let you live?"

"I can't let you be, Special, that would go against everything I've ever been about. So, do what you got to do, *mami*. If you love me like you say you do you won't be able to pull that trigger anyway."

She shook her head. "You just don't get it, pretty man. I love you, yes, but I love me more! Good-bye, Pussy Monster." She raised both pistols and aimed them at Papio and pulled the triggers.

THE END